WICKED WAGER

BEVERLEY OAKLEY

SANI
PUBLISHING

NOTE ON MY NEW GEORGIAN ROMANCE SERIES

WELCOME TO MY NEW SERIES!

Wicked Wager is the first in a collection of novels laced with romance and intrigue, set during the Georgian period in the late 1700s.

Full of secrets and intrigue with a nod to an old favourite — *Dangerous Liaisons* by Choderlos de Laclos, first published in 1782 — **Wicked Wager** pits virtue and innocence against the cruel and wicked parlour games played by a couple of bored and dissolute aristocrats.

I was captivated by the 1988 period romance movie, **Dangerous Liaisons**, starring Glenn Close, John Malkovich and Michelle Pfeiffer, however, in my book, **Wicked Wager**, the motivations on the part of the handsome libertine and ruthless society beauty, who plot to ruin my innocent heroine, are very different.

And as it's a romance - laced with mystery and intrigue - it has a happy ending. (I do love a redeemed rake!)

ALSO, COMING UP IN MY GEORGIAN ROMANCE series is a post-French Revolution romance, set in a London ballroom, called **Her Valentine's Secret**.

I'll tell you more about it later.

NOTE: **WICKED WAGER** WAS FIRST PUBLISHED BY Harlequin Escape under my Beverley Eikli name. It has since been revised.

Would you like to hear when I have a new book out?

Then sign up to my newsletter and get a FREE copy of
Her Gilded Prison!

CHAPTER 1

$\mathcal{L}$ord Peregrine liked a wager. The cards, the horses, occasionally a pair of spiders, could whip up his blood and tip him out of the lethargy and *ennui* which characterised his usual state of being.

This wager, though, was different. He could feel it in the sudden stillness into which he'd been plunged; the colour, vibrancy and chatter that had washed about him from the moment he and Xenia had stepped into their box at the theatre, sucked into the void.

Xenia's seductive purr as she put her head close to his was as sweet as a feather skimming his heated, naked flesh.

And as dangerous as a black widow's bite.

'Come, Perry, it's not like you to have scruples.'

He blinked to clear his mind and as his gaze raked the breathtaking contours of London's most beautiful widow—and probably its most immoral—he wasn't sure if the thrumming of blood to his extremities was due to outrage or titillation.

Slowly he exhaled, acknowledging almost sadly that it was the latter, which would of course confirm society's opinion of him as a bored and dissolute libertine who'd done nothing but wallow in his father's wealth, living a life of scandal. A man totally without redemption. Indeed he would deserve every uncomplimentary epithet hurled at him if he accepted darling Xenia's outrageous wager.

He surprised himself with his hesitation. A sudden flowering of moral fibre? Or fear? Clearly Xenia was surprised by his lack of enthusiasm, for she glanced at him askance, before her lips curved into that devastating smile that never failed to render him no better than her unruly, slavering hounds of whom she was so fond, who rutted with anything that crossed their paths.

And there was the rub. Yes, he was immoral, he was dissolute, but at thirty-three he couldn't believe he was totally beyond redemption.

Lord Peregrine sighed, abandoning the daydream he was better than he was—for that's all it was—and met Xenia's ice blue gaze while he schooled his features to betray no emotion. A lifetime's practice under the brutal tutelage of his uncle had made this easy. He could appear unmoved when it was true to say that he still was capable of *some* feeling. Whether that was a good thing or not was a matter he'd not yet decided.

And then he took another sip of his champagne. Around him the theatre once again pulsed with the energy he'd been conscious of before Xenia's carefully calculated whisper.

Oh, she was good. She knew exactly how to stir his blood.

Xenia gave a soft, throaty laugh. 'She's over there, if you want to look.'

He followed the direction indicated by her elegant finger, towards the stalls where two society beauties, with painted faces and elaborate pomaded coiffures two-feet high, were making eyes at the gentlemen over the top of ivory pointed fans.

'No, not there!'

Peregrine smiled. He enjoyed teasing her.

Xenia was quick to irritation. Quick to anger, and quick to passion, too.

The high-pitched inducements of the girls selling oranges in the pits almost drowned out the wavering top notes, which concluded the opera singer's aria; and as Peregrine searched for the object under discussion, his thoughts revolved around the usual litany of: 'Diversion, diversion; anything for diversion'.

No, certainly these were not the thoughts of a gentleman; more like a wolf wearing the trappings of one.

'She's a beauty, isn't she?'

He was aware that Xenia was watching him carefully, but again Peregrine schooled his features into a mask of indifference, even before he'd assimilated the scene before him.

And then the blurred images coalesced into one and as he regarded the handsome couple seated across the gallery, something in the graceful movements of the young woman stirred his senses, triggering an emotion not dissimilar to the energy that surged through him as he followed the hunt, charging with the rest of them after the wily fox.

By God, it was good to feel *something* that wasn't boredom.

Xenia, or rather Lady Busselton, as she'd become, lowered her opera glasses, her arched eyebrows and pursed lips showing how much she was enjoying Peregrine's reaction to her suggestion.

Her *wicked* wager.

He hooked one elegantly shod foot over his black satin pantaloons, regarding her over steepled fingers as he considered his response. The heat and smell from hundreds of bodies pressed close to enjoy tonight's production was making his head pound.

Or was it excitement? Revenge wasn't usually a game he played. Well, not with a woman as the spoils.

'You, of all people, Perry, know that the incomparable Miss Celeste Rosington is as far removed as is possible from the celestial virgin she is painted.'

Xenia raised her shoulder slightly in the direction of the couple across from them who, heads bent together, hands almost touching, represented the epitome of lovebirds on the eve of their nuptials.

'Your poor sister knows it, to her eternal cost.' She gave a husky laugh; the same laugh that for ten years had never failed to make Peregrine harden with instant desire. 'Come, my dearest Perry, it's not like you to allow your scruples to get in the way. After all, *she* has none.'

She was prodding, and would continue, until she got her reaction. Xenia, the tearaway cosseted only daughter of a ruthless and successful sea captain who had gone to extraordinary lengths to ensure she got her heart's desire—including two husbands with fortune and title—had changed little since Perry had become acquainted with her in her first season out. Back then she'd put financial and social considerations above their mutual attraction, accepting an earl that trumped a lowly viscount. He suspected—hoped—she'd rued the day.

'Scruples? I hope I have *some* at least, Xenia. And no, it's not scruples that give me pause. It's whether I have the stomach to further an acquaintance with a jezebel like Miss Rosington, even if I have every reason to see her revealed for what she is.' There. He'd just proved himself a gentleman before any unflattering epithet could be added. 'For a start, what do you suppose my sister would say if she heard I was sniffing after the woman who ... well, destroyed her life, to use Charlotte's own words?'

Xenia pursed her mouth and raised one thin, charcoaled

eyebrow. Though no longer in her first flush of youth, she continued to exude the most potent sexual allure of any woman Peregrine had met. With or without powder and rouge she was still a beauty, with the delicate bone structure of her long-dead mother, an impoverished aristocrat who'd married the coarse, bluff ship's captain after he'd amassed a fortune with his growing fleet plying a lucrative trade with the Far East in spices, slaves and silks.

Not that her heritage was something Xenia discussed. Though she eschewed her links with trade, she was quick to utilise the benefits of a seemingly endless supply of funds, even when husbands were not so forthcoming; and to prod the captain's more ruthless streak when it might be of any benefit.

She continued to fix Peregrine with her calculating blue stare. 'Your sister is no fool. Why, Charlotte would understand perfectly well that the only reason you could possibly show an interest in Miss Rosington was because you were avenging her; doing what any loyal brother would for his unjustly treated dear sister.'

For some reason Xenia's little wager seemed to have fired her blood. She patted Perry's shoulder, her expression a mask of false sympathy.

'Poor Charlotte has been made to look a fool. Surely *you*, Perry, wish to know why Miss Rosington was discovered, half undressed, by your sister in Mr Carstair's saloon before the two of them rushed guiltily into the night? Surely, *you*, Perry, know that the only way you're going to help Charlotte is to get close to that designing Miss Rosington—' she jabbed a finger at the unaware couple, 'who's looking moon-eyes at her betrothed—and find out for yourself. *Why* did she do it? Boredom? A wager? The fact is, your sister is heartbroken, her reputation tarnished ... while Miss Celeste remains society's darling, soon to wed her cousin in the match of the season.'

She breathed deeply, a provocative motion since it brought into greater evidence her full, lush breasts, revealed to ample advantage in her low-cut confection of gold embroidered silk and lace.

Her eyes slid over Perry's elegantly turned-out form and settled on his face, her lips pursed in a suggestive *moué*. 'If you wish to sample what you've always wanted, Perry darling,' the unexpected insinuation of her body as reward made him harden even more, 'and discover for yourself what has enthralled my long list of lovers, then call it amusement, but also atonement, that I attach this condition.' She sat back, fanning herself languidly while her bosom strained against her bodice. Another glance at her face revealed her suppressed excitement: eyes bright, her neat, curvaceous body quivering. 'Reveal to the world the truth of what Miss Celeste really is. Let the public understand it so that they might revile her for the woman who stole your sister's happiness. And at the same time, you can find out where Harry Carstairs is. After that, I will make you very happy.' The candlelight reflected off her pretty, pearl- like teeth, her look a mixture of lustful intent and daring. As she leaned back, eyes brimming with promise over the tips of her fan, her final words sealed the deal. 'After so many years' friendship, Perry darling, I think it's time to raise the stakes

—don't you?'

THE SHRILL ENTICEMENTS FROM THE ORANGE SELLERS TO BUY their wares faded as Celeste put her head close to her cousin's to murmur in his ear, a dull sense of dread permeating her soul. Never had she known anyone as determined as her cousin, Raphael, but now he was custodian of her happiness and she didn't fancy her chances that he would relent. Since they'd been children Raphael had to prove himself the best, the one in charge, and his honeyed tongue and sharp wits always won the day.

'Please, Raphael, it's not fair to hold me to this marriage if you cannot love me as a wife would wish to be … at least revered,' she whispered, the familiar grief clawing its way up her gullet.

Since Celeste could remember, they'd been destined to marry. As a child, this knowledge sat comfortably with her. Raphael was handsome and accomplished. She knew she had to marry someone with the wealth and lineage to satisfy her parents, so it might as well be the cousin who was generous and handsome in a careless sort of way. He'd always taken a general interest in her wellbeing and defended her on occasion during their childhood games. The marriage made sense for so many reasons, not just dynastic, and Celeste had had no objections.

That is, until Raphael's tinderbox revelation three weeks ago.

With a glance over her shoulder to reassure herself that her elderly chaperone was still gently snoring away in her seat in Raphael's opera box, Celeste returned to the topic that had been at the forefront of her mind every waking moment since Raphael had told her that his heart belonged to another.

'For the hundredth time, I'm begging you to release me. Let me find someone who will place me first in his heart.' As the words spilled out, she realised how pathetic she must sound. Her arguments had no basis in the decision agreed upon by Raphael and Celeste's uncle, her guardian since her father's death five years before. But she had to try; to say what was in her heart. 'Don't tell me I seek a fairytale that doesn't exist. I know I'm surrounded by men and women bound together in marriages that are hateful to them, but I would want to *begin* mine with hope.'

He was restless as usual, his dark, moody eyes scouring her face as if searching for her chink, her weakness; confident, ultimately, that the force of his will would mean her ultimate acquiescence, in words at least.

His thin lips pursed and his glance made no secret of his contempt. 'How many women would dream to be in your position,' he muttered. 'I am offering you the chance to take any lover you choose. All you have to do is what our parents, custodians—and I—wish. Marry me. Once you have done your duty, you can follow your heart, indulge your passions, explore a world of sensuality you have no idea even exists. '

'As you have?'

'I know what I want, I've explored it and I like it. Do you not see, marriage to each other is more than just expedient, it offers us everything we want: companionship and respect for each other, and ultimately the freedom to pursue our every desire beyond the domestic arena.'

'My desire is to be loved by my husband.' She spoke woodenly, despite knowing it would inflame him. Fortunately, he was more on show here. He had to temper his responses.

Still, it was clear he was irritated. Only the fall of lace at his sleeve softened the severity of his expression as he raked his fingers through his hair, though he was careful not to disturb his well-groomed queue. 'Celeste, it is all very well to ask me to release you, but do you suppose your uncle and your Aunt Branwell would countenance your absurdities? Why can you not simply go through with what's expected of us, provide the necessary heir, and then you're free to do whatever you wish—within reason?'

Tears stung her eyes and her throat thickened, making it

hard not to choke on the sob she must hold at bay. In a low voice she muttered, 'Three weeks ago, I proved my love, Raphael—'

She was not expecting the vituperative response. Raphael's eyes blazed with a different intensity now, though his voice was a controlled hiss. 'Yes, but where is Harry Carstairs *now*, my love?'

She'd heard it before. Unable to bear his reproach, she squeezed shut her eyes and clenched her fists. 'All right,' she whispered, 'if it matters neither way to you, and it's my uncle whose absolution is required, would you agree if I found a match that would exceed even a match with you?' Somehow she had to hear him give ground. Ignoring his barb, his reproach that she'd failed in the mission he'd sent her on three weeks earlier, she continued to plead her case. 'What if a contender suddenly emerged with title and estates that eclipsed yours, and I loved him and wished to marry him, what then, Raphael? Would you release me?'

Her cousin made a noise somewhere between a laugh and a snort as he tossed his handsome head and fixed her with his compelling gaze; the gaze she'd once thought indicated his unconditional affirmation for her and her best interests. Now it was hard, though she knew it wasn't anger at her, but at the situation that had suddenly ensnared them so recently. 'That's not very likely within a month, is it, my dear?'

She shook her head, sadly, and her shoulders slumped. 'No,' she replied, defeated. 'It isn't.'

THE LAST OF THE APPLAUSE DRIFTED AWAY AND FOR A FEW seconds the shrill cries of the orange sellers held sway. Rising from his ironic bow for the benefit of his companion, Lord Peregrine held back the red velvet curtain that had afforded them privacy so that Xenia could pass through and join the throng of theatregoers descending the sweeping staircase.

He saw that she had fallen into conversation with a club-footed general whose more than interested eye swept appraisingly over Xenia's abundant assets, and once again Perry felt the familiar heating of his loins that only Xenia could inspire with a mere incendiary glance. The contours of her sack-back gown, adorned with a row of bows the length of her stomacher, recalled the more lascivious of those thoughts he'd entertained for the past decade: what it would be like to undress her, layer by layer by layer. He could only imagine *how* many layers there might be, but the prize would be worth the exquisite torture of restraint. He'd not revealed quite how much her proposition tonight had taken him by surprise, and the fact he'd agreed fuelled him with an odd combination of conflicting sensations: raging lust tempered by the knowledge that he'd just sunk to depths of moral depravity that might make even his uncle squirm in his grave: seduce an innocent on the eve of her nuptials. Except that Xenia maintained the young woman's ingenuousness was a ploy. Still, Miss Rosington retained her standing in society as a paragon of virtue. What right had he to assume otherwise, just because it was convenient?

He was diverted by a squeal to his left. Xenia was moving ahead, caught up by the crowd, her head bent to absorb the admiration of her club- footed general. Peregrine meanwhile found himself unable to continue, due to the fact the young woman in front of him had snagged her skirts on what appeared to be a nail or splinter protruding from one of the supporting beams. No one could move until she'd freed herself, and as Peregrine was directly behind her it was incumbent upon him to act the gentlemen and so enable the rest of the pulsing crowd to forge ahead.

'Please be careful, sir, it'll tear and it's the first time I've worn it,' the young woman warned as he took a handful of stiff silk in one hand. 'It's my finest.' She twisted her head round to address him.

As her lips parted, revealing a set of near perfect small white teeth, and her worried blue eyes bored into his, Peregrine felt a jolt of something unidentifiable plummet like a stone to the pit of his stomach. No, further than that, for without a doubt his groin was reacting with something akin to roiling hunger. And, surprisingly, with an intensity that exceeded the dull throb of ten years of wanting Xenia like a frustrated schoolboy.

Close to, Miss Rosington was exquisite, her pale white and rose-blushed skin far more lustrous than when seen from a distance through opera glasses. Her powdered coiffure, dressed to fashionable heights, accentuated high, rounded cheekbones; and with growing excitement he followed the sweep of her graceful neck to a bosom that was rising and falling with surely greater rapidity than fear of what peril her gown might face. He liked to think that was so, as her candid look met his and the connection between them seemed like the sharp tug of some inner cord, forcing him forward, his hand brushing hers, nestled beneath a froth of silken furbelows, as they both reached for the undamaged silk petticoat, now released.

'No harm done,' he murmured as she drew herself up, her companion, the black-eyed viscount to whom she was affianced, returning to claim her, drawing her away with the barest of thanks.

All over in a matter of seconds, and at what cost? For while silk skirts and dignity had escaped with minimal damage, Peregrine was the first to concede, as he watched her graceful back with pounding heart and aching groin, that a great deal of harm had indeed been done.

'ANY DAMAGE?' RAPHAEL ENQUIRED OVER HIS SHOULDER AS HE drew Celeste level with him. Ridiculously, she felt as if she'd run half a mile, for she was finding it difficult to breathe, constricted as she was by her stays. Not that they were tightly laced for she had the right shape naturally, for the fashions of the day. But Raphael's creased brow sent fear coursing through her as she was reminded of the night three weeks ago when he'd sent her after Harry Carstairs. She stopped and ran clammy hands over her wide skirts. Skirts supported by so many petticoats and layers, tied around her middle; dressing seemed sometimes to take forever. As did undressing, she thought with sinking heart, another image of that fateful night intruding: a room strewn with petticoats, Harry fumbling with the ties, before Miss Charlotte Paige's shrill cry had sent them fleeing in fright. Harry had snatched Celeste's hand, dragging her with him as they passed his horrified betrothed on his way to the front door; then down the passage and through the front door.

Celeste wondered if the young woman still had those discarded petticoats or whether she'd burned them. At the time she'd wanted to say something. To apologise. Explain. She'd thought it might come to that; a full accounting of her actions, but when Miss Paige failed to name her, Raphael had applauded Celeste for a mission accomplished in part.

His satisfaction was short-lived. Weeks later, no word had come from Harry, and Raphael's growing agitation and bursts of anger were increasingly directed at his cousin and future wife, Celeste.

'I asked you if you were unscathed, darling,'

Raphael repeated, an edge of impatience to his voice as Celeste recovered her wits and returned to the here and now.

Unscathed? 'My skirts, you mean?' she asked, hooking her

hand into the crook of Raphael's elbow and patting a curl into place as she affected the unruffled demeanour of the lady of fashion.

'I think that is all I could be referring to, my dear Celeste, for you did not take a tumble, though you certainly look as dazed as if you'd hit your head.' He flicked her an impatient smile. 'You didn't, did you?'

She felt as if she had. The brief glance she'd exchanged with that unknown gentlemen had affected her like no other encounter. His dark penetrating gaze had been more than just unsettling. He'd felt the connection, too. She was sure he had.

Celeste glanced at her skirts and shook her head.

'Good, then I daresay it's time to call it a night. I shall see first you and then Lady Drummond home.' He was brisk and businesslike, as usual, ascertaining her movements for the morrow. 'At noon you'll have the fittings for your wedding finery and I shall see you at nine in the evening at Vauxhall with the rest of our party.' He withdrew a snowy linen hand-kerchief from his coat pocket to flick across the seat of his carriage, before offering his hand to Lady Drummond and then Celeste to help them into the carriage. Such fastidious-ness might appear as solicitous care to some, but Celeste found it irritating beyond extreme, sometimes. Now being one of those occasions. Raphael said he cared deeply about her— and she believed him—but not so deeply that he'd put her feelings above his own, much less on the same level.

She glanced at Lady Drummond, whose wizened face was etched with lines of weariness and whose shoulders sagged, and took a chance. The old woman was all but deaf, she knew.

'Raphael, I want you to release me from this marriage,' she whispered, pretending interest in her ivory fan. 'I am trapped. I cannot cry off. Uncle will never allow it, and the

13

whole world believes you are mad for me. I once thought it, but I cannot marry you, knowing what I know now. Please, release me from this marriage so that I might find a husband who will love me as I would wish to be loved.'

The tautness around Raphael's lips indicated far more than his tone, that he was mightily displeased. 'I don't believe this is a conversation for our short journey home in present company, my dear. Perhaps tomorrow evening we might discuss in greater detail the joys we can look forward to during our long and fruitful union.'

Celeste slid her eyes away from his thunderous expression. 'Of course, you're right as always, Raphael,' she said softly.

And wondered how many times she was condemned to say those exact words in the decades that stretched ahead of her.

CHAPTER 2

*P*eregrine rubbed thoughtfully at his left knee with the sea sponge, careful not to slosh water over the side of the bathtub. Two candle sconces above the mantelpiece cast long shadows across the chamber, which was silent but for the crackle of the fire and the ebb and flow of the bathtub's contents as Peregrine reached up to place his scoring markers on the cribbage board.

'Ha! Trump that!' he muttered softly, as his giant, broad-shouldered Negro manservant, Nelson, bent to study his own cards.

Nelson frowned. 'I accept your challenge, *master*.' The corner of his mouth quirked at the oblique reference to the ambiguous relationship between the two men.

Nelson could not in fact be free under the current legislation, yet it was on account of this slave's heroic actions that Peregrine was still alive today.

Cursing as he conceded a loss at Nelson's next play, Perry relaxed back into the soapy water, stiffening when Nelson, remarked, glancing up from his cards, 'I gather there's trouble a-brewing with Miss Paige, m'lord.' Nelson's English was as impeccable as his master's.

Perry considered the question. In no other servant would he have countenanced such impertinence, but Nelson was not the usual servant.

Until the dramatic incident five years before, when footpads had set upon Perry one night, Nelson had been a silent, obedient footman acquired some years previously to form a matching pair.

However, since Nelson had hurled himself into the fray and succeeded in disarming to the blackguards, and doing a great deal of damage besides, before assisting a seriously wounded Perry back to his home, an unusual bond between the men had been forged. Nelson had been promoted to valet and there had been a great many mutually enjoyable conversations since then between master and servant over the cribbage board in the bathtub.

'Trouble, yes. And more than just a-brewing,' Perry admitted, glad of the opportunity to unburden himself. With the game concluded, Nelson held up a strip of linen to wrap about his master and Perry elaborated. 'It's not just my sister. There's another young lady.'

'There is usually another young lady.' Nelson nodded sagely, the candlelight highlighting his noble features. Nelson had been groomed for the chieftainship before he'd been snatched from his coastal village by slavers.

Clad in his banyan and seated in his dressing room, Peregrine picked up a nail file from his grooming box and toyed with its smooth mother-of-pearl handle. He wondered if Miss Rosington's pale skin would feel as smooth beneath his hands. The mere thought of his immoral wager made his breath quicken with desire but his conscience gave him pause. The woman had the face of an angel, but what of her morals? Xenia would have it seem they were as corrupted as his own.

'I've just returned from visiting my sister who has got it into her head that a certain young lady is the source of all her troubles.'

Charlotte's hysteria had been disconcerting when Peregrine had ventured to suggest she might have been mistaken in identifying Miss Rosington as Harry Carstairs' accomplice. 'Ask her if she knows anything of this, then!' she'd screamed, hurling a gold locket at his head. 'I tore it from Harry's neck as he ran past me.' Peregrine was aware now of the locket's oval contours against the lining of his pocket as he watched Nelson consider the matter. To be sure, the cryptic, half-torn message the locket contained was perplexing, but it was not enough to convict Miss Rosington of the charges Xenia had laid at her door.

'Miss Paige has no husband.' Nelson looked up from folding his master's clothes and his mouth stretched wide in a slow grin. 'If she blames another woman for the fact, I pity that woman. Perhaps you will have to protect her from Miss Paige's ire, m'lord,' he added suggestively. Charlotte was, after all, famous for her hot and cold moods.

Peregrine grunted. 'I'm ashamed to say I'm involved in a scheme to discredit this other young woman, yet the truth is, even if she *is* guilty, I've lost the appetite.'

'Lost the appetite?' Nelson's face contorted into an expression indicating great disgust. 'So she is not a woman you'd care either to besmirch *or* champion?'

'God, no!' Peregrine shook his head emphatically. 'She is angelic. There's the rub. I should be flayed for entering into such devilry.'

'You are an honourable man, m'lord. If you have doubts, I suggest you relinquish your involvement and leave this possibly innocent young woman be,' Nelson said with another sage nod, pausing on the threshold, having brushed and put away Peregrine's coat.

It was as if Nelson was dismissing *him*, Peregrine thought with a mixture of irritation and amusement as Nelson offered him a bow before stepping gracefully backwards.

'I shall do nothing of the sort.' He floundered for a plausible excuse, aware that his motives for furthering his acquaintance with Miss Rosington were cloudy at best. 'Indeed, she may, as you suggest, need my protection,' he added, feebly.

'Then if this young lady is worthy of your protection, my lord, I wish you great joy of her.'

An ambiguous remark, Peregrine reflected as he climbed into his carriage a short while later, and took the short journey across London to Vauxhall Gardens where he was to meet Lady Busselton.

Joy of her? Well, he was fully anticipating more pleasure than pain at the end of all this, but he'd rather he was protected by the usual indifference that ensured he never lost his heart or his head. The truth was Miss Rosington, up close, had unleashed a veritable storm of emotions that denied rational explanation. A visage of such purity surely could not belong to a woman who'd betray her cousin and the man she was to marry. Hers was not the guise of a hardened strumpet capable of destroying his sister's happiness.

Now he was in danger of becoming mawkish. He turned his head away from the gathering group of beggar children chasing his carriage, frowning deeply at the extraordinary conundrum beginning to consume him. A moral dilemma? That would be a first.

Yet if there was more to her behavior than met the eye, Miss Rosington did need to be revealed. And if Perry went through with Xenia's wager and Miss Rosington did indeed throw herself at Perry, as Charlotte claimed she'd done to

Harry Carstairs, then Miss Rosington deserved everything she got.

Suddenly filled with charity, Peregrine tossed a handful of coins out of the carriage window, the corners of his mouth lifting as he looked back to see the children throw themselves upon the spoils like starved animals, their shouts and wails fading as the carriage rounded a bend by the river.

Yes, if the spoils were worth it, he didn't mind getting a little dirty along the way. For ten long years he'd wanted Xenia.

Yet as he drew in a breath laden with anticipation, it was not Xenia's heaving bosom that speared him with excitement.

Ah, Xenia, he sighed, closing his eyes to savour the thought of what shared delights would soon be his for the taking, irritated that instead of Xenia's creamy, sculpted perfection, it was Miss Rosington's fresh-faced visage that nagged at him.

XENIA WAS WITH A GROUP OF FRIENDS. HE HEARD HER trilling laugh before he saw her, causing him to stop as he rounded the Serpentine Walk to admire her confident carriage and the way she threw back her head to respond to a joke made by her companion, the notorious libertine, Sir Samuel Wray.

Sir Samuel had been much in Xenia's company lately. The man fancied himself a poet and was in the habit of composing sonnets proclaiming the virtues of whoever happened to be his latest ladylove. Peregrine could hear him reciting something that suggested Xenia now filled that role. Well, Sir Samuel was to be disappointed. Xenia, for reasons that went further than merely exhorting Perry to prove his brotherly love by unmasking Miss Rosington, had turned her focus upon Peregrine.

And Xenia, he reminded himself, was his sole reason for consorting with Miss Rosington. The ship captain's beautiful daughter was the only woman he'd ever truly desired, and now that she'd offered him the key to her favours, he was not about to be diverted by a fresh-faced ingénue who either was complicit in his sister's shame or, if not, was an innocent who'd not yet cut her teeth on sophisticated society and so could hold no interest for Peregrine.

As Peregrine approached he noted that the only disguise Xenia wore tonight was a masque. Amidst her hair, powdered and ringletted as was the fashion, nestled a replica galleon, a tribute to her papa; or more specifically, her papa's generosity. Though Xenia's lavish wardrobe was, to all intents and purposes, funded by two wealthy late husbands, Peregrine suspected money was going to be a problem if his beautiful friend continued her spendthrift ways. Fortunately, if rumours were to be believed—and the increase in her father's fleet suggested they were—Captain Alfred Higgin's trade appeared to be going from strength to strength. As long as the captain was alive there'd always be someone to indulge Xenia's rapacious appetites.

Perry stopped and smiled as Xenia pushed away from her coterie of admirers, having locked gazes with him. She'd had too much to drink and as she draped herself upon Peregrine she hiccupped, kissing his ear untidily.

'Darling Perry, I thought you'd never come and rescue me,' she crooned. 'I've been bored to distraction, surrounded by oafs.'

'Very poetic oafs. I heard Sir Samuel's ode to your matchless beauty and divine purity. Have you set your sights on making him your next husband?'

'Silly man. You and he, both.' She hiccupped again and

took his hand, resting it against her heaving bosom. 'See what you do to me. Perhaps *you'll* be my next husband.'

He laughed, not imagining she could be serious. 'I've known you too long, Xenia. Your foibles and extravagant fancies would make a poor man of me.'

'But I would be worth it,' she murmured, her breath tickling his ear before he felt the whisper of her fan unfurling, her eyes gleaming with promise over the top.

'I've no doubt you would, Xenia.' With a wry grin and an unsteady tattoo of his heart, Peregrine pushed her gently aside before she could deepen the display of intimacy. Curiously, he was unsettled by her words when once he'd have crossed crocodile-infested waters for it to be so.

'I will be more than worth it once you're done with little Miss Rosington.' She wasn't ready to let the subject go. 'She's here tonight, did you know? A water sprite and very pretty with her dark hair tumbling down her back. No doubt that's what Harry Carstairs thought too before she burned him at her flame. Don't forget to ask her what has become of poor Mr Carstairs while you're busy with your little seduction.' She put her face close to his. 'There has been neither sight nor sound of him since he fled like a coward into the night. Perhaps he jilted Miss Rosington too and she's had him murdered.' She drew in a ragged breath and pointed, her words slightly slurred. 'Why, there she is, Perry. Over there by the fountain. Her cousin is taking her into the rotunda to dance. What a handsome couple they make. So in love, everyone says. But you and I know better. Let's show the world the truth, shall we? Go on, Perry, ask her for the next dance. Pretend you're new in London and have no idea who she is. I'm sure she'll not know you as Charlotte's brother. No, this is her first season out. She'll never suspect *you*.'

PEREGRINE NEEDED NO URGING. HE WAS CONFIDENT MISS Rosington would not know him as Charlotte's brother.

But would she remember him after their brief meeting at the theatre? The thought intrigued him as he bowed before her when he caught her alone. Her betrothed was procuring her something to drink while the old woman he presumed was her chaperone was nodding her chin companionably with another old crone in the gloom a few feet away.

Perry surmised Miss Rosington had been about to snub him, but as he rose from his bow her startled gaze and sudden stillness revealed she clearly recognised him; and his own heart echoed what he surely saw she felt: the jolt of surprised awareness. Her rosebud mouth dropped slightly open and her eyes brightened.

He saw, also, the quick glance she sent over her shoulder and he followed her glance in the direction of her cousin, who'd been detained by a rotund and voluble gentleman in a bag wig and a gold-figured red and cream coat and black silk pantaloons. Perhaps Miss Rosington considered he would keep her betrothed occupied, for with a slight incline of her head she put her hand on Peregrine's arm to allow him to lead her several steps into the shadows.

'Thank you for the service you rendered me last night, sir,' she murmured. 'Naturally we must pretend to have been introduced.'

'Call me your rescuer incognito, but let me say you were very brave, Miss …?' He ended on an enquiring note and she supplied him with her name, before Peregrine suggested, 'But we *have* met, Miss Rosington. Do you not recall the terrible snowstorm from which I plucked you and your aunt when your carriage axle broke? Why, you'd have frozen to death had I not been able to provide you with the sanctuary of my equipage.'

Instantly she caught on. 'It seems you are always on hand

to render me assistance, sir. And indeed it was a fine tavern to which you conveyed us while the wheelwright was called. The innkeeper's daughter brought the lightest madeleines I've ever tasted, while the conversation was uncommonly diverting. I don't believed I offered you sufficient thanks for your chivalry; and for your company in general, which I might say was brought into sharp relief by having to endure that of my dreary aunt for the next four hours.'

He liked her quick humour. 'Then now is your chance, Miss Rosington, for I *shall* think of some way you can thank me. In the meantime, might I be permitted to compliment you on your raven locks? I barely recognised you, and may not again once you defer to the powder puff to which all you ladies seem addicted.'

'It is not only the ladies, sir. You also look very different without your wig. You have very fine eyes. I could not miss those.'

'A very pretty compliment.' He grinned, feeling ridiculously pleased by this little exchange. But he was also aware of Miss Rosington's cousin in the distance, looking over his shoulder. He bowed. 'Sadly and with huge regret, I must retire before I am chased away for making unwanted overtures.' An unexpected thrill surged through him as he turned away from the sight of Miss Rosington looking after him with such clear interest in her lovely blue eyes.

Had Xenia not been watching, he might have been less guarded in his response. But now his old friend was gliding up to grip his wrist as he returned to her orbit, whispering in his ear, 'She is smitten, if ever I've seen a woman lusting after a man, Perry. Ah, but you were lucky. She will be a nice, easy fish to reel in. Watch her closely, for I believe she'll look for any opportunity to elude her gaolers and you must be waiting.'

CELESTE HADN'T REALISED SHE'D BEEN STARING INTO THE darkness like a moon-eyed green girl until Raphael reclaimed her attention with a tug at the lace at her wrists.

'Worshipping the stars, my dear, or have you seen a vision?'

Somehow he managed to imbue everything with an irony that implied she was lacking in some way. As a child they'd played and tumbled together, but when Raphael had come down from university he had developed a worldly air that suggested his cleverness was not easily matched. And certainly not by Celeste, whom he treated with condescending fondness, as if she must be cared for, and by him, like any of the other vacuous females of his closer acquaintance he loved to ridicule.

'Perhaps I have seen a vision, Raphael.' She smiled as she brought her attention back to him. 'Perhaps it was a shining vision with a golden wand, dispensing words of wisdom.'

'Well, tell me? What words of wisdom did it dispense, then?'

'It said I must follow my heart.'

'You have a perfectly sound head, my dear. I think the sensible thing would be to follow the voice of reason. Hearts have a habit of behaving erratically. They are not to be trusted. Not like common sense.'

Celeste sighed and declined to pursue the topic. He would not sanction her desire to end their betrothal and besides, what choice did she have? She was to be married within three weeks to the man she'd happily accepted as her husband-to-be before she was old enough to understand.

What foolishness was it that she should imagine an alternative future?

THE NIGHT WAS STILL AND WARM WITH A TWINKLING OF STARS overhead. Celeste took comfort in their constancy as she told herself Raphael would be a good husband, regardless of whether he pledged his heart to another. That was the tragedy of it. She believed *she* could train her heart to take her marriage in good part, if she'd not learned the truth of exactly what a sham this marriage would be from the start.

Murmuring her intention to return shortly, as Raphael was caught up in conversation with a lively group of gentlemen, she took a couple of steps away, intending to greet an acquaintance she'd met at a number of her aunt's *salons*. A glance at her chaperone reassured her that the old woman was thoroughly engrossed in gossiping with a stout matron by a tree.

'Miss Leddings,' Celeste began, only to find the young lady she'd intended to address gone. Unexpectedly alone, she turned on her heel as she prepared to resume her position at Raphael's side. 'You appear lost, Miss Rosington? No chaperone? Perhaps you'd allow me to return you to your friends, though being alone in my company for even those few seconds might be dangerous. I would strongly warn you against it.'

A hanging lantern revealed the now familiar face of the gentleman she'd met earlier, cast in shadows and planes, his admiration apparent. It thrilled her, forbidden though it was. Of course she should smile politely, to soften her rebuttal, then take a few steps into the light towards Raphael.

Instead she said softly, 'Sometimes a dangerous offer is too tempting to resist—if it were but for a moment.' Such words had never issued from her mouth and she trembled violently as she observed the surprise with which he offered her his arm.

'Ten steps to the left would have you amidst the milling crowd and is where I strongly suggest I lead you.' He paused, his voice suddenly husky. 'However, I can recommend a pleasant detour with little more than ten steps into the darkness in the opposite direction. It would be dangerous to choose this direction, but it's the one *I* strongly favour.'

For a moment common sense swept aside her rash daring, for what possible reason could he have for leading her to a secluded part of the gardens than to take liberties that, if discovered, could ruin her?

She was not such a fool. But oh, she was tempted.

Unable to make a clear decision, she wavered. 'Why are you always at my shoulder, sir? I could almost imagine you are following me.'

'And why should that come as a surprise to the most beautiful woman in the gardens tonight? I thought it when you turned and gazed at me at the opera on Thursday. When you'd gone I believed I must have imagined such luminescence. Now my eyes assure me I did not.'

'A very pretty speech, sir. Do you use it on all the ladies?'

'Only those whose acquaintance I wish to further. You are not … attached to that gentlemen with whom I saw you earlier? I might think your beauty unrivalled but I am not a libertine. I would wish to know if you are free to bestow your attentions upon me.'

She hesitated for the merest second before replying quickly, 'Raphael is my cousin. He often accompanies me to such places.' She tilted her head to smile at him. Artless and encouraging, and Peregrine felt a curious surge of excitement, but disappointment too. For she had lied to him. By omission, at any rate.

Drawing her, unresisting, a short distance away into the darkness, he murmured, 'Then if you are so bold as to court the attentions of a dangerous stranger, I would be so bold as to ask for a kiss.' Her transparent, clearly unfeigned shock heightened his desire. So she was not in the habit of making conquests, as Xenia suggested her dealings with Harry Carstairs implied.

Her eyelids fluttered closed as she ran the tip of her tongue across her top lip. Experimenting? Priming it? He gave her barely a chance to do either before he swooped to seize the moment, nestling her against his chest while he gently traced the line of her beautiful mouth with his thumb.

Her body tensed before she melted in his embrace, responding with fleeting but impassioned ardour when her mouth fused with his, sealing his desire with a kiss of such incendiary passion he could almost believe it sufficient to incinerate them both.

Brief as it was passionate, for suddenly she was pushing him away, spinning on her heel to gain distance, her shocked face illuminated by the lantern hanging from the branches of a nearby tree.

'I don't know what came over me. It defies rational explanation.' She put her fingers to her lips, as if she could not believe what they'd been subjected to. 'Please excuse my reckless behavior.'

'I would prefer to encourage it.'

She opened her mouth to say more, then added simply, 'Goodnight, sir.'

When Peregrine blinked again she was gone and he was left standing alone beneath the spreading branches of a plane tree, his brief elation swept away by disappointment and another feeling that he was not prepared to identify. One he'd felt when his older and favourite cousin no longer had any wish to deal with him. But surely devastation was too strong a word for what was a calculated conquest that took no account of the heart?

CELESTE CRESTED THE HILL TO FIND HERSELF ALMOST UPON Raphael and his cohorts. He was laughing, in fine humour, and so fortunately responded to her slight disorder with careless concern.

'Communing with the Vauxhall ghost, my dear? Here, a glass of champagne will have you up to the mark. My friend Sir Samuel has just been telling me the latest *on-dit*. Apparently Lord Peregrine's sister is about to take Holy Orders after she was, to all intents and purposes, jilted at the altar.' Raphael clapped Sir Samuel on the back in a gesture of uncharacteristic bonhomie, which Celeste recognised for what it was: a deliberate attempt to wheedle more out of Sir Samuel.

'Jilted at the altar? Yes, I heard it, but this is old news. Poor young woman. Have you any idea why?' Dry-mouthed, Celeste asked the question required of her, relieved when Sir Samuel raised his palms in a gesture of helplessness. 'The question is on everyone's lips, Miss Rosington.'

'As is the whereabouts of the prospective groom, no doubt.' Celeste, though still highly discomposed by her recent encounter, was sharp enough to seize her opportunity. It would be one less matter to displease Raphael when he called her to account later that evening.

Sir Samuel raised his eyes heavenward. 'The man has not yet settled his account after I won a tidy sum from him just before he went to Jamaica. Now he is back, but disappeared within a day of disembarking upon English soil. Miss Paige is not the only one who would like to know where Harry Carstairs is.'

Celeste was aware of Raphael's eyes trained on her. Waiting. Obediently she asked, 'Has there been no word from Mr Carstairs at all? I believe he was visiting his plantation in

Jamaica and had returned to England to claim an inheritance and marry Miss Paige. Perhaps he received a chilly reception from Miss Paige and decided to return to warmer climes.'

Sir Samuel smiled thinly. 'I hope not. If he's on the high seas then I will not see what's owed me, will I?' He changed the subject. 'You're looking uncommonly fetching this evening, Miss Rosington, if it's not too bold to say in front of your intended. I'm sure the end of the month can't come soon enough, when you'll become mistress of estates, both here and in Jamaica, and the envy of half the women of the realm.'

This time it was Celeste's turn to offer what was, at best, a thin smile in return. 'Indeed, Sir Samuel,' she replied, touching her lips, which still burned from the most exciting, illicit kiss she'd ever experienced.

CHAPTER 3

*D*uring a brief moment of solitude in his dressing room, Peregrine leaned over his desk, searching for answers in the puzzling ruins of the message contained in the gold locket his sister had thrust unceremoniously at him. He'd have preferred to have remained in his red velvet upholstered armchair, enjoying the quiet and the warmth of the fire in his dressing room, but soon Nelson would be on hand to dress him for a dinner he was to attend in honour of his old friend, Lord Cowdril, for his elevation to the House of Lords. A house party attended by more guests would follow.

Straining to see the letters more clearly in the weak light, he traced his forefinger over the crumpled, partly destroyed parchment: 'este immediately ...'

Charlotte maintained that 'este' referred to the last letters of Miss Rosington's Christian name, but Perry was not convinced. He tapped the tiny locket, which had also contained the miniature of Charlotte behind which the scrap of paper had been hidden, stuck to the glue when the rest of the note had presumably been torn out. When the time was right he'd find a way to bring up with Miss Rosington the subject of that night, when the locket had been lost. First, though, he had to gain her trust.

He smiled, savouring the image he had of her, all wide-eyed horror at the scandal of the month—for of course she'd deny involvement initially— before he once again plundered her mouth.

While she, of course, would be entirely amenable. No ... he smiled. Delightfully responsive.

His mood was lightened by the arrival of the dignified Nelson, with whom he struck up a lively conversation on the evils of strong liquor. Nelson made him laugh like few others of his acquaintance. Nelson's keen eye also ensured Perry appeared a cut above the rest, which tonight had him dressed in a brocade coat, richly embroidered in cherry and silver, a cream and buff waistcoat and navy pantaloons.

Reluctant to venture out into the cold once his toilette was complete, Perry paused longer than usual to admire his reflection in the cheval mirror. Idly he asked, 'Do I appear the Devil Incarnate, Nelson?' He ran his finger around the inside of his stock. 'Do you shudder when you behold me, knowing that my sins go deeper than mere fondness for strong spirits?'

'The Devil Incarnate, my lord?' Nelson asked in his precise English, his eloquent shrug conveying as much as his words. He looked as imposing as his lordship in his gold and royal blue livery. 'To me, you are a fine master. To the rest of the world, you are who you choose to be.'

Nelson's response took him aback and Perry sighed with the closest he'd come to genuine regret, as a picture of past exploits and future, equally underwhelming examples of moral behaviour, flashed before his eyes. 'I fear that it was written in my stars the moment I was born that I am beyond redemption, Nelson. My father counselled me to resist the temptations of the flesh, of greed and jealousy, though I was only nine when he died. He said I must be a better man than he; that like himself, I might realise this truth through the unexpected offices of a good woman. It happened when he met my mother.' He sighed again. 'But it's not going to happen to me, Nelson. No *good* woman with a brain likely to interest me would touch me with a ten-foot pole. My uncle confirmed it.' He smiled wryly. 'Alas, I cannot change fate.'

'Fate is changed by those brave enough to battle the more difficult road, my lord.'

But Peregrine was not ready to go down this particular philosophical path. 'See if my carriage is ready, Nelson,' he said, smoothing his queue as he turned away from his reflection. 'And don't wait up for me. I anticipate a late night.'

Half an hour later, strolling the length of the family portraits lining the walls of Lord Cowdril's Long Gallery, he halted when he spied Xenia's elegant coiffure above the gold and cream striped sofa.

'Lady Busselton, why am I not surprised to find you here?'

'Indeed, why should you be surprised over anything after my cleverness in setting up yesterday's little Vauxhall tryst?' Her bright blue eyes sparkled as she twisted her head. 'But, Perry, there are a few matters you'd do well to bear in mind if we're to ensure the outcome is as satisfactory as required.'

'As satisfactory as required ...' He repeated her words in a thoughtful tone as he took a seat beside her after a perfunctory bow. 'What exactly do you consider satisfactory, Xenia? I'm curious, for reflection has me wondering if there might be greater depths to your interest in all this.'

She looked indignant. 'I am a dear friend of Charlotte's. Indeed, your sister is like the sister I never had, so of course I want to see her avenged."

Peregrine nodded slowly. 'A thousand pardons if I have

insulted you, but Xenia, there is usually some ulterior motive —deeper than would appear—behind everything you do.'

Xenia fluttered her fan with even greater enthusiasm. 'Have I not been transparent, Perry? I want Miss Rosington exposed … I want to see her reputation in tatters as part payment of the terrible cruelty she's imposed on your good sister. And then I want you.' Her smile was more a simper, and for the first time Peregrine wasn't felled by a spear of lust at the mere thought of Xenia's naked body writhing beneath his own. Rather, his mind was occupied by the conundrum occasioned by the mixed responses he had to Miss Rosington and the consequences of … exposing *her*.

Harlot and husband-stealer? She'd certainly been responsive to Peregrine's overtures, but not in the way that suggested either epithet applied. And Peregrine was certainly speared by lust at the very thought of having *her* naked body writhing beneath his. Yet ruining her publicly was another matter.

He took up the dish of tea Xenia offered him and smiled at her pique over the rim. Yes, it was true that the last time anyone had seen his sister's betrothed was in a tumble of Miss Rosington's petticoats. It was also true that the last four letters of Miss Rosington's name were written on a note found concealed in the locket Charlotte had ripped from Harry Carstairs' neck that fateful night.

Certainly, if Miss Rosington needed to be called to account, Peregrine was very happy to be just the man to do that. But he would not do so without conclusive evidence.

Xenia raised one finely arched and darkened eyebrow as she patted the seat beside her. 'I have it all planned. Won't Miss Rosington's heart be aflutter when she's introduced to the handsome stranger who whisked her into his arms at Vauxhall the other night? What a surprise that you *both* find yourselves house guests of Lord and Lady Cowdril?' She gave a little laugh. 'Well, I will confess to a little meddling, but *you* will be the one to discover everything you need to know about the circumstances surrounding Harry Carstairs' flight into the night.' She held out a languid hand in invitation for Perry to come closer.

In other circumstances Peregrine would have caged the dainty little ring-encrusted hand she placed upon his thigh as he obeyed her summons, but today he felt a very real disinclination for contact.

Xenia raised an eyebrow, as if she sensed his reserve. 'Just remember, my dear Perry,' she said softly, 'that it's not worth falling in love with the little baggage.'

One glance at her hard, beautiful face reminded Peregrine that Xenia was not one to cross.

CELESTE WAS RELIEVED AT THE OPPORTUNITY HER AUNT Branwell offered to be away from the stifling scrutiny of her betrothed for a couple of days.

Her aunt and her mother had been childhood friends of their hostess, Lady Cowdril, who had surprisingly, at the last minute, extended her invitation, saying how delightful it would be to include 'little Celeste' in the small house party at their riverfront estate.

Celeste was now enjoying her couple of days' respite from Raphael's unrelenting pressure, her mind occupied by handsome dark-eyed strangers as she sat beside her aunt, both in heavy, straight- backed chairs that had been hauled outside by the servants and set up on the grassy bank. Several other guests lounged nearby, drinking tea, while her aunt dispensed advice.

'So you might not be as overwhelmingly enamoured of your husband-to-be as we would all wish, but it is mayhap a blessing in disguise.' Lady Branwell had correctly surmised the reason for her niece's lack of spirits and was pursuing a topic Celeste would rather have left alone. Her marriage was inevitable; discussing it was akin to worrying a wound with a thorn.

Aunt Branwell fluttered her sandy lashes over thoughtful hazel eyes. She'd always been kind to Celeste. 'I had much for which to be grateful in my marriage to poor Joshua, so recently carried away by that terrible fever. I never loved him—nor wished to, as you appear to deem important—but as a husband he offered me freedom I could not have enjoyed as a spinster.' She gazed a moment at a family of ducks breaking the surface of the smooth water, then directed Celeste a candid stare. 'Now, as a widow, I've secured all the freedom I could wish for. I can think of no better husband than Raphael for one of your flightiness, Celeste.'

Celeste merely raised an eyebrow. If her aunt considered her flighty there was nothing to be gained by objecting. Aunt Branwell did not like to be contradicted. Her aunt had never been a beauty, but she'd been clever at cementing a position of relative power and influence within her own household. Celeste suspected her late uncle Joshua was enjoying a lot more freedom six feet under than he had when he was living.

'It's time to take a turn about the gardens. Come, Celeste.' With an imperious nod of her head the older woman rose and put her hand on her niece's forearm. 'You are young and beautiful with the world at your feet, if you only knew how to engineer matters to your own pleasing. Do not make too much of your objections to Raphael. If he's formed other interests, disregard them. It's a wife's duty to turn a blind eye, but do not forget that it also bolsters your own position when can follow your own interests after the line is secured.'

Celeste cast a horrified look at her aunt but was

prevented from responding by the arrival of Lady Cowdril, who had left her indoors guests.

'The weather is smiling on us, ladies. Come, let us walk. Cowdril is with the gentlemen, no doubt settling up after last night. I've been assured the damage is not too dire, though my husband declares he's determined to win back what he lost at the whist table. Not that I have any great hopes on the matter, especially with the arrival of our new guest. Lord Peregrine is a notable player.'

Celeste froze. Lord Peregrine. The brother of the woman Harry Carstairs was to marry? *Here*? Her heart began to hammer and her throat closed up. She'd never met the gentleman who was considered a prize catch and a notable philanderer, and she never wanted to. Especially not now, for what if his sister had indeed recognised Celeste as the woman who'd rushed into the night with her betrothed, Harry Carstairs?

'My dear, you look pale,' remarked Lady Cowdril with furrowed brow. 'Perhaps you're not up to a walk.'

Celeste shook her head. 'I think a walk is just what I need,' she replied faintly. She certainly didn't want to be indoors, where the gentlemen would be on hand to greet their anticipated guest. Perhaps she could find some excuse to miss dinner. Though surely if the viscount had been made aware of Celeste's role in his sister's predicament, he'd have called her to account by now.

It was all she could take comfort from.

LORD COWDRIL'S FAMILY SEAT DATED BACK TO ELIZABETHAN times, with neat gravelled paths and formal gardens providing a charming venue for gentle exercise.

Lady Cowdril, who was easily exerted, never went

beyond the second tier of rose bushes, she declared, due to her palpitating heart. However, the opening lines of her sentence, suggesting a return to the house, was truncated by a start of clear delight and rapid *volte face*.

'Perry will give me his arm,' she declared in robust tones, and they all turned to observe a figure issue from the front portico and down the steps, advancing towards them.

Perry? Celeste raised her eyebrows in a silent question regarding the identity of their new visitor, but as he was nearly upon them she followed the cue of the rest of her party: curtseying as she inclined her head in greeting of the arrival whose tall frame was coming into focus. Though to be sure, no one's heart could be pounding as fiercely as hers, even Lady Cowdril's in the midst of one of her palpitations.

She ventured a glance from beneath lowered lashes. He was impressive, even from a distance. Unusually, he wore his dark hair naturally, tied in a queue at the back, with informal country attire: knee breeches and knee boots with a dark wool coat. Yes, even from a distance she saw his eyes were very piercing.

Swallowing with difficulty, she was alarmed to observe, as he approached, that they were focused on her. Could it be that this gentleman, whose features were gaining greater distinction with every step, did indeed know her for her role in his sister's distress?

She frowned as she noticed his full lips were curved in a smile; a smile that seemed *only* for her; and her heart did a skittering dance at the clear interest of this inimitable Viscount Peregrine as he rounded the rose bushes and finally came to stand in full view before them.

Dear Lord. Cognisance was like a stone dropping to the pit of her stomach. Those lips had covered hers not two nights before in a secluded arbour at Vauxhall Gardens. Those arms had held her against him in a lust-filled moment of abandonment. Sweet Mercy, but Perry—whoever he really was to Lady Cowdril—was Celeste's handsome stranger.

She stood aside in rigid panic as the formalities were conducted. It only grew worse. This was Viscount Peregrine? Her heart rate ratcheted up several more notches. What would he say? How would he respond? Would he reveal her for the bold strumpet he no doubt thought her? Would she still be able to hold her head high by the end of the house party?

When, by some strange rearrangement of pairings, she found herself walking by his side, having no choice but to rest her hand on the forearm he offered her, she had completely lost the power of speech.

Lady Cowdril had managed one more turn around the rose bushes before seating herself with Celeste's Aunt Branwell. However, the viscount, or Perry as everyone called him, had evinced a strong desire to admire the roses, calling upon Celeste's recently lauded expertise.

The kindling look he sent her as they paused by the blooming bushes brought a surely far more vibrant bloom to her cheeks.

Lowering his head, as if to elicit some opinion on a deep red, velvet rose, he murmured, 'Ah, the Apothecary's Rose.' He raised an eyebrow. 'Now I have you all to myself.'

She wasn't sure what to make of his words. Should she start with an abject apology for her behavior? A *declaration* she was not in the habit of consorting with strange men? Neither seemed appropriate when his eyes were twinkling with suppressed humour. Bending to smell the rose, she managed, 'I prefer to call it by its less pedestrian name, the Red Rose of Lancaster.' Self-consciously, she brushed an escaped strand of hair from her cheek. Then, summoning up all her courage, she whispered as she cast him an appealing look, 'Should I be afraid?'

The look he levelled upon her was one of singular calculation. He chuckled. 'Woe betide The House of Lancaster, for they did not prevail, did they? Hmm, Miss Rosington, your question depends on your assessment of our unexpected little encounter the other night. Was it pleasing, or were you never more relieved than when I melted into the dark? I must say, it really is the most extraordinary coincidence to find you here, when I'd thought never to lay eyes on you again.' Plucking the rose, he handed it to her with a bow. 'Perhaps the Rose of Lancaster will one day be an emblem of victory, but for my purposes right now, please accept it as a token of peace.' He straightened, that wicked, difficult-to-interpret smile tugging at the corners of his mouth. 'Nevertheless, to return to the subject of our little encounter … As I'd planned to rectify that little matter and ensure I was in a position to lay more than my eyes upon you again, Miss Rosington, perhaps you could say that fate has played into my hands most unexpectedly. You are even more ravishing in the harsh light of day than you were when last we met.'

Celeste shot him a startled look, mixed emotions roiling within her as she found him smiling down at her with both amusement and calculation.

'You are too kind, my lord,' she murmured, dropping her eyes as she took the rose, stepping forward to resume their walk. His words were both shocking but curiously exciting. She glanced at the ladies to ensure she was not likely to become the latest subject of their gossip, but they were well occupied with their own gossiping, and half obscured by the rose bushes.

'A very pretty blush for a maiden who must be accustomed to having praise lavished upon her. So you are a friend of Lady Cowdril? Or your aunt is?'

'I've known Lady Cowdril since I was a child. I did not

know who you were, my lord. I don't know what you must think of my—'

He stayed her rush to lay bare her shame with a finger upon her lips. His lips quirked and his dark eyes seemed to smoulder with everything that swirled between them. Again she felt the sharp rush of sensation spear her belly; the sensation that was familiar to her only in the presence of this gentleman.

'Your behaviour came from the heart, Miss Rosington, for if you did not know who I was, then I can only be delighted that you found my attentions so pleasing based purely on your honest reaction to me as an ordinary man. You have no idea how delightful that is to a gentleman such as myself, who is constantly fielding off advances.'

His smile, warmer now, more sincere, made Celeste's heart hammer even harder. So he didn't condemn her? Nor, it seemed, had he drawn any association between her and his sister.

Thank the good Lord.

He also seemed to misconstrue the extent of her relief for something else, together with her apparent willingness to pursue that which began by a hanging lantern on a plane tree in Vauxhall. For now he had taken her hand, a gesture concealed by the lush greenery, and one that was doing extraordinary things to Celeste's equilibrium.

He put his head close to hers and she closed her eyes and inhaled with excitement the fragrant breeze bearing the scent of roses. 'I can't tell you how much I anticipate the following two days,' he murmured, 'now that we have been thrown together in this singular way.'

Celeste opened her eyes to see him straighten, a regretful smile tugging at the corner of his oh so kissable mouth. 'Now, your aunt is signalling to you, but before you go to her ...' He hesitated, bending slightly to take her hands. 'I'd like you to know that I shall be admiring the daffodils beneath the mulberry tree by the lake just before dinner. Ten minutes before we are due into the dining room, in fact.' He straightened, dropping her hands, and for one thrilling moment Celeste imagined he was about to brush her cheek with his fingertips.

'Until later, Miss Rosington ...'

Celeste blinked stupidly as he offered her an elegant bow before turning on his heel as Lady Branwell came to claim her.

She was still in a daze when her aunt began describing the details of some titillating *on-dit* to which she'd just been made privy, no doubt intended as a salutary warning on the need for becoming chasteness in her niece.

Celeste was not in the mood to heed any kind of moral guidance right now. Clearly, there could be no misinterpreting the viscount's single-minded interest. If she had half a brain, or at least any consideration for her reputation, she knew she should nip this in the bud. She should certainly not for a moment consider meeting Lord Peregrine alone, anywhere, under any circumstances.

But her heart hammered nevertheless at the interest this handsome, raven-haired scion of elegance and refinement showed in her; and she felt the tug of something deeper than superficial desire, although that on its own was compelling enough to throw caution to the winds.

'Celeste, are you chasing after fairies or are you coming indoors with us?'

Celeste raised her head to attend to her aunt. Was she chasing fairies, she wondered as she trailed after the two older women?

Or was Celeste chasing after the first very real prospect of something that might flourish from her barren heart and offer her a happiness she would never know with Raphael?

CHAPTER 4

*C*eleste paced her bedchamber in an agony of indecision. There was nothing to be gained other than exposure and ruin should she indulge in this wicked, clandestine meeting just before dinner.

Unless it was to make clear to him that under *no* circumstances would she risk her good name by indulging in wicked, clandestine meetings with the presumptuous said viscount, now or in the future. Obviously she'd overstepped all notions of proper behaviour at Vauxhall Gardens, and she needed to ensure he understood she would on no account be up for such adventures again.

It was that which determined her, for the truth was she was too restless to remain in her dressing room and hope that her failure to materialise would send the required message. No, far better to see the viscount in person and make it clear that she was betrothed, that she deeply regretted her shameful impropriety but that she could never find herself alone with Lord Peregrine again.

The trouble was that ten minutes later, beneath the mulberry tree, at the requisite moment, midway through spouting her rehearsed little speech, the deeply interested, smouldering look of that gentleman almost completely undid her. His close proximity made the constriction of her stays almost unbearable, while her throat thickened so much she could barely push out the words, though she tried valiantly enough.

As she floundered while trying to explain that she could never see him alone again, he considered her words thoughtfully, his long shadow easier for Celeste to focus on than his face, which she now thought the handsomest of any she'd gazed upon.

'What you're saying, Miss Rosington, is that you allowed your heart to rule your head. That while you are pledged to your cousin you were swayed by your physical impulses, which is your excuse for kissing me.'

She knew she must appear like a gaping fish, yet still the rest of the words needed to make sense of her sentence refused to come.

'Kissing you *back*, my lord,' she finally corrected him. 'I am not in the habit of such rash and inexcusable behaviour. In fact, I have never been so close to any gentleman stranger, alone, in such circumstances.'

He took a step closer and circled her waist, and though the she gasped with surprise she did not move back. No, she closed her eyes and swayed in his embrace, her mind drinking in his words, delivered in a compelling, husky murmur, as if they were some drug.

'So despite your nuptials nearly upon you, you are telling me that when I strayed into your orbit you were impelled by impulses beyond your control to seek alternative excitement. Namely, that which I offered?'

She opened her eyes briefly, registering a flare of indignation, for he made her sound no better than a strumpet.

But with his face only inches away from hers, her

defences crumbled. With a brief incline of her head she opened her mouth to admit that this was exactly the case; and then his lips were on hers, a sweet touch that instantly turned her into a melting puddle of desire.

Raphael had never kissed her and Celeste knew he never would. So she savoured the moment, surrendering entirely to the soft, teasing touch of his hand that cupped the back of her neck, offering no resistance when the arm about her waist pulled her closer. The feel of his hard chest pressing against her breasts fired off desires she'd never experienced, strong and confusing, coursing through her body which seemed to succumb to an almost mindless, euphoric ecstasy. It was this which galvanised her into pushing him away; this unfamiliar lack of self-control when she had spent a lifetime obeying strictures.

Her future was arranged. It was only now she realised how foolish and impossible were her ideas of marrying to please her heart. The gorgeous philandering viscount embracing her knew she was to be wed in two weeks. This alone was well nigh the reason he considered himself safe in making up to her. He was certainly not about to declare he couldn't live without her and make her a marriage offer within the requisite time to free Celeste from a lifetime bound to Raphael.

Moreover, he was dangerous; not just for the feelings he unleashed in her but the fact he was Miss Paige's brother.

So what was Celeste doing out by the mulberry tree, alone...yes, with a man reputed to be a libertine? Sheltered she might be, yet she had heard the stories—she should be deporting herself with the decorum required as Raphael, Lord Ogilvy's future wife. Hadn't Raphael said he would give her license to follow her heart? Well, that was only on the basis that no hint of scandal be attached to her for the first years of her marriage. Later, with Raphael's family line secured, she could do as she wished. Her future husband had said so in just those words. Though what desires she might choose to pursue in Jamaica was another matter.

Oh Lord, but it all sounded so sordid. She didn't want such affairs to be her only means of satisfying the needs of her heart.

'Where are you going?'

He sounded surprised when he yielded sufficiently to look into her face. She might almost have believed he was genuinely disappointed as she shook her head, pushing completely out of his arms and saying over her shoulder as she turned, 'I've made a terrible mistake in coming here, my lord,' before she fled back to the house.

CELESTE HAD GAINED SUFFICIENT COUNTENANCE TO FACE THE viscount over the dinner table during dinner, though she avoided his eyes. It was the only way she could keep the heat from her cheeks and form coherent sentences as she was engaged in conversation by the vicar on her left.

When the subject turned to trade in Jamaica, she felt the blood thrum through her veins and, glancing down, the blush that spread from her bosom upwards. She only hoped that what was noticeable to her would be dismissed as the heat by everyone else.

What if Harry Carstairs' name were to be brought up? The disappearance of the wealthy Jamaican plantation owner was bound to become a topic of discussion.

Especially when he was to have married the sister of the man sitting across from her, Lord Peregrine.

With sinking heart, Celeste picked at her food. He'd not know that she had just as much reason for finding Harry as he did.

'I hear the captain of the *Batavia's* put in a hefty insurance claim for the loss of so many slaves on the high seas,' Lord Cowdril remarked as he tucked into his beef. His deep voice cut across the tinkling conversation, which dulled to a murmur before all ears were on what was apparently the latest *on-dit*.

'Slaves?' His wife raised her eyebrows. 'An insurance claim? Well, a lucrative commodity whose loss would surely hurt the captain's pocket, to be sure.'

'Yet a human being, with all due respect, Lady Cowdril?' Lord Peregrine looked more enquiring than combative, though Celeste heard the edge to his voice. She was surprised to see that the lips, which had claimed hers with both tenderness and passion so recently, were set in a hard line.

Lord Cowdril dabbed at the goose fat dribbling down his chin. 'Ain't your manservant a slave, Perry? Don't know how you can sleep at night for fear he'll cut your throat.'

Lord Peregrine raised an eyebrow as he carefully put down his cutlery. 'I've never had a more loyal manservant than Nelson.' The cold cast of his features made Celeste think suddenly how much she'd dislike crossing him. The passionate, interested viscount she knew was not in evidence now.

'Nor do I fear for my life, since it is due to my manservant that I indeed still have a life,' Lord Peregrine went on.

'So he valiantly snatched you from the jaws of death. From footpads, I recall. Of course he did what he needed to secure his position with you.' Lord Cowdril waved a dismissive hand. 'You disapprove of slavery, Perry, and of calling them commodities, and yet do you not concede that you've bought this man—or rather his loyalty?' He looked triumphant.

Celeste watched Lord Peregrine obviously choose his words with care. 'I won Nelson at cards and yes, I admit it, I considered him a commodity at the time. Only since I've come to know him as a human being have I come to disapprove of slavery.'

Lady Cowdril's vermillion-stained lips curved into a thin smile as she patted her pomaded locks. 'Your conversations on slavery with Lady Busselton must be diverting, Perry. Her position was secured entirely through her father's reliance on the slave trade.'

Celeste felt herself go even pinker while a certain horror rose within her. She hadn't known Perry was a friend of the captain's daughter. She studied him covertly. His answer was imperative to what she'd have to report to Raphael.

'Lady Busselton occupies a place in society which, as you correctly point out, is thanks to her father's trading success, but I assure you, our conversations do not encompass trade. Especially not her father's.'

Lady Cowdril shuddered, as if the idea of trade were more repugnant than slavery. Lord Cowdril looked satisfied. He drained his wine glass and smiled. "Course not, Perry, and no intention of lancing you at the table like that. Unpardonable.'

The conversation appeared to be headed for less controversial waters, but there was still too much Celeste did not know.

Boldly, for she was not yet married and speaking up at the dinner table was not sanctioned for one in her position, she ventured, 'How did these slaves die?'

Five shocked faces turned to her, as if she'd uttered blasphemy.

'Good Lord, girl, what does it matter?' her hostess replied. 'They're slaves.'

The vicar on her left patted her hand and sent her a warning look, as if counselling her to hold her tongue. Only Lord Peregrine eyed her with more sympathy and interest than hitherto as Lord Cowdril said, 'Disease, Miss Rosington. Once the first one succumbed, the rest went down like flies.'

'Like flies, my lord?' She repeated his words, imbuing them with the faintest scepticism. Lord Cowdril appeared to take offence, but Lord Peregrine, she noticed, looked surprised.

Interesting, she thought, assuming the subject was about to be turned to another topic by Lord Peregrine's thoughtful silence. She was just responding to a murmured question from the vicar when the viscount suddenly remarked, in a tone he'd use to address a girl barely out of the nursery, 'Miss Rosington, you are very young but you do understand that as Lord Ogilvy is a notable slave owner in Jamaica, you, yourself, will lose many of the wretched creatures through disease, and no doubt your husband will rail at the financial impost.'

Lady Cowdril put down her fork with a clatter. 'Come now, Perry, you are being unfair on my poor guest. What does she know about slaves? She is an innocent, not yet married, and you are making her the focus of the entire table by your remark. Miss Rosington has no interest in whether her husband's slaves succumb to disease or any other such nonsense.'

Disregarding his hostess, Lord Peregrine went on, 'She will most certainly care if the loss of such an investment impacts on her dress allowance.'

Celeste raised her chin as anger needled her. 'It is true that I had not considered the fact that my husband is a slave owner, my lord. I gather from your tone that you are an abolitionist. Well, I can only hope that you and my future husband do not lock horns on the issue.'

Lady Branwell gave a nervous titter. 'Of course not, Celeste. Let us turn the topic, for it is not one for young ladies, besides.'

'And why is that, Lady Branwell?'

Celeste had to hide her smile at her aunt's patent discomfiture.

The older woman shifted uncomfortably. 'Well, slaves… We're discussing trade, and what can you know of trade? They're slaves, not human beings.'

Lady Cowdril clicked her tongue. 'Please don't encourage Perry, my dear Mariah,' she murmured. 'As you can surely tell, our esteemed Lord Peregrine begs to differ.'

Lord Peregrine smiled. 'The hare which changes colour in snowy conditions is still the same creature whatever its outward appearance,' he quoted. 'Black or white, we are the same creatures underneath. But for the sake of everyone's comfort I shall redirect the conversation. Miss Rosington, might I say that the shade of pink you are wearing has become a fetching camouflage. The porcelain hue of your complexion when you sat down to dinner is now nowhere in evidence.'

Celeste stared at him a moment, horrified, then dropped her eyes as Lady Cowdril said indignantly, but with a coquettish smile, 'And dearest Perry, the colour of your black coat is the very same as your eyes and, I've been told, your heart.'

PERRY SIPPED HIS PORT, RESPONDING DISTRACTEDLY TO questions put to him by his host after the ladies had retired from the dinner table. He knew he had to atone. He'd been unpardonably rude by focusing attention on Miss Rosington and insinuating she was somehow diminished by the fact her future husband owned the slaves that would garnish her lifestyle.

Future husband. When Miss Rosington had wondered aloud if he and her future husband would lock horns, the thought had evoked some confusing responses. He didn't like the idea of Miss Rosington belonging to another man... though there were certainly advantages for Peregrine if she were safely married—and dissatisfied.

The niggling thought returned that Xenia's self-righteous condemnation of Miss Rosington relied to a large extent upon the young lady's apparent hypocrisy. But that charge could not be levelled at her if she were not in love with her betrothed.

Of course, her involvement with Harry Carstairs was an entirely different matter.

It was the very—and supposedly only—reason Peregrine was furthering his acquaintance with her. Instantly he banished doubt and guilt by reminding himself that he was charged with the task of ascertaining whether or not Miss Rosington really was the demure virgin she presented to the world. She had been caught enjoying intimate relations with Harry Carstairs, and her enthusiastic responses to Peregrine's overtures belied the wide-eyed innocence she maintained for the rest of society.

She was his sister's nemesis.

Oblivious to the conversation between Lord Cowdril and the vicar, he ran his finger round his cravat to let in a little air as his glass was replenished by a smart footman in powdered wig and livery. If Peregrine chose, he could entertain like this, and supplement his rich, if sedate, lifestyle with *amours* as he chose.

All he would need was a wife.

He sighed. There was the rub. Perhaps there was a kernel of honour lodged in the depths of his depraved heart. He would, at least, like to *begin* his marriage in full faith that he would stay true.

Yes, he did nurture the faint hope that he could be like his father, the reformed reprobate whose life had been claimed by the muddy Thames during his foolish and ultimately futile attempts to rescue his beloved wife.

What must it be like to love a woman to such distraction, so deeply, that one would take the risk his father had that fateful day the three of them had gone boating?

Peregrine shuddered. Now was no time to torment himself with failure. He'd been only nine, a poor swimmer, but he had tried. Nor could he blame his father for his foolishness, for hadn't Peregrine done the same? Attempting to save his mother when their boat upturned was the last heroic action he could ever claim before his uncle became his guardian and his soul went to the dogs.

Suddenly he was aware of Cowdril and the vicar's eyes upon him. He raised an enquiring brow.

'I said, what do you really think is behind this business with Carstairs?' his host asked him. 'Rumour has it he was found by your sister with a woman the last time he was seen. Can you confirm it? Everyone is close-lipped and I've no intention of making public something that would further distress poor jilted Miss Paige, but what do *you* know, Peregrine?'

There was a very good reason Peregrine was an excellent poker player. 'A false rumour, my lord,' he murmured, 'otherwise Charlotte would have said something.'

Indeed, his hysterically-inclined sister had said a great deal, though Perry had been glad when Charlotte reported that Xenia had counselled her not to make public the fact that she'd clearly identified Miss Rosington as the woman in question.

The caveat, though, was now making Peregrine increasingly uncomfortable. Xenia had reassured Charlotte that when the time came for Miss Rosington to be revealed for the marriage-breaker she truly was, it would be done in 'spectacular fashion'.

But at the time Peregrine had agreed to becoming involved, Miss Rosington had been nothing more to him than a jezebel whose crime against his sister needed to be publicly exposed.

However, each encounter with Miss Rosington seemed to suggest the case was not as clear-cut as he'd presumed. Certainly, there was something she wasn't telling him, but Peregrine was becoming increasingly sceptical regarding Xenia's adamant charges against the young woman.

Not to mention increasingly susceptible to Miss Rosington's damnably effective manner of combining sweetness and supposed innocence with an allure that promised a world of unknown delights, if he only trod carefully with her.

Without a doubt, she was an enigma.

Without a doubt, also, Miss Rosington must have had *some* knowledge as to where Harry Carstairs had been heading the night he jilted his sister, even if there was a plausible reason she'd been caught alone with him in a room strewn with petticoats. He had to acknowledge, also, that Harry Carstairs and Miss Rosington's cousin and betrothed, Lord Ogilvy, were friends. The three would be well known to one another. Could there be some as-yet unknown explanation behind the apparently mad scramble that night? One that had nothing to do with the conclusion to which Charlotte and Xenia had jumped and which he'd meekly accepted before he'd become involved with—he took an uncomfortable swallow of his brandy—*exposing* Miss Rosington.

Savouring the heat that coursed down his throat, but not the direction his thoughts were taking him, he repeated, blandly, 'Not heard a thing, Cowdril.'

'Well where in God's name *is* Harry Carstairs?' his host said with uncharacteristic vehemence, followed by an apologetic glance at the vicar. 'The man owes me five hundred pounds.'

'I'd be more concerned with what has *become* of Harry Carstairs,' the vicar mumbled. 'His aunt is beside herself with worry. She's not heard a word from her nephew in three weeks. Did he see his lawyer and collect his inheritance, only to fall foul of cutthroats in some staging inn? Not that I suggested as much to Mrs Carstairs.'

'What's his lawyer have to say about it, Peregrine?' Lord Cowdril demanded in his most insistent tone; the one he used whenever he'd had too much to drink. 'A mighty hefty inheritance it was, from all accounts.'

Peregrine shook his head. 'His lawyer knows nothing of Carstairs' intended movements, either.' He was not going to mention the locket containing the cryptic, half-torn message.

With the mystery surrounding Carstairs assuming ever increasing proportions, Peregrine wished heartily he could have directed his focus towards winning his wager with Xenia so that, in good conscience, he need not worry about the whys and the wherefores behind the mystery of which Miss Rosington was at the centre. His role had been to simply persuade Miss Rosington into wrapping her white, elegant limbs around him in mindless passion, but he was now caught up in a moral dilemma.

Miss Rosington might be damnably tempting and easy on the eye but clearly her involvement with Harry Carstairs was more complicated than it first appeared.

Dammit, he thought, as he downed another brandy, his conscience really was getting in the way if the truth was a prerequisite for following through on his carnal desires.

Though perhaps a little *persuasion* might induce Miss Rosington to be more forthcoming with the truth surrounding her involvement.

After the guests drifted off to play whist or were repairing to their respective quarters, Perry awaited his opportunity. He knew he had offended Miss Rosington over dinner but he was confident she would not stay angry with him for long. She was far from immune to his charm; anyone could see that, he thought with a degree of smugness. And she certainly would not be once he'd offered her the most elegant apology he could formulate.

Nevertheless, she faced him coldly as he detained her in the Long Gallery. Lord Cowdril was a keen collector and during his Grand Tour of the continent had amassed an array of treasures from busts of roman senators to coats of armour from all corners of the globe. The sight of Miss Rosington standing level with a Mongol warrior was an incongruous one but clearly the brief amusement he allowed to show on his face did not go down well.

Goodness, she could appear formidable, he thought, a spear of excitement heating his loins and shooting up his spine; for he'd expected Miss Celeste to be all forgiveness once she'd gathered that he clearly intended to seek her pardon. No doubt, though, the pretense was for show. She'd not want to appear too transparent. And regardless of whether or not she bore any guilt in her dealings with Carstairs, Peregrine knew that she definitely was not in love with her betrothed and most definitely was susceptible to Peregrine's charms.

'You do not look as pleased to see me as you clearly were when we met by the mulberry tree just before dinner.' He smiled as he took in her delectable form with an unashamedly lascivious eye.

She stared regally through him, her body positioned for a hasty departure. 'After all but insulting me at dinner, are you not done with your sport, my lord?' Now, if you'll pardon me, I must go to bed.'

Had she not been so haughty he might have joked an insinuation that alluded to the fact that's where they both intended to end up—together—at some stage before the weekend was over.

But the conviction of her current performance had him suddenly doubting the foundation on which he'd built her up, for there was nothing in her manner to suggest the experienced jade. Her mouth trembled and she kept casting decidedly frightened looks in the direction of her now-departed chaperone.

He moved close and put his forefinger beneath her chin. As he tipped her head a little, a sudden, unexpected tenderness washed over him. Miss Rosington looked terrified and, quite frankly, as if she were about to cry.

In the next moment he caught himself up. No, surely he was being hoodwinked, just like every other susceptible man would be in this instance. She'd honed this helpless act to a fine art and he was about to fall victim like a lovelorn fool. If Miss Rosington and Harry Carstairs weren't exactly lovers, Miss Rosington was definitely on the hunt for pastures greener than her current marital prospects.

Clearly there was more to her than had initially met the eye and he must discover what it was. His sister's happiness depended upon it. Yet Miss Rosington was guilty of *something* that belied her wide-eyed innocence.

So, while his mind hardened, he maintained his tender look for her benefit, and was rewarded by her softening expression.

Slowly, he brought his face towards hers. 'All this talk of slaves is not talk for gently reared females such as yourself. I was wrong to focus the attention on you, Miss Rosington,' he murmured. He was nearly there, his soothing voice like a drug, he thought confidently; one she was clearly unable to resist. Soon his lips would be on hers and he'd feel her body sag against his as he conjured away all her resistance.

'My deepest apologies, Miss Rosington. If I could but atone.'

The stinging slap on his cheek brought him up short. Outraged, he glared down to find her equally outraged face glaring back.

'Did you not hear me, my lord? I said I had forgiven you and there was no need to kiss me into resistance,' she hissed.

He shook his head. 'You said that? Why, every indication —first meeting me at the mulberry tree, and just now— suggested that you were very happy to further what was started in the *darkness* at Vauxhall.' He was dismayed by the turn things had taken, though still confident this was part of her play-acting. Of course she wanted to heighten his desire and, while her slap had been rather a shock, it had certainly been a very good ploy. No innocent debutante knew how to balance indignation with subtle encouragement. She thought he wasn't onto her but now he understood exactly the game she was playing. His cheek stung but suddenly he'd never felt more desire for any woman.

He considered his next move as he focused on her furious, beautiful little face. Miss Rosington put on the appearance of being upset extremely well. Her bosom, deliciously in evidence beneath her laced-edged rose pink gown, heaved with emotion and her dark blue eyes flashed fire, twinkling like the jewels in her high coiffure.

All he had to do was say the right thing and she'd be his for the taking. He calculated the distance to his bedchamber to be only a hundred yards to the right along a corridor that was dimly lit and away from the rest of the guests. They would not be discovered, though clearly Miss Rosington was a risk taker. She'd have to have been to have risked so much to meet a single man at the mulberry tree and to have kissed him at Vauxhall with her betrothed not ten yards away. No, he decided, Miss Rosington was not averse to making lovers of the men she found attractive.

'Then I am even more of a cad than you thought at dinner and there *is* only one way to atone.' Swooping, he brought his mouth to hers, covering her lips as he held her tight, the sweet, unutterably desirable flavour of her feeding through his veins as she went limp in his arms and her arms twined around his neck. He hardened as she cleaved to him, just as he'd imagined she would. His breathing became erratic as her little tongue touched his, drawing from his very depths a groan of frustrated desire, for he must have her now or he would explode.

Quickly he scooped her into his arms, but to his surprise she wrested herself free of his embrace, stumbling to regain her balance as unwillingly he let her go.

Her face was wild, her eyes wide with something he couldn't define: terror, disappointment, the remnants of her own frustrated desire?

'I must beg your pardon for giving you every reason to think that I had forgiven you for taking liberties, earlier, my lord.' Her voice trembled. 'I do not! Nor can I be alone with you, as I have gone to great pains to make clear! Ever!'

She looked about to turn on her heel and flee down the passage. Confused, but above all disappointed beyond belief, he waylaid her with an honest question.

'Is that because you don't trust me, Miss Rosington, or because you don't trust yourself?'

She crinkled her brow and bit her lip, gestures of confusion, which he found more irresistible than any practiced piece of outright seduction. 'Both, my lord, now please don't detain me further—'

He reached out his hand as if trying to coax a small

animal. Now he didn't feel like he was play-acting. He truly wanted to banish her resistance, which sadly, he realised, was very real.

'Come Celeste, if I may call you that. Forgive me. Let us start again. Let me kiss you, one more time. Please? That's where it'll start and end.' It was ridiculous how fear and disappointment were making a fool of him. Suddenly he wanted her, not as a conquest, but as a delightful surprise he could unwrap, layer by layer. She was as sweet and innocent as she was fiery and mysterious. He'd never been confronted by such a potent mixture in a woman.

'You know that's not true, my lord,' she whispered, stepping backwards. 'And that's why it must end ... why everything must end ... between us. Goodnight.'

End? Oh no, this was not how it was going to end. Calling on every reserve for the means to supply him with the necessary inspiration, Peregrine found himself saying urgently, 'If it's Harry you want, then it's not over between us.'

Cryptically phrased, but the words found their mark as he'd grasped for straws. Her eyes widened and her mouth fell open as she took the bait, supplying him with more information than he could have hoped for as she whispered, 'You *know* where Harry is?'

Oh, but he was clever. Why had he not understood before that she'd been casting around in the dark for news of her lover—or whatever he was to her— who'd gone missing the night they'd both fled together? Xenia thought Miss Rosington was keeping his location secret, but the truth was that Miss Rosington was seeking Harry, just as he was.

He was just congratulating himself on matching her wits when she asked suspiciously, 'What proof do you have?'

'My word is not good enough?'

She hesitated. 'Why should I trust you when I suspect you are toying with me, my lord?' Her shoulders slumped and a look of great distress crossed her lovely features. 'Clearly you knew from the outset that I ... was acquainted with Harry.'

Well, that was true enough. But the more he toyed with her the more he wanted her. He ran his hands over his coat, thinking.

And felt the locket in the lining of his pocket.

'Perhaps this will persuade you,' he said, holding it out.

For a moment, he thought she was about to faint.

CHAPTER 5

*C*eleste had always been impressed at Raphael's ability to hide his real feelings. Lord, she hoped she was succeeding even moderately at concealing the confusion and fear that churned in *her* breast following her late-night encounter in the Long Gallery with Lord Peregrine.

The whole nature of their relationship was now turned on its head. How long had he known of her interest in finding Harry? She thought back to their first encounter. That had been pure chance, she was sure of it. But after that? Why, coincidence had continued to throw them into each other's orbit until suddenly, at Lady Cowdril's house party, he'd produced the one thing Raphael would sell his soul for —or rather, Celeste's.

Celeste shivered. She was almost beyond caring for the whys and wherefores. Whether Lord Peregrine was a philanderer or had set his sights on Celeste for reasons relating to his sister, the fact was that every time Celeste found herself in Lord Peregrine's arms, she was speared with the consciousness that *any* chance was worth taking if it resulted in a happier alternative to marrying Raphael.

Lord Peregrine might have started out with ulterior motives, like she had, but he was just as affected as she by their closeness, she was certain.

This evening, following her return from the lovely Jacobean estate by the river, Celeste watched her betrothed amidst his own surroundings. He appeared the most languid and carefree of gentlemen as he lounged with his guests, between walks in the gardens or over refreshments in the saloon, discussing local events and entertainments. His mother had engaged Celeste for the last hour on matters pertaining to the forthcoming wedding. There was the wedding breakfast to organise and the order of the day.

Celeste's heart was never less engaged, but she did her best to appear dutiful. She didn't dislike her future mother-in-law. Lady Margery had always been kind to her and seemed somehow to understand Celeste's inability to be truly excited. After all, it wasn't as if Raphael had ever evinced a great enthusiasm to wed Celeste, either.

But there were protocols, and once it was over and done with they could all get on with their own lives and interests.

Finally the saloon was cleared of all but Lady Margery and Baron Rutherford, a constant companion these days of Raphael's widowed mother. When these two were ensconced on chairs in front of the fire, Celeste glided over to her betrothed and, seating herself with her handiwork, said the words she knew would test his ability to hide the state of his heart. Oh, but it would be good to be the one to cause disharmony in his breast.

'Lord Peregrine knows where Harry is.'

The flare in Raphael's eye and his involuntary gasp told her more than his measured tone. Though her head was bent in apparent concentration of her needlework, she was secretly thrilled by his agitation and the tic at the corner of his mouth.

'You have *met* Lord Peregrine and he has told you all this? How remarkable.' He raised an eyebrow while his right foot tapped the floor.

But of course there'd be more and why had she not thought of the ramifications of her foolish words?

Celeste tried to rein in her growing fear. Now he'd begin the questions and she needed to have the answers that would please him. Or rather, not *dis*please him.

Raphael rose in his usual languid fashion and began to pace. A deep furrow ran between his eyebrows as he ran his thumb along his lower lip.

Celeste hunched further over her work, working the stitches through blurred vision, desperately wishing she'd approached the conversation with more care; that she'd practiced her answers so there was no chance he'd suspect how her own feelings had been engaged.

'So Lord Peregrine knows where Harry is and he told *you* this.' Raphael spoke under his breath, turning his inquisitorial gaze upon her. The topic was not one to be overheard. 'What I would like to know, my dear, is *why* Lord Peregrine should have divulged such information to you. It seems a rather extraordinary coincidence.' He looked steadily at her, and Celeste felt the unspoken threat like a cold shard of metal worrying more than just her conscience.

She swallowed and glanced at her future mother-in-law at the far end of the room, glad now of her presence as Raphael went on, 'What—in our esteemed viscount's eyes— do you suppose could possibly connect you with Harry? Miss Paige has not identified you. Surely you did not lie to me when you said you'd destroyed the message contained within the locket? The locket went missing the night of Harry's disappearance, you assured me, though you knew so much depended upon it.' His pale, searching eyes needled her very soul as he added warningly, 'Perhaps you did not tell me everything about that night, Celeste.'

Celeste forced herself to meet his look. 'I did not lie, Raphael, when I assured you that I removed the message as you instructed me …' She took a breath, adding bravely, 'after your … *oversight* … in forgetting to destroy Harry's communication before you thrust his locket—and me—into the night to provide him with the salvation he requested.' Should she reveal the full truth? The fact that she'd stuffed Harry's desperate plea into the seam of one of the petticoats she'd removed for Harry? Surely the tiny missive could not possibly have been found, else Lord Peregrine and his sister would have been trumpeting Celeste and Raphael's sins all over town long before now.

'I must be truthful, Raphael.' She couldn't keep it from him and indeed, he would continue to needle her until she confessed. A dampening thought indeed. Raphael was adept at making her feel as helpless as a butterfly on a pin. 'A tiny fraction of the message was caught in the glue behind Miss Paige's picture when I tore it out. Just a few letters only—'

'And how might that be sufficient to explain Lord Peregrine's interest in you, my dear?' He was breathing quietly, but heavily. 'Since you have just assured me the message could not have fallen into his hands.'

Celeste glanced across at Lady Ogilvy staring out of the window in the distance and wished she were closer. Shrugging, she regarded him miserably, unable to find a reason that would satisfy him.

'Curious, my dear.' Raphael shook his head, choosing to appear more sorrowful than angry, though perhaps it was easier to adopt this course since his mother and Baron Rutherford were approaching. He lowered his voice. 'I hope you have not been indiscreet, Celeste, for I find it difficult to understand how you can have gained a philandering stranger's trust to the extent he would so willingly divulge information that is, let us say, not in the public domain.'

Celeste's cheeks burned though she tried to bravely hold Raphael's look. 'As you know, Lord Peregrine was a guest of Lord and Lady Cowdril during the weekend and ... we were much thrown together.' She swallowed. 'Naturally I was terrified of speaking to him, in case his sister had indeed recognised me that fateful night at Harry's townhouse, though it appears I am safe on that score. Nevertheless,' she took a deep breath, 'at dinner the talk turned to slaves and later, we were in discussion regarding you being a slave-owner while Lord Peregrine is in opposition to slavery—'

Raphael interrupted her with a sigh. 'Please get to the point, Celeste, and tell me how you managed to charm the abolitionist libertine Lord Peregrine into revealing to you this extraordinary information. No doubt you flirted shame-lessly with him.'

Celeste dropped her eyes and nodded. 'I did, Raphael, for I thought that where Harry is concerned ...' She raised her head and finished defiantly, 'you'd not care what I did as long as you discovered the information you were looking for.'

Raphael appeared unperturbed by her charge. 'As long as you are discreet, Celeste, I don't care what you do.' He smiled as he leaned against the mantelpiece. 'Now tell me, where *is* Harry? That is all I am interested in, though I am somewhat surprised you did not tell me this news earlier.'

Celeste licked dry lips. Her eyes blurred as she stared at the black and white work she'd nearly completed, deeply afraid now of Raphael's reaction and wondering how she might mitigate any possible damage she'd done by venturing along this ill-chosen path. 'Well, Lord Peregrine didn't tell me exactly *where* he is,' she said slowly, 'however, he showed me the locket.'

'Good God!'

She hid her smile, terrified though she was. He was as shocked as she'd known he would be and by all that was holy it felt good to spear Raphael with something that wasn't cold indifference or irritation, even though the consequences for her could be dire.

'How on earth …?'

Celeste had never seen him lost for words. Indeed, she, too, had not known what to say when Lord Peregrine had held out the sparkling treasure in the palm of his hand. As Celeste had gaped at it, she'd nearly fainted at the memory of watching Raphael receive it from the breathless street urchin before, without a thought, he'd sent Celeste, protesting and terrified, into the cold dark night. But the oversight in forgetting to remove the damning words, which Harry had penned and concealed in the locket, was his alone, and he knew it.

Nevertheless, Celeste knew now he'd have no compunction in risking her safety once more, though this time her feelings were mixed. Certainly it would be dangerous. In fact, she felt sick at the churning of her susceptible heart to any future encounters with Lord Peregrine. Her fingers tingled and her head swam at the prospect but still there may be compensations, she thought with wild hope as she waited for him to formulate a predictably measured response to her extraordinary news.

'Did he give it to you?'

Celeste shook her head.

Raphael was silent a long moment as he studied his manicured hands. A log exploded in the fireplace and the sap hissed from the heat. Slowly he raised his head. 'Well, my dear, how do you propose to prise this locket—and more information—from Lord Peregrine?'

Celeste put down her handiwork and sent him a curious look, her fear now under control, despite the fact that Lady

Ogilvy and the baron had quit the room. He was less threatening when she knew she could be useful to him.

'What do you suggest, Raphael? I shall soon be your obedient wife and it'll be your duty to direct me as you see fit. Though that hasn't stopped you from doing so already.'

He ignored the jibe. Clearly he was too busy thinking. And appearances suggested his thoughts were in turmoil. Very uncharacteristic. But then, Raphael's feelings for Harry were singularly uncharacteristic, to her mind.

He shifted, the continued nervous tic revealing what his habitual cool tone did not. 'What do I suggest?' He repeated her question as if he were surprised she should ask. 'Why, Celeste, you will do what you must to persuade the viscount to impart whatever he knows about Harry. You must encourage him to surrender the locket to you. I am sure he has no idea of the real meaning of its contents, but without that locket, Harry is lost.'

'Perhaps he's already lost. Lost to us, anyway.'

Raphael chose to ignore her inflammatory suggestion though his look was cold. 'You will find a way to persuade Lord Peregrine to give you that locket. I just hope you are equipped with the skills and enticements—' he shrugged as he stared dispassionately at her décolletage, 'to persuade him to do your bidding.'

'What if he is difficult to persuade?'

Her cousin shook his head, his expression pained. 'Well then, Celeste, you must find the resources that *will* persuade him.'

'WHAT A CLEVER BOY YOU ARE, PERRY. PERHAPS YOU DESERVE part payment on your very … unexpected information.'

Pouting as she gazed across from the blue velvet sofa in

the saloon, Xenia looked at Perry as if she'd like nothing more than to devour him. Once, Perry would have enjoyed nothing more than to be devoured by her, but as had been the case lately, the usual surge of desire that accompanied her suggestive comments was absent.

In its place was simple curiosity.

Toying with his glass of Madeira, he raised his head to look at his old friend with a frown.

'It's not like you to offer rewards before your bidding is done, Xenia.'

She gave him a playful smile. 'In business, judicious encouragement can sometimes be … helpful to ensure a job is satisfactorily completed.'

'And what would you consider a job satisfactorily completed? You want Harry Carstairs. Why?'

Xenia looked hurt. 'Why, to avenge your sister, of course. You are just as eager to do that as I am, surely?'

'Will that reverse the damage done? Do you really think finding Carstairs will mean his marriage to Charlotte will go ahead?' Perry sighed, his thoughts switching between Xenia's real motive—avenging Charlotte was a convenient excuse for something else, he was now quite certain—and Miss Rosington. Miss Rosington was hiding something, he was sure, but regardless of whether or not she was, or had been, Harry's lover, he would not see her ruined.

No, Perry had now become fixated upon the idea of making her *his* lover, and not so he could ruin her, though of course, he could not hint at this to Xenia. Clearly, Xenia had her own unstated reasons for wishing Miss Rosington brought down, which Perry must discover. Xenia was a formidable opponent. No one would wish to make an enemy of Xenia, and Peregrine most certainly did not.

However, he needed to learn exactly what motive Xenia

had for seeing Miss Rosington effectively destroyed if he were to have any chance of protecting the young woman.

Strangely, he rather liked the novelty of playing the knight in shining armour ... albeit one who would ultimately seduce the delectable object of Xenia's evil ploy. Now, though, was not the time to pretend he was better than he was. He'd worn the mantle of careless libertine and conscienceless philanderer for too long to know how to change his spots.

Carefully he put down his wine glass and crossed his legs. He'd come to pay Xenia a supposedly social visit in the palatial home she'd occupied since her second marriage, though really he was here to apprise Xenia on his progress pertaining to Miss Rosington. And most definitely, what Xenia must not suspect, were Perry's growing feelings for the young woman.

Deep in his coat pocket he felt the outline of the locket and wondered at its significance. A token of Carstairs' love for Miss Rosington? She'd certainly blanched the shade of parchment when he'd shown it to her. Yet when he went over their various encounters, he was sure Miss Rosington's attraction to him had been unfeigned.

Perry liked to think he was adept at reading the situation correctly but, of course, he couldn't discount the possibility that he was proving to be as easily duped as the other men in Miss Rosington's life.

Nevertheless, the fact the young woman was hiding something did not mean her crimes warranted what Xenia clearly had in mind for her.

Xenia's voice was brittle as she examined the half moons of her fingernails, and then her soft, white hands. 'Surely the reasons behind Harry's defection are what we need to find out. Why did he disappear? Where did he go? Is he still alive? Charlotte knows nothing. She talks of taking Holy Orders.

That is not the Charlotte we love and know. She is distraught. Surely it is our duty to do all within our power to furnish dear Charlotte with the reasons her life suddenly fell apart?' Xenia affected a sympathetic smile as she rose and made her leisurely progress across the patterned carpet. 'We *need* to find Harry Carstairs.' Pausing before Perry she placed her hand on his shoulder, then very slowly trailed it down the lapels of his brocade coat.

Uncomfortable, Perry rose and began to pace. 'I don't think Miss Rosington can help you, Xenia.'

Her silence was telling. So was her clipped tone. 'Don't tell me the little baggage has hoodwinked you, too.'

Perry was careful to make his reply noncommittal. Right now he felt a great affinity for a fly caught in a spider's web, helplessly facing the homeowner. The feeling, though, was fleeting. Xenia thought herself clever, but she was not clever enough to blackmail him. Careful to suppress his fury, he murmured, 'It is *because* Miss Rosington holds such little interest for me that that I am loathe to pursue further investigations through the vixen.'

The fire crackled and the steady tick of the clock marked time in the silence. Slowly Xenia raised her head, her cold blue eyes boring into his. 'Is that so, Perry?' she asked softly.

CHAPTER 6

*C*eleste's hand shook as she reread the neat handwriting on the note she'd received only that moment from her unlikely admirer. She leaned back on the little chair Mary had placed in front of the fire for her in her bedchamber and closed her eyes while the maidservant waited before her.

Would she really entertain such madness?

Bringing the note up to her chest, she rested it against her strongly beating heart.

What possible reason would Lord Peregrine have for wishing to meet with her alone, unless it were to pursue a dangerous, illicit agenda no proper lady would consent to being involved in?

She swallowed with difficulty, aware of Mary hovering, but having no answer for her yet. She needed to weigh up her options with care. Certainly, Raphael had sanctioned her to do what she needed to in order to reclaim the locket and to discover knowledge Lord Peregrine possessed.

But at what cost?

Undeniably, Celeste was strongly attracted to the gentleman, but she also was not a fool. Allowing herself to get any closer to him would only confirm her as such, for during their last encounter he had indeed proved himself the libertine society—and Raphael—painted him. Yes, she sensed that her attraction was returned, but he'd been interested in her only as his latest conquest.

And what, if anything, *did* Lord Peregrine in fact know? It was true, he had the locket, but what value was that on its own?

It was in this mood of miserable reflection that Raphael found Celeste, and when he'd at last needled out of her the reasons for her state of confusion, he laughed.

Mary had scuttled out of the room and Raphael now leaned over the back of Celeste's chair, his hands resting on her shoulders. The heat from his breath warmed her cheek and froze her heart as he murmured mockingly, 'So the fact of the matter is that you don't know if you should accept Lord Peregrine's clandestine invitation to meet you at Romsey's studio because you fear he has designs upon you, my dear?'

Celeste kept still, terrified of revealing her revulsion. Raphael rarely touched her and now the gesture was not one of tenderness, which his next words confirmed. He stood up suddenly and came round to stand in front of her, blocking her heat with his elegant, threatening bulk. Reluctantly Celeste met his cold, implacable look. How much he reminded her of Michelangelo's *Statue of David* albeit with his clothes on, though the thought of the alternative made her tremble with horror. Physically perfect but utterly cold. 'There is no contest for your susceptible emotions to win, my dear,' he said crisply. 'You will meet with your apparently lovelorn libertine, for that is the only way you will gain possession of the locket. Is that not so?'

Celeste raised her chin and forced herself to meet his eye

as he rested his arm against the mantelpiece and stared down at her. In a small voice she whispered, '*Is* the locket so important, Raphael? After all, it's Harry you want, isn't it?' She sighed, crumpling the paper in her hands. 'Besides, how will I gain possession of Harry's locket without danger to myself? To meet Lord Peregrine alone is perilous. Surely you would not sanction such a thing.'

Raphael rubbed his chin, thoughtfully, then shrugged. 'Clearly you've devised a winning strategy already, else the viscount would not be so taken.' He smiled a little. 'And taken he is, though whether that's because he's fallen desperately in love with you in a remarkably short time or you've been somewhat blatant in advertising your availability, I daresay you're in a better position to tell than me.'

'You're a cruel man, Raphael.' Celeste dropped her eyes as she straightened in her chair, his words finding their mark. 'I've done no more than you required of me.'

'Not yet, Celeste. You've not *yet* done what I require of you, and in sending you off to meet his lordship I very much fear that your foolishness risks all the gains you have made.'

Angrily Celeste jerked her head up. 'How dare you insult me like this, Raphael,' she said in a low voice, rising to her feet and striding over to the door in a froth of skirts. 'If you don't trust me, then I will not meet him. You're right, he's dangerous, so why would you thrust your future wife into the lion's den?' Gripping the doorframe, she met his impacable look. 'Henceforth I shall have nothing more to do with wicked Lord Peregrine, for what you say is true; his goal is seduction and I am risking my reputation every time I'm with him, alone or otherwise.' She didn't know whether to cry from relief at having made such a decision or wilt from despair at having acknowledged the truth of it. Raphael's words cut deep. Lord Peregrine *was* only interested in her because she'd flagged her availability.

Or ... she trembled at the alternative reason for his lordship's interest to which Raphael had alluded. If Lord Peregrine believed she was the last to see Harry Carstairs, was that the sole reason he'd pursued her from the start? Briefly she touched her lips. Had the passion and excitement during their several illicit encounters been on her part alone?

Now she really was going to cry, for the truth was it would be pure folly to have anything further to do with a gentleman whose clear aim had just been revealed as no more real and admirable than her own. The trouble was, *her* heart had well and truly been engaged.

Raphael's voice drew her out of her reverie. 'You are my best chance of regaining Harry's locket, Celeste, and if you didn't realise it already, I must make clear that Harry's entire future rests on its return. Why do you suppose he used it as the vessel containing the note telling me of his danger? So that if he fell foul of his would-be attackers I would be able to use it to claim his inheritance.'

A fit of trembling seized her and Raphael smiled as he ran his eyes down to her feet before fixing his gaze on her face. 'I know you are frightened, Celeste, and I know you are attracted to Lord Peregrine. But you are sensible. You know the risks you run in being caught alone with him just as you know that whatever happens, you can *not* allow even a whisper of scandal to damage your reputation. Nevertheless, you must accept his invitation. I insist upon it, with the caveat that you behave with your usual modesty and good sense. After you return Harry's locket to me, with no unfortunate repercussions or any lapse on your part, you will be well rewarded, my love.'

Celeste put her hands to her temples and shook her head, resting her brow against the doorframe as she struggled against the tears that threatened. The more Raphael revealed of his feelings for Harry, the more she realised the barren life to which she would be condemned after she became his wife.

Wearily she looked up at him. 'I once thought you cared for me, Raphael.' Her voice caught. 'But how can you when you subject me to such ... danger? I understand the risks, but what if I miscalculate and it's not my fault? What if my reputation is besmirched because Lord Peregrine is more dangerous than I'd believed? Raphael, release me from this madness, for I don't know if I can safely follow through what you would have me do.'

Before she'd finished speaking he was in front of her, gripping her wrists, lowering his face so that she could smell the brandy on his breath. Now that it had come to this, Raphael was quick to show where his true feelings lay; she should not have been so disappointed.

A surprised, haunted cast to his ascetic features made him seem more human in that moment. 'Forgive me if I've insulted you, Celeste. I regret it now.' His voice was urgent as his eyes searched hers. 'Surely you realise how much I care for you? Lord, we've grown up together, but is my honesty not to be commended? No, I cannot love you as your foolish heart seems to require but as I shall have the care of you, I swear that I will treat you with the respect and kindness you deserve.' He brought their clasped hands up to his face and kissed her fingertips. His dark eyes sought hers with feverish intensity and his nostrils flared. 'Celeste, I *need* you to gain possession of Harry's locket. It contains valuable information Harry depends upon if he's to stay safe. Do this one thing for me and I shall ask nothing more of you. Immediately upon our marriage we shall sail for Jamaica, where you will be mistress of vast estates. Give me a son and then I shall grant you the liberties to follow your heart. All I'm asking in return is that you fulfil this one simple task.'

She knew how much Raphael hated it when she cried, but

as the tears fell he chose not to notice. Releasing her, he left swiftly, saying abruptly over his shoulder as he entered the sanctuary of the passage, 'Call Mary in so you can give her your answer. You can tell Lord Peregrine that you'll meet with him as soon as he desires.'

CHAPTER 7

*L*ate that afternoon, accompanied by Mary, Celeste entered the viewing rooms of the celebrity painter whose work she admired and who'd recently enjoyed wide public acclaim for his series of vignettes featuring a beautiful society matron. For Celeste to view them in the company of her maid and on the eve of her marriage would not be considered beyond the realms of respectability. Her conversation with her secret admirer, however, might well be. For what Raphael had requested of her would require a level of coquetry and skill she feared she did not possess.

The smell of turpentine and oils struck Celeste with force as she raised the pink and green striped skirts of her fashionable chintz *à la Française* to step across the threshold and into the long gallery, which was located in a lofty attic lit by large skylights. She'd dressed with care —or rather, Raphael had overseen with care the way Mary had dressed her—in a new season's gown that was cut low across the bosom, and filled with a lace fichu. She'd felt beautiful when her toilette had been complete and she'd stared at her reflection and seen hope luminescent in her clear blue gaze, her powdered hair topped with a somewhat rakish straw hat festooned with flowers.

Raphael had poisoned that image when he'd declared, 'Innocence and experience,' as he'd assessed her critically. 'What designing rake would not be intrigued?'

The fact that these words came from the man who would soon be her husband and who, himself, felt nothing of such sentiments should not have pained her so greatly. After all, her heart was equally without desire for Raphael. She'd gracefully inclined her head in response to his bald stipulation that she needn't return until she'd completed her mission.

Yet it pumped with a different sensation. Did the locket have such meaning that Raphael would truly sanction her to do *anything* to reclaim it? She felt ill with excitement; still, this was not how she wished matters were ordered.

The fact that Raphael was using her, trading her, without compunction, was one thing.

But what of Lord Peregrine? He did not love her. In all likelihood he'd sought her out due to his suspicion of her involvement with his sister's betrothed; which of course meant his motives were as calculating as Raphael's.

But each time she returned her thoughts to the combustion of their brief, passionate exchanges, she could not rid herself of the feeling that Lord Peregrine *had* felt something for her that was real and pure.

Even if he had not intended such feelings to intrude.

Tugging nervously at her gloves, Celeste tried to adopt an expression of distant admiration for the works of art surrounding her. She was a lady of fashion with a love of art and must not draw attention to herself.

Canvases in various degrees of completion leaned against the sides of the walls, and on easels, while a gauze-draped chaise longue in the far corner suggested where the artist's model might repose when she sat for the artist.

A well-dressed couple at the far end of the room speaking with the painter were the only other occupants, she noticed with beating heart, as she searched for Lord Peregrine.

She was unsure if she were relieved or otherwise that he was not here, but the possibilities so tantalisingly within reach made her mouth dry and her palms clammy as she gazed at the serene visage of the artist's beautiful muse and wondered what it must be like to enjoy such freedom.

Perhaps one day Celeste might know peace when she'd done all that Raphael required of her; though what entertainment would be on offer after she was married and gone to Jamaica were another matter. This afternoon's little jaunt, sanctioned by Raphael and with such clear instructions on what she must achieve, was the most license she'd been granted since she'd worn her hair loose and unpowdered.

Taking a few regal steps towards a cluster of oils, she glanced about the room. He was still not here.

Oh dear Lord, she felt sick with anticipation. Soon she'd have to put to the test her abilities to extract information from someone far more experienced than she in the arts of sophisticated obfuscation. She bent towards a painting of a girl on a swing, closing her eyes as her thoughts whirled.

Then a rustling beside her and a familiar murmur made the blood rush to her head.

'The beauty of the artist's muse is but a pale imitation of yours, Miss Rosington.'

So he was here. She tried not to be discomposed by his words, not batting an eyelid as she took the arm the viscount offered her, inclining her head in polite appreciation as he indicated a painting of the titian-haired beauty dressed in Grecian robes appearing to rise up from the sea.

'You flatter me, my lord,' she replied under her breath, as

she obediently allowed herself to be led to the most secluded part of the room. 'There is no need for it, though. I came, didn't I?'

'You came, and I can't tell you how pleased I am, though we did not part on the best of terms,' he conceded, strolling past painting upon painting with barely a glance. 'This time, I promise to be better behaved.'

'I feel relatively safe in such a public place,' Celeste replied with a wry glance at him.

So far, so good, she thought. She'd managed to hide the visible signs of her palpitating heart.

He stopped and stared thoughtfully ahead. For the moment, all trace of the infamous seducer had vanished. His contemplative gaze was full of intelligence, his mouth cast in a pleasant curve and her heart lurched a little. But when he looked down at her, his eyes were suddenly hooded and there was speculation in his expression.

Celeste turned away, disliking what she saw. He regarded her as an opportunity or a conquest, rather than an attractive woman, and the knowledge was deeply dampening. How thrilling life had been when she believed Lord Peregrine genuinely entranced.

Misery swamped her. 'You think I'm guilty in my dealings with Harry Carstairs, don't you, my lord?' She slanted a desperate look at him, as much surprised by her spontaneous candour as clearly the viscount was, but before he could answer she forced herself to go on. Now she knew how she must proceed: with the truth! Without transparency there could be nothing gained from this association. Yes, Raphael had counselled her to use every feminine wile at her disposal to prise the locket from Lord Peregrine, but Celeste was a poor liar. She'd stumble at the first post. And oh it was a bitter pill to understand the real reason for Lord Peregrine's interest.

'You pursued me, my lord, both at Vauxhall and at Lord and Lady Cowdril's house party—after you learned I was the woman last seen with Harry.' The breeze through the open window ruffled the tendrils of hair at the nape of her neck and she shivered, for now there was no turning back. Squaring her chin she added, 'So either you are intent on punishing me, or there is some other means by which you believe you can profit by our association ... is that not so, my lord?'

She observed the flare of surprise in his eyes, followed by a more thoughtful look as he straightened his queue, the froth of lace at his wrists obscuring for a moment the working of his features. 'Come, Miss Rosington. Step over the threshold into the next room for but a moment. Your maid will not miss you.'

He took her hand and led her into the gloom beneath the low eaves. A room clearly not intended for visitors. She should not go, of course. He would try and kiss her and maybe she would let him; yes, and fondle her and make her feel things that would serve forever as a reminder of how much she was missing in her real marriage.

She should not go when she knew his intentions went no further than base seduction, but oh, just to *feel* for a few moments would be worth all the years of loneliness that stretched ahead of her; even if he was just a grubby seducer with such different motivations from the ones she'd originally attributed to him.

Obediently she allowed him to lead her over the threshold, her nod to Mary leaving the girl in no doubt that they were not to be disturbed.

In the darkness she could just discern the outline of his face as he loomed above her. He held her hands up to his lips and gently kissed her knuckles.

'You are an honest woman, Miss Rosington,' he

murmured, 'and brave too. Yes, you are right, I did seek you out after I learned from my sister of your association with Harry.'

She heard his gentle sigh as he stooped to bring his head closer. 'An association which has brought her great torment and which you've not begun to explain.' He released her hands and gently cupped her face, his expression searching as he whispered, 'Miss Rosington ... will you explain to me your interest in Harry Carstairs before I am candid about my interest in you?'

Celeste closed her eyes as he began to caress her cheek, surrendering herself to his gentle touch as he traced the outline of her lips with his forefinger, mesmerised as he went on in a low murmur, 'For I am more than interested, but I must know if Harry is your lover.'

'My lover!' She jerked her head away, stepping back quickly as she shook her head. 'Harry Carstairs is *not* my lover!'

A shaft of light from a grimy skylight spilled onto the floorboards between them. Across the pool of dancing sunbeams, Celeste faced him squarely. Raphael would wring her neck to hear her speak so plainly but Lord Peregrine was not a fool or likely to be easily deceived. Nor, fortunately, was he looking at her as if he suspected she was trying to deceive him.

She took a deep breath, focusing on a dancing sunbeam rather than Lord Peregrine's face. In that instant she determined that she *would* tell him the truth: everything she knew, Raphael be damned. Clenching her fists she took a deep breath and prepared herself, wondering if Lord Peregrine would manage to contain his inscrutable mask by the time she was done and wishing she were as practised at keeping her real thoughts to herself.

'Harry Carstairs is a friend of my cousin and intended,

Lord Ogilvy,' she said carefully. Lord, honesty was one thing but she must ensure no hint of scandal attach to any of them by the time she was done. It wasn't just Celeste's reputation that hung in the balance, for if she were responsible for tarnishing Raphael or Harry, her existence would be intolerable. Choosing her words with even greater care, she went on. 'When Harry disappeared mysteriously shortly after arriving in England, Raphael was beside himself with worry. More so when he learned Harry was in danger.'

'In danger?' Lord Peregrine raised an eyebrow.

So he had not known? That was some small relief. Celeste nodded. 'Harry had been supposed to meet Raphael, that is, Lord Ogilvy, immediately after visiting his lawyer but he never turned up. When Raphael made enquiries, he was told Harry had not returned to his townhouse which, if you did not know, was engulfed by fire only a week ago, though whether that has any bearing on what happened to Harry cannot be known. Then finally Raphael received a message from Harry.' Celeste sighed, remembering Raphael's relief when he learned that his friend was safe.

'Go on,' Lord Peregrine signalled with a slight nod.

There was nothing to be gained by keeping anything back. 'The note had been written in haste by Harry to Raphael, telling him Harry had been held captive on the way back from his lawyer's. He said he'd escaped and was in hiding in the basement of his townhouse and that his life was in danger; that those who would see him dead were just waiting for him to come out.' She had to tread carefully now, for the truth was one thing but the reasons behind it could not be divulged. She slanted a look up at Lord Peregrine. 'He said he truly believed that unless he could escape, in disguise, his throat would be cut.'

'Good God! Harry Carstairs must have had some formidable foes if he believed that ... unless he were not of rational mind.' Lord Peregrine lowered his head. 'Have you any idea who these cutthroats were and why they wanted Carstairs?'

Celeste was glad of the gloom. Lord Peregrine would be less likely to discern the nervous working of her features and suspect she was not telling him everything. 'I think these men felt they'd been cheated. Harry owed a lot of people rather a lot of money.'

She was relieved when that seemed to satisfy Lord Peregrine, who said, 'And I presume the message came in the locket asking you to bring him clothes to effect his disguise?'

Celeste nodded, glad he could see the connection and hoping he believed it exonerated her.

'But why send the locket?' He straightened and gripped her forearms, frowning. 'And why did Lord Ogilvy send *you* to rescue Harry, my dear, if such danger threatened?'

Celeste dropped her head. 'Raphael believed I was the only one he could trust to do what needed to be done.' She remembered her own dismay at being faced with such a terrifying situation. Mary had accompanied her to the basement door after Raphael had walked them silently through the streets, ensuring to the best of his ability that no one saw Celeste enter. He'd hired a street urchin to create a minor disturbance a few yards away, pretending the lad had stolen from him so all attention would be diverted from someone entering the Cadogan Square premises.

'The locket was very valuable apparently,' Celeste added. 'Harry knew Raphael would understand the graveness of his situation if he sent it rather than just a note, which might go astray. He also suggested that I be sent as I could discard my cloak and several petticoats and so effect his means of escape without compromising mine.'

'What a brave young woman you are.' Lord Peregrine

smiled wryly but Celeste was unable to see the humour. The events of that night were still too raw.

She squeezed shut her eyes. 'A judicious combination of threat and inducement served to do the trick.'

'Well, *I* shall start with inducement.' Suddenly Lord Peregrine's breath was tickling her ear as he gently wrapped his arms about her. The warmth of the contact seeped through her as she rested her head against his chest, revelling in the rare sense of sanctuary as he murmured, 'Your betrothed has certainly sought to profit from you before you're even married. Do you love him so much that you'd so willingly sacrifice your safety?'

Or my reputation? she thought with despair, replying with resignation as she buried her face in his striped waistcoat, 'As I said, a judicious combination of threat and inducement works wonders when one has little in the way of bargaining power.' Celeste did not resist as his hands stroked her cheeks before trailing down her throat, sliding beneath her fichu to explore the sensitive skin above her décolletage. The human touch he offered so soon after she'd revealed the terror of that night was cathartic, laced though it was with danger.

'And of course I know the rest of the story, my dear,' he murmured, as he continued to caress her with gentle fingertips. 'My sister chose an inopportune time to pay a highly inappropriate visit and she found you divesting yourself of your petticoats to help Carstairs and so jumped to her own conclusions.'

'That is the truth of it, my lord,' Celeste whispered, nuzzling closer against him as she twined her arms about his neck, to deepen the contact.

This moment would be the pinnacle of all she'd ever enjoy; she realised that in the dark recesses of her brain as she only half consciously tried to draw from him all the sensations her affection-starved body craved. 'You sought me out to punish me for destroying your sister's happiness, as you believed it, but I have told you the truth.'

Whether he believed her or not, she'd never know, but she could enjoy this. In a darkened room in an artist's studio she'd be safe from straying too far from the boundaries of what was acceptable. But for now they had the privacy to indulge in the kissing and fondling that she was all to ready to throw herself into, body and soul.

In days she'd become Lady Ogilvy, after which her life stretched into the barren unknown. She'd be living in a country she had no desire even to visit, away from all that seemed safe and that had sustained her until now. Allowing Lord Peregrine the liberty to kiss her and stroke her in the darkness would not trouble her conscience, while he'd be only too happy to be given such licence.

'I could never reconcile the impression I gained of you with the hardened jezebel my sister—and others—would have you painted.' She heard the suggestion of humour in his voice. 'And I would never have asked the question of a hardened jezebel, but I would ask it of you, sweet Celeste ...'

She opened her eyes and her heart flowered to see him staring down at her with such desire. 'May I kiss you?' He moved his head closer. 'I thought the precaution of asking wise, in view of the repercussions last time I attempted such liberties.'

Celeste blinked open her eyes. 'I promise I won't slap you this time, my lord.' With a smile she primed her lip with her tongue. 'It's true; before, I felt you were indeed taking liberties, but this time I very much want you to kiss me.'

His smile was so full of tender humour she nearly dragged his head down to begin the kissing herself.

Instead, closing her eyes with a shiver, she surrendered to the sweet touch of his lips bearing down on hers with gentle and growing urgency. Her heart was free of guilt and her body ready to receive the love and desire Lord Peregrine was ready to communicate.

Even when his hand strayed to her décolletage, slipping beneath her tight bodice, she did not withdraw. She was hungry for the physical, revelling in the spears of sensation that shot from the point of his touch to somewhere in the pit of her roiling belly. Her breathing quickened, sudden short, sharp breaths leaving her starved of air and something just out of reach that she could not articulate.

It was forbidden, fascinating, all-consuming and it may be the only opportunity she'd have in her lifetime to experience the desires of body and heart.

'Ah, my lord, but you do exquisite things to me,' she murmured, shifting slightly to accommodate his change of tactics.

A moment before Lord Peregrine had been toying with her nipple. Now suddenly he swooped, pushing her left breast out of its confines and taking it into his hot, greedy mouth.

Celeste squeaked and held him tighter as he suckled her nipple. She felt the cord of connection between them grow tauter and her brain reel into the ether on a cloud of rapture as her body succumbed to unknown pleasures.

If only Lord Peregrine were her husband, then this and so much more would be sanctioned.

If only he were her husband?

If pigs could fly …

Miserably she dragged her mind back to reality.

There was as much likelihood of Lord Peregrine making her his wife as there was of Raphael loving her.

CHAPTER 8

*S*incerity was not an emotion with which Perry was much familiar or that, until now, he'd particularly esteemed. His relations with women had taught him that one never said what one really felt.

Now, with Miss Rosington responding to his overtures with all the enthusiasm that he might once have regarded as the hallmarks of an experienced jade, he could think only of how he might protect her and her innocence.

For this was enthusiasm born of innocence. She truly had not experienced the sensations he was delivering, and clearly with such success.

Xenia would say he'd been hoodwinked.

He didn't care, but nor did he believe it. He did, however, believe Miss Rosington's story.

Voices growing louder nearby suggested they would be wise to halt their lovemaking, though Peregrine was reluctant to relinquish Miss Rosington at the same time as he was careful to hold her away from the possibility of being recognised should by some chance an intruder appear.

He caught her smile as he shifted her gently.

'That was even nicer than I'd expected,' she whispered, straightening her fichu and ordering her hair. Her smile grew wistful. 'It shall sustain me when I'm in my new island home.'

He was shocked by the jolt of alarm that speared him. 'You are leaving London?' He'd not expected that.

She blinked, looking surprised. 'You did not know? Raphael and I sail directly after we've said our vows. I don't know when or if I shall be back.'

The idea that he'd not see her again was suddenly untenable. Peregrine had fondly imagined many future such trysts, stolen moments when Celeste's new husband, whom she'd roundly declared she did not love, was otherwise occupied.

Now the thought of never seeing her again left him curiously bereft.

He leaned forward to cup her face, strange thoughts he'd never imagined entertaining chasing themselves around his brain. Call him a fool but surely there came a time in a man's life when he'd be a fool to act counter to *every* instinct that screamed at him?

'You can't leave.' He shook his head, not caring that the trappings of the careless philanderer he was so at pains to cultivate had well and truly fallen from his shoulders. *She was leaving the country? No, he could not let this be.* Contouring her face with his hands he looked deep into her eyes. 'I had not realised your departure was set in stone. That it was so imminent.'

She dropped her gaze. 'In a little over a week I set sail for Jamaica.'

'There's not much time. Truly, Celeste, I cannot bear the thought that you shall be parted from me.' Her smooth shoulders shrugged out of his grasp as she stepped back, shaking her head. 'I am to be married, my lord. Much as it's true I ...' she swallowed, clearly finding the words difficult to say, 'desire to enjoy more of your attentions, I do have some honour. Raphael is to be my husband and I must submit to my duty towards him alone.'

'Submit. What an ugly word.' Pulling her close once more, he rested his chin against the jaunty straw hat nestled in her coiffure, his thoughts in turmoil. She couldn't leave, just like that. It was not possible that his heart had been so engaged; that he, a grown man and a rake to boot, should be acting like a smitten schoolboy, unable to accept the departure or defection of his apparently one true love.

'Celeste, I *can't* let you go.' It was true. The notion left him bereft. Ridiculously, surprisingly so. 'And you've said you don't want to leave. What if I could offer you an alternative—'

'I will not be your mistress, my lord!'

His mouth dropped open as she flung out of his embrace. Surely she must have seen this was the last thing he was proposing. But he was well and truly put in his place, and it took him a moment to reconcile the truth of what he felt in this moment with the manner in which he was publicly painted. It took him a moment to gather himself before he said with quiet intensity, 'You believe that a man with a reputation such as I have is incapable of making an honourable offer?

She contemplated his words. Lord, but she had the face of an angel, he thought, with lips and limbs like Venus. Now, though, he really was acting like a mooncalf. He gave himself a mental shake so as to attend to what she was saying.

'Your reputation as a rake is known throughout London, my lord. I heard of it long before I met you.'

'A rake with scruples,' he muttered feeling uncomfortable.

Her slow, spreading smile truly warmed his heart, and he knew with even greater certainty that he had to have her if she could make him feel redemption was within reach under circumstances like this.

'Raphael didn't trust me with you when he saw me go.' Her lovely mouth quirked. 'I didn't want to meet you either when I knew how little I trusted myself.'

Her words caught him by surprise and he glanced over his shoulder, for a moment wondering if this were a trap and he were about to be emasculated by a furious Lord Ogilvy.

Half laughing, the wonderful girl opposite reached across the distance between them and gripped his wrists. 'Raphael doesn't care about anything beyond my getting the locket. I'm not sure why it's so important, or if it's even just a test he's set me. But that was the entire purpose behind my coming, and my lord, for all your wonderful words, the truth is I can't see you again.' She looked so sad as she dropped his hands and took a step towards the light, her head bowed, as if she truly had the weight of the world to carry. Stopping at the threshold she smiled at him over her shoulder, 'I don't expect you to give it to me, my lord, but you have no idea how much easier my life would be if I could deliver Harry's locket to Raphael.'

Unconsciously his hand was already closing around the item inside his coat pocket, while his mind was in turmoil. Was this really what everything was about? A tawdry ingot of gold that signified who knew what but meant nothing to Peregrine.

And everything ... for without it he was of no interest to the woman he now knew he wanted more than he'd ever wanted anything.

Slowly he held it out, the disappointment in his breast spreading throughout his body and weighing him down. 'The locket is yours, Miss Rosington ....' He took a difficult breath. 'With no conditions attached.'

She was surprised, her smile eager and laden with gratitude as she hurried back a few steps to take it. She opened her mouth to speak, perhaps to thank him, but he cut in, the words too important, too fuelled with urgency to be held back.

'I do however have one request, Miss Rosington. Before you go I would like ...' He stumbled over his words, knowing she already had her sights on the door and that within moments she'd be gone. Perhaps forever.

And he couldn't bear that.

'Miss Rosington, my request is that I see you again, for the truth is I can't bear to let you go ... like this.' He stared, possibly as surprised as she was. Reaching out to draw her gently back towards him, his heart rate quickened and his palms tingled with the fear of what her response might be to the most outrageous question he was ever likely to ask.

'Go on, Lord Peregrine.'

He needed no further urging. The words that had tumbled about his brain just a second ago now formed coherence and a great sense of calm banished his turmoil.

Yes, this was the right thing ... the one thing that was guaranteed to bring him happiness and a deep contentment during the years that stretched ahead. How could he have hesitated before now?

She was waiting expectantly and he wouldn't disappoint her.

Clearing his voice he said quietly, 'Miss Rosington, I didn't realise it until you told me you were leaving the country, how much your departure would affect me. Quite frankly I don't think I can bear the idea that I'll never see you again.' He considered her, a deep sense of pleasure seeping through him to watch her surprise turn to something he truly hoped was anticipation. His own anticipation threatened to swamp him and he struggled to keep his voice steady as he went on, 'The only way that I can ensure that doesn't happen, Miss Rosington, is to make you a respectable offer.' Lord, but he hoped this was up to scratch. He'd never made a respectable offer to anyone before. Certainly he'd made roguish offers that had been roundly rejected and earned him a slap about the face. Those hadn't mattered.

But an offer that was sufficiently compelling and delivered with the right degree of gravitas was suddenly more important than any proposition he'd ever uttered.

He certainly had her attention and her expression filled him with hope. But he'd not finished.

'My desire to secure my happiness with you is, I realise, more important than anything else in my life has ever been. Please, Miss Rosington, I'm asking if you'll marry me.'

A great joy began to overtake him as he contemplated the possibilities of a shared future with this lovely, innocent creature. She, too, was smiling at him like a veritable angel.

Then suddenly her interested look turned inwards, and with sinking heart he realised a woman of such purity and virtue would not wish to throw in her lot with a man of his character.

Yet when she replied her reasons were not quite along these lines, although she failed to address them adequately, to his mind.

'Lord Peregrine, you do me the greatest honour. It's what I've desired up until this very moment, but now I realise the futility of such dreams.' Her mouth trembled and tears gathered in her eyes. 'It's simply not possible.'

'Not possible?' He pushed back his shoulders and stared down at her, indignation swamping him. How could she think of rejecting him? Why? He'd never honoured a woman like this before.

Ashamed, he realised his inner rake had taken over; this may be the very reason she chose to continue on her current, perhaps safer, path.

Still, he had to push her for a reason at the same time as trying to persuade her. 'Miss Rosington, I desire above all to marry you and you've just admitted you desired me; that you *wished* for such an outcome. How, then, is a union between us not possible?'

He waited, ready to counter any reason she might have, for he was determined now.

She hung her head and her shoulders slumped. 'For so long I've begged Raphael to release me from our contract, even though there were no other contenders, and knowing he does not, and will never, love me. But he has always refused.'

'You are not his wife *yet*. You don't need his approval.' If this were all, it could be easily fixed. But she'd not yet indicated the extent of her feelings for him and suddenly nothing was more important that he be assured that what was in her heart echoed the desperate roiling to be together that churned in his.

'You've not told me you would accept me … if I could arrange matters with Lord Ogilvy and your uncle.'

'Oh, but I would—'

'And you love me? As I love you? For I do, Miss Rosington … Celeste. Indeed I do!'

'Yes!'

He would have kissed her again had he not heard voices on the other side of the door and been reminded that time was of the essence. 'Then I shall consult with your uncle and a contract pleasing to all will be drawn up.' He clenched his jaw. 'Whatever terms he has made with Raphael, I shall ensure my offer trumps your cousin's.'

'You make it sound as if I'm the spoils of a game of hazard,' she observed sadly, shaking her head. 'No, my lord, there is no chance matters will run in your favour, for Raphael has too much invested in marrying me. Please do not press me on my reasons but the truth is that I realise now my cousin will hound me to the ends of the earth to ensure that I do my duty by him; that is, that I honour my promise and marry him—as I'm due to do in just a few short days.'

The more she objected the more determined Peregrine became that he would have her.

'Miss Rosington, you have captivated me. Entranced me. The idea that I will wake up in a week, knowing I will never see you again, is untenable.'

The voices of the others in the gallery, which had become muted with distance, now grew louder, signalling the need for even greater urgency. He caught her by the hands, pulling her quickly away from the door as he said in a low, hurried voice, 'Then we shall elope. In three days' time I can secure a Special Licence and make the necessary arrangements. You say you'd marry me if it were not for your fear of your cousin making your life intolerable. Well, dear heart, in three days' time you shall be *my* wife and there'll not be anything he can do about it. What do you say?'

She stared up at him, the fear in her eyes slowly turning to luminescent delight while his own heart beat out a joyful tattoo to witness the transformation that, yes, *he*, had effected.

'I accept, Lord Peregrine.'

He wanted to swoop down and kiss her once more but first he needed to ensure he'd covered every contingency.

'I will contact you as soon as I have something secured,' he told her, thinking as he spoke. He gripped her hands tight and held them to his lips, punctuating his sentences with kisses upon her knuckles. 'Have a small bag packed with your valuables at the ready in case it's not possible to take your trunk in the first instance. Tomorrow I shall write to you with an address. In all probability it will be easier if you pretend you are taking your maid to visit an acquaintance, therefore I shall choose a respectable meeting place at a respectable time. I do not wish to chance your reputation by whisking you off in the middle of the night.'

'You are most thoughtful, my lord.' Her mouth trembled with suppressed laughter and her eyes danced, and as he gazed upon the delightful reordering of her features he felt an overwhelming happiness, accompanied by a spear of lust.

Perhaps she was thinking what a surprise turn of events this marriage offer was compared with the illicit night of passion she must have suspected he'd originally planned.

Certainly his mind was consumed by the night of passion that was now so imminent, and so worth waiting for.

Their wedding night.

AND INDEED, WHEN CELESTE'S LEGS BUCKLED UNDER HER AS she took a seat in the drawing room of her aunt's townhouse later that afternoon and accepted a dish of tea, her mind was wholly occupied with wicked thoughts of what it really would be like to be Lord Peregrine's wife, not Raphael's.

She was finally stirred to more a robust awareness of her surroundings by the arrival of Raphael who swept into the elegantly appointed room like a sleek black cat, tossing his *tricorne* hat onto a nearby footstool before taking her free hand and brushing the back of it with his lips.

She tried not to recoil.

'How pleasant to see you,' she lied, tensing as she prepared for his inevitable inquisition.

He ignored the pleasantry. 'How did you find Romney's portraits?' He pulled away, raking his hand through his queue, his pinched handsome face showing his strain as he paced before the fire with his usual restlessness.

She knew he wasn't the slightest bit interested in whether

she'd enjoyed them or otherwise, though she was concerned he might have had her trailed.

Still, she'd not behaved with immodesty in public, so even if Mary had been quizzed the girl could honestly say her mistress had met Lord Peregrine at the studio, and farewelled him there, too.

She opened her mouth, still unsure what words to utter, for she did not know how much Raphael knew of her movements, when he cut in.

'Lord Peregrine is clearly taken with you. Did you succeed in drawing information from him?' His thoughts were obviously focused on Harry, not Celeste. 'Perhaps you entertain the same suspicions I do over Lord Peregrine's involvement. He met the *Batavia* when Harry was disembarking, and Harry was one of only a handful of gentlemen passengers onboard. Perhaps Lord Peregrine had him followed to the lawyer's and what he learned there prompted him to have a hand in what happened later? Did you think there was more he wasn't telling you, Celeste? Is it possible Lord Peregrine could in some way be responsible for what happened to Harry? That *he* sent the cutthroats, perhaps, or is in fact holding Harry himself?'

Celeste hoped Raphael's preoccupation with these various conspiracies was enough to draw his attention from the indignation she was unable to hide. What a ridiculous notion that Lord Peregrine was involved with Harry's plight.

Raphael swung round to look at her once more, a faint smile marring his handsome face. 'But mayhap these are matters he's only prepared to divulge with a little more … persuasion. After all, a rake such as Lord Peregrine is used to enjoying the audience of a beautiful woman. No doubt you are simply one more conquest for him. And Lord Peregrine obviously hasn't an inkling of your real interest in Harry Carstairs.'

He moved behind her, his hot breath on the back of her neck as he lay his hand on her shoulder and bent to whisper in her ear, making her squirm in discomfort. Raphael knew more than she did. But Lord Peregrine involved in wrongdoing? No, certainly not that. He wanted to *marry* her. He was sincere. She might not be the experienced jade he'd thought her when he first pursued her, but she had no doubt about his sincerity in this important matter.

Struggling for inspiration, Celeste cast about for what snippets that might satisfy Raphael. What could she tell her betrothed that would make him retreat, leave her alone, drop his hand from her shoulder this moment? Release her forever.

Or at least for the next couple of days so she could wait in peace for the letter that would arrive from …

Her future husband, Lord Peregrine.

She put her hand to her heart to still its wild palpitations, though pretending languid boredom while her mind raced for an answer that would solve her current distress.

'Lord Peregrine was disappointing when it came to information regarding Harry's exact whereabouts, however, it would appear that Harry has ….'

Even in her self-imposed darkness she was acutely aware of Raphael, tense and waiting. He was like a coiled spring or the bow of an arrow drawn back, ready to leap to life the moment she satisfied him with her response.

'… Communicated.'

Celeste stared into the dregs of her tea, immediately wishing she'd thought of something else to tell him as she tried to dampen her restless excitement. Why this? A lie she could not substantiate? It had been prompted by foolish desperation when she was surely cleverer than that.

Yet she'd had to think of something. She was not rid of Raphael's hold over her yet, and until that time she needed reasons up her sleeve for her cousin to sanction future freedom.

'He's sent a letter?' Raphael smoothed the snowy linen at his neck, his voice infused with sudden pleasure as he began to pace once more. 'Then he's not dead?' At the window embrasure he flung round, his countenance so radiant with joy that Celeste nearly wilted in the face of it, knowing how consumed with rage he'd be when he learned of her treachery.

Oh Lord, but she was so ready to escape him.

'And Lord Peregrine gave me … this.' She swallowed, holding out the locket.

In two strides Raphael was before her, towering over the little gilt chair Celeste occupied and staring down at her open palm.

'This is … incredible, Celeste.' He held out his hand for the locket then, frowning, began to study it, both on the outside and the inside. His voice was full of wonder. 'Why, my dear, you have achieved a success I'd strongly doubted. I was certain his lordship would place certain … conditions upon its return.'

He quirked an eyebrow and his lips twitched. 'I shall not ask if you were forced to trade a kiss at Romney's studio, Celeste. I had you followed, you know, but nothing untoward could have occurred during such a brief interlude.' His smile grew wider as he gazed upon the locket. 'So Harry is alive and well yet you have not told me how he has communicated and from whom you received the information. Lord Peregrine, I presume. Well, I shall soon find Harry and then you and I will be married, and Harry will accompany us to Jamaica. Joy will be in the ascendant and no more will I subject you to the dangers this unconscionable libertine Lord Peregrine poses.'

Celeste was unable to meet Raphael's inquisitorial gaze.

'Lord Peregrine gave the locket to me … as a token … of what else he's prepared to tell me, knowing my interest.'

Raphael stilled. His look narrowed and his voice dropped. 'And what did you suggest to Lord Peregrine *was* your interest?'

Nausea rose up in her throat. She was not in the habit of lying. Lord Peregrine knew nothing further he could add to the mystery.

'I told him Harry was my lover,' she whispered, shrinking from Raphael's uncertain reaction; but this lie, based on Lord Peregrine's initial suspicions of her, was her only inspiration. Quickly she went on in the silence, 'I made clear my interest in Lord Peregrine but said that naturally I was concerned, in view of my past association with Harry, that he was safe.' She clasped her hands together to stay their trembling as she went on, 'I suggested to Lord Peregrine that he might be induced to tell me what information he'd hinted to me he had pertaining to Harry's whereabouts.'

To her astonishment Raphael let out a roar of laughter. Sobering, he raked her with the critical gaze she was so used to and which never failed to make her feel like a piece of meat or a partridge on a hook, curing in the larder. 'Why, my dear Celeste, I truly did not believe you capable of such subterfuge. You told him you were Harry's lover? Well, that's what Lord Peregrine has believed of you from the start, I daresay. But why did you suspect Lord Peregrine had knowledge or involvement in Harry's disappearance, might I ask?'

Celeste couldn't meet his eye. Staring into the fire, she whispered, 'It was a chance remark he made …' *What, oh what, could she say?* Then she remembered Lord Cowdril's comment at the dinner table and on a wave of inspiration she added, 'Harry owes him a lot of money. I believe Harry owes a lot of people a lot of money, and something you said earlier and something else Lord Peregrine said hinted that someone may be holding Harry either as revenge or until he recouped what he was owed.'

This certainly got Raphael's attention. 'But Lord Peregrine gave you the locket, Celeste. Why? The locket was his means of recouping what he was owed, yet he clearly didn't know it.'

'What do you mean, Raphael?' She cocked her head. 'I am confused. You've said this locket is meaningful, but you've not said exactly how its value extends beyond its value in gold, or indeed its sentimental value.'

Raphael grinned. 'There are six numbers engraved on the inside, behind Miss Paige's picture.' He sounded smug. 'These are the numbers to a security box containing Harry's aunt's fortune. That is why Harry sent the locket to me and why he needs it so much.' He chuckled. 'But now you have it. Oh my dear, that was masterful. If Lord Peregrine wishes to receive what is owed him he need have looked no further. Clearly when Harry entrusted the locket to a message boy, he believed at the time he could escape or that he'd not be killed rather than be forced to give up his fortune, but *I* would do anything to secure Harry's release. Now it is up to you, Celeste, to determine the terms of his ransom.'

Celeste shook her head slowly. 'It's true, I traded a kiss for the locket, but I denied Lord Peregrine what he *most* wanted.' If honesty had worked so well for her last time, it stood to reason it should be the basis of her next lie. 'He therefore refused to tell me further details, though he has promised to reveal all if I agree to meet with him again.'

'The arrogance!' Raphael pulled out his snuffbox and took a pinch. 'London's most celebrated libertine truly believes that on such bare acquaintance you'll happily divest yourself of your honour—and your virtue—in return for the information he chooses to give you.'

'It's what you've all but asked me to do, Raphael.' Celeste

tried to keep the spleen from her tone, just as she was careful to hide her indignation at the object of her obsession—no, her love—being painted in such terms.

Nevertheless, she'd say and do what she had to. All she needed was another couple of days quietly left to her own devices before she could respond to Lord Peregrine's instructions and slip into the night with a few possessions ready to begin her new life ... as the handsome viscount's wife.

The thought galvanised her with renewed hope and energy and she straightened in the face of Raphael's taunts. 'I shall not meet with him, of course. As your future wife, I know the importance of ensuring no hint of scandal attaches—'

'Oh, you will meet him, Celeste.'

She glanced up at his gritty tone. Raphael was not laughing now. No, his face was a mask of determination. As it would be, Celeste supposed, for he was as close as he'd managed to get in finding Harry since his friend had disappeared and there was absolutely no way he was going to squander his best opportunity.

He certainly didn't care about squandering Celeste's virtue, if that was the price that had to be paid, though no doubt Raphael had a plan in place. He would not want to be saddled with an impure wife, or one to whom scandal attached.

'You will extract everything Lord Peregrine knows but I don't need to tell you to be careful. He might be Lady Busselton's lover but such loyalties won't stop such a man from taking advantage of *you*, my sweet innocent.'

The world stilled. Raphael continued talking.

Celeste was no longer attending.

Lady Busselton was Lord Peregrine's *lover*? She clenched her fists in her lap and prayed Raphael would not observe her trembling as she digested this bombshell. She'd heard they were old friends at Lady Cowdril's dinner table ... but *lovers?*

Feverishly Celeste tried to remember if she'd been aware of anything to suggest this was so, and could not. Lady Busselton was handsome to be sure, but she was a good ten years older than Celeste, and the widow of two husbands. There was an air of world-weary boredom about her that Celeste supposed some might find intriguing but which Celeste found cloying and repugnant.

Devastation lodged in her breast. How could Lord Peregrine find such a jaded creature attractive?

No, she reminded herself, he did not; else he'd not be marrying Celeste in three days. He'd made her a proper offer. He was not toying with her as he'd done in the beginning. True love had blossomed between them. She might be an innocent but she knew reciprocated love and passion when she stumbled upon it.

Raphael had made that comment in an attempt to ensure Celeste was even more on her guard with him.

Surely that was how it was?

Though discomposed, she nevertheless adopted a mask of mild interest while Raphael went on, 'Clearly his lordship knows more than he has told you, meaning you must spend whatever time you need with him to learn exactly what has happened to Harry. You must discover the truth, Celeste. I truly believe you can, though of course you must be on your guard. He will do his best to seduce you, I can assure you.'

Doubt flooded her. Was she no more than an innocent little fool the viscount found a pleasant diversion? She had, after all, advertised her availability with all the discretion of a Union Jack atop a flagpole in a strong wind.

But that aside, Lord Peregrine had asked her to *marry*

him. This very moment, in fact, he was arranging matters in order for them to spend the rest of their days together.

This was not a cruel hoax. He was sincere. She was certain of it.

So certain, that when Lord Peregrine's hastily scrawled missive with instructions to meet her at a respectable Cadogan Square address the very next day was delivered to the faithful Mary in the street by a breathless street urchin, and then into Celeste's trembling hand, Celeste nearly burst into tears for joy.

Lord Peregrine was sincere and clearly so eager to be with her he'd managed to organise matters in an even shorter time than the three days he'd estimated it would take him.

Carefully burning every last scrap of the note in the fire, after giving the boy a coin and a monogrammed handkerchief as proof she'd received his lordship's message, Celeste immediately set about rearranging her day and, with pounding heart, preparing herself for the most daring act she'd ever embarked upon.

Her elopement with her wicked, wonderful, *reformed* rake, Lord Peregrine.

The risks of discovery were so great that she would not even tell Mary what her plan was just yet, although Mary's chaperonage was needed for the moment.

Aunt Branwell believed Celeste was visiting a friend's house that afternoon to play cards, with Mary naturally accompanying her. The carriage had been brought round to take her to a very respectable address a short ride across London. There was no incriminating note and no servants entrusted with her secret who could possibly expose her before she had achieved her goal.

And as she waited on the top step of her aunt's townhouse for the footman to open the carriage door, her heart was full to bursting with all the possibilities that lay ahead.

For this would be the last time she issued down these stairs as simply Miss Celeste Rosington.

Before midnight struck, her world would be tilted on an axis far more disposed towards her happiness and she'd be venturing forth as Viscount Peregrine's new wife.

She wondered if it were possible to die of happiness.

CHAPTER 9

*T*wilight was casting a golden sheen upon the cobbled streets when Celeste, hidden by a concealing cloak, arrived at the stipulated address. As if by magic, the front door opened the moment she raised her hand to knock. A small, round-faced woman dressed in black, who introduced herself as the housekeeper, welcomed her into the grand hallway, then led her to a small drawing room where she offered Celeste refreshment while another servant led Mary downstairs to join the staff.

For a moment Celeste was confused by her reception, wondering if she'd perhaps walked straight into Lord Peregrine's own townhouse. Then she realised that the décor and general air did not accord with the kind of abode a single gentleman was likely to inhabit when in London. There was a distinctly feminine touch to the furnishings, while several family portraits of a pretty young lady and a well attired, if serious-faced, gentleman stared at her from the walls. They seemed familiar, and yet Celeste could not place the likeness. As she'd become acquainted with so many new people since she'd arrived in London, though, it was perfectly reasonable she'd not remember them all.

She smiled her thanks as the parlourmaid brought her some Madeira, excitement and nervousness raging war as she tried to imagine how she could properly order her features once Lord Peregrine appeared.

For she'd never been more sure of anything when it came to choosing which man offered her the brighter future: Raphael or Lord Peregrine.

Lord Peregrine might be a libertine but somehow she, innocent, artless Celeste, had found a way to breach the careless, louche barrier he'd erected against overtures to his heart.

He loved her and she loved him. It was incredible. Astonishing and miraculous and she'd never forget the sense of wonder and excitement she now felt, knowing that her whole life was about to be turned upside down.

Finishing her Madeira, and with the silence beginning to play on her nerves, she continued to indulge her girlish daydreams. Soon she would be Lady Peregrine, wife to a handsome, humorous, highly intelligent man. There would be sparring matches and there would be passionate trysts.

There would also be exciting bedroom activities. She was not exactly certain of the details involved, however her bodily responses to the preliminaries of such lovemaking filled her with confidence that she'd thoroughly enjoy the proper act if Lord Peregrine were in charge.

The thought of sharing a bed with Raphael filled her with shame and disgust; but when she replaced Peregrine in such imaginings her body flowered with want.

More time passed. Hiding her impatience, Celeste studied the room. On a stand in the corner a Sevres vase had pride of place. A collection of Royal Doulton china figurines lined the shelf of a walnut-inlaid cabinet against the far wall, while around the Aubusson carpet was ranged a cluster of finely made Chinese-style furniture with latticework and lacquer, bearing the hallmarks of the famous cabinet-maker Thomas Chippendale.

The draperies were of the finest, imported, Celeste suspected, from the Far East.

Clearly the home belonged to someone with contacts in far-flung parts of the world; someone possessed of a great deal of money.

But whose house could it be? As she finished her second glass of Madeira and her mind continued to roam, she wondered why Lord Peregrine was keeping her waiting so long.

Presently she heard footsteps in the passage and the door opened to another rosy-cheeked woman with neat grey curls, wearing a dark blue floral saque-backed gown, who rushed forward, greeting Celeste as if she'd not expected her.

'My dear, how long have you been waiting? Mrs Warner did not tell me you were here. But you are alone?' She looked about her with a frown, as if unable to believe Celeste had come unaccompanied. Then she blinked rapidly, lowering her voice as she whispered, 'Ah, but it's because of Harry that you're here! You are a friend of Charlotte's, of course. I've only just this moment returned and was not expecting you, but I wonder why my housekeeper did not fetch my nephew down to speak with you?'

'Harry?' Celeste could only blink stupidly for a strange lethargy was permeating her bones. 'Harry is *here*?' She forced herself to sit up straight, silently chastising herself for having drunk that second glass of wine, which seemed to have gone straight to her head.

The woman opposite was making no sense.

She spoke as if she were Harry Carstairs' aunt and this was her house.

Why had Lord Peregrine sent her *here*?

The answers were too difficult to tease out. She made to lift her hand to her cheek but her limb felt like lead. Horrified, she tried to stand, but her legs would not obey her. Celeste blinked, her neck feeling like a fragile stem unable to support the heaviness of her head, and it was difficult to raise her chin as the parlourmaid entered the room in response to Mrs Carstairs' urgent summons. The fright in the woman's voice pierced Celeste's numbed brain, though everything else happening around her was confused and muted.

'Miss Rosington, what is it? You are unwell!' cried Mrs Carstairs as, together with the maid they supported her on her little gilt chair so she'd not fall to the ground.

Then Mrs Warner, the housekeeper was rushing into the room, though Celeste noticed she didn't appear quite as shocked.

Celeste opened her mouth to speak but her words came out a jumble of slurred nonsense. Her limbs did not obey her woozy exhortation to respond and she was only vaguely conscious of the housekeeper's demand that the footman be summoned to help convey Celeste to one of the chambers, 'for Lord knows, we can't do it alone, the state the poor miss is in.'

Despite being nearly insensible, Celeste had enough cognisance to be horrified by her situation.

This really *was* the Carstairs' residence? Did Harry live here? It made no sense.

She tried to object when they lifted her but as she had no strength to resist, she suffered herself to be carried up the stairs and deposited on a large four-poster in a lavishly appointed bedroom. A large, stuffed monkey in a glass box grinned from a table in the corner, while the draperies were richly embroidered and clearly not of English design. How strange that her mind seemed unable to cope with the more urgent matter of what possible reason someone would have for wanting her here but, instead, dwelled on irrelevancies.

'Unlace her, Mary, I'll remove her shoes.'

What a relief it was to see Mary by her side. She heard the two servants discuss her disrobing as if she were a mere doll, but she was unable to do anything for herself. Strangely, she was not consumed by terror, now; merely a mild distress, and a great desire for sleep.

All would be right, she tried to assure herself. Lord Peregrine would come soon. He would help her, comfort her … and explain.

He'd bring the Special Licence. She might feel unwell but that wouldn't stop her from being married.

When she was laid out in a lawn nightrail, her clothes neatly folded on the kist at the end of the bed, she forced open her eyes one last time as Mary and the housekeeper retreated, closing the door the behind them, their whispered concern overlaid by the high-pitched tones of Mrs Carstairs, whose confusion was clearly as great as Celeste's own.

Still Lord Peregrine did not come. Celeste tried to keep her mind alert and her eyes open for as long as she could. Where was he? What could be keeping him?

And why was she lying in a bed in the house of Harry Carstairs' aunt?

Finally she could cling to consciousness long longer. Her eyes fluttered closed as she drifted gently upon a tide of heavy lethargy until she was claimed by sleep's comforting embrace.

All would be well, she reassured herself. Lord Peregrine would ensure her safety. Beneath the exterior he chose to show the world he was kind and loving.

And he loved *her*.

An eternity later Celeste awoke to the quiet turning of the doorknob. Opening heavy lids, she blinked at the silhouette of a tall gentleman against the dim light of the corridor. For a moment he stood there, simply looking at her, then quietly he closed the door behind him as he stepped inside the chamber.

'Lord Peregrine?' Celeste whispered, immediately chastising herself for her lack of discretion with what few wits remained to her, for her limbs were so heavy she could barely move.

He did not answer, and despite her condition she felt a jolt of alarm.

If this was not Lord Peregrine, then what gentleman would be admitted to a lady's private chamber in a respectable house?

But of course. It must be the doctor.

The stranger took a few steps towards the bed and lowered himself onto the chair at her side. In the darkness, Celeste heard his heavy breathing while she waited for the inevitable question that would begin the examination.

She was surprised by the sound of a gentle thud upon the floor, followed by another.

She forced open her eyes and her mind struggled to assimilate the man's actions, for what doctor would remove his boots?

And what gentlemen would then divest himself of his coat, and waistcoat, and cravat? she wondered in growing alarm as these items of clothing were followed by his pantaloons and stockings. The gentleman loomed over her, his expression utterly indiscernible in the dim light, while his voice conveyed both great reluctance and regret.

She opened her mouth to scream, but not sound came. Whatever lethargy had taken control of her body had also rendered her voiceless.

'Forgive me, Miss Rosington. I wish this as much as you,' he muttered, as he removed his shirt and climbed, naked, beneath the covers.

His next words were both shocking, inexplicable and of no comfort at all. "But please don't be afraid for I shan't hurt you.' He sighed deeply as he drew the covers up to his chin while Celeste struggled to move away from him. 'You may not believe me now,' his voice was grim, 'but distasteful though my actions are to both of us, they are done to ensure your safety, and preserve the lives of those we love.'

And then with the horror, darkness swept over Celeste and carried her thankfully into oblivion.

CHAPTER 10

*D*amn! But the wait was challenging his patience. A distinctly testy Lord Peregrine was in no mood for pleasantries as Nelson struggled to find him a waistcoat to suit his finicky mood.

'Not the pink and gold,' Perry grunted as he rejected the finely worked brocade garment Nelson had just handed to him, tossing it to the floor. 'Far too cheerful for one as black as I am today.'

'Pink and gold is very good with black, *sah*,' commented Nelson calmly, bending to retrieve the offending garment and stroking it almost reverently.

Peregrine raised one eyebrow and almost smiled. Whenever Nelson believed his master was behaving like a petulant schoolboy, he reverted to the ironic address of 'sah'—a dismissible impertinence except that, of course, Nelson was a slave. Certainly, such a gross lack of respect would have many masters relegating their errant slaves to manual labour below slaves, but Nelson was obviously well aware his position was secure.

'Watch your tongue, my good man,' Peregrine grunted as

they both stared at the waistcoat in Nelson's arms. 'You're in debt to me to the tune of two hundred pounds and if I choose to pursue it ...' He raised an eyebrow, not quite smiling at the preposterousness of coming after a slave for money he'd never realise. Last week, during their regular cribbage sessions when Peregrine took his bath, the situation had been reversed. But of course Nelson was too well trained to allude to this in so many words.

He merely bowed his incongruously powdered head and replied with heavy deference, 'Very good, my lord.'

Too much deference, Peregrine reflected, when he was ready for some verbal sparring with his slave. Nelson could switch his mood from serious to amused like no one else he knew. And Perry was in the mood for being diverted, now that it was taking longer to obtain the Special Licence he'd hoped, and that soon he must pay court to Xenia, something he relished less and less these days.

'So, pink and gold is very good with black, eh? Said by one with an eye to the dusky ladies, Nelson? Does this pink and gold palette set off the midnight shade of your favourite negress? Do you speak from experience, or are you suggesting it to counterbalance my black mood?' He finished the remark on a suitably severe note.

'A slave gets no opportunity to enjoy the pleasures of the ladies, my lord.'

Perry conceded this with a shrug. 'Then the implication can only be that you think me in a vile humour. Well, I'm sorry you have to suffer for it. I shall try and mend my ways before I proceed where duty calls.' Lord but he had no wish to see Xenia tonight.

Not when he was on fire to whisk Miss Rosington— Celeste—far away from this sordid city before her fresh ingenuousness could be tarnished by the vile tongues of people just like Xenia.

For once nobleness beat strongly in his breast, forcing a reluctant smile as he regarded himself, for the first time, with pride.

Most certainly he was pleasing himself by making her his bride, but he was doing so in the knowledge that he was saving her from desperate unhappiness. He would give her a good life.

He just wished arrangements weren't taking so damn long, for much as he'd like to scoop her up and devour her this very moment, he had to prove that he'd laid the ground-work for how he intended to go on. With measured care contrasted with robust and sinful enjoyment!

The moment they were married he'd transport Celeste to a delightful abode he'd secured only this morning and which she'd find strewn with rose petals as she crossed the thresh-old. And that was before she even reached the bedroom. There, he'd arranged for roses in abundance across the white and gold counterpane. The Lancaster Rose, to be exact, for hadn't she triumphed indeed?

Her sweet charm had well and truly breached his calcu-lating, dissolute exterior and she needed to know how highly he held her in regard, for that—and for so much more.

And then he'd show her what it *really* was like to be loved and revered.

He licked his lips as his manservant worked his way around him, his body on fire as he contemplated discovering his new wife's wondrous delights. He must restrain himself, though, in the beginning. Prove himself a lover with finesse and take things slowly, for she was a virgin and he'd never bedded a virgin. He wanted her to enjoy herself as much as he certainly was going to.

'Have I forgotten anything, Nelson?' he murmured, staring at his reflection.

Nelson stepped back and regarded him with a critical eye.

'I do not think so, m'lord. You look every inch the gentleman of fashion.'

'No, I mean with regard to tomorrow. The moment I have the Special Licence in my hands and the parson on hand I'll send a note round for Miss Rosington to meet me at the townhouse I've secured for us. No one will be the wiser if we spend the first night there before we embark for France.' Excitement filled him but he frowned as he dusted a speck of dust from his sleeve. 'She'll need someone to attend her in the beginning, of course. You've seen to that, I take it?'

Nelson nodded.

'But you've been discreet. No one knows anything of our plans?'

Nelson shook his head, but he did so with the faintest crease between his brows and immediately Peregrine demanded, 'Well, what is it?'

Nelson paused, uncertainly. 'Discretion has been the order for the day for both of us, m'lord, but I did fancy one of the under housemaids was stoking up the fire at the far end of the room when you made mention of something pertaining to arrangements. I do not believe she could have heard, but I did become aware of her only as she quitted the room.'

Peregrine swung round. Lord, he wanted Celeste this instant like he'd never wanted anything. Now that she was so close to becoming his, and chosen to throw in her lot with absolutely no reservations to be with him, he had to protect her. Like a bear.

'We can take no chances.' His throat felt dry just at the thought of holding her against him tomorrow, not to mention all the other things he would do. Strange, he'd thought his emotional state would calm in the interim, but the opposite was happening. He was like an impatient schoolboy. 'See that Miss Rosington receives a message not to go out this evening. She intimated she would not, but I would prefer to reiterate that, to make certain she comes to no harm. Nelson, I'm charging you with this. Find someone reliable to pass on my concerns and to tell Miss Rosington I will send her full details in the morning.'

Nelson inclined his head. 'You are determined, my lord.' His large mouth stretched into a rare grin. 'It is good to see you charged with a noble mission.'

Peregrine raised an eyebrow and forced himself to stand straight and not to sag with the onerous duty thrust upon him tonight. 'Yes, Miss Rosington is a noble mission. A noble, *worthy* one. She'll be good for me, Nelson.'

For the first time, as he stared critically at his reflection, he was not speared with disgust at his failings. Even his pathetic attempt at nine years old to save his drowning mother was imbued with a different light, for hadn't he *tried*? Since he could remember, his uncle, into whose care he'd been thrust after being orphaned that dreadful day, was wont to regard the attempts of Peregrine and his father pathetic failures. 'You lost her. You let the prize get away,' he'd slur with that twisted lip when he was in his cups. 'And hell will claim you for it ... here, have another drink with me.' He'd burdened Peregrine with his vices and his misery for almost as long as Peregrine could remember.

Recently Peregrine had learned that his uncle had made Peregrine's mother a marriage offer she had rejected in favour of Peregrine's father. Perhaps his uncle never forgave his brother for having won what he had wanted.

And Peregrine had let his uncle's bitterness poison Peregrine's sense of self.

Miss Rosington had changed all that.

Now, as Peregrine drew back his shoulders and stared into his eyes in the looking glass, he saw a handsome, dark-haired man with an honest face. No irony marred the resolve of his mouth or the clear intent of his gaze.

Indeed, he'd never been more resolved and intent on doing good in his life than now. Miss Rosington needed rescuing. Miss Rosington was worth fighting dragons over.

Miss Rosington would redeem him because she would inspire him to be the man his father—not his uncle—regarded him.

With a sigh he turned. 'And now I must pay my respects to Lady Busselton.'

FINALLY OUTFITTED IN A BLACK VELVET ENSEMBLE, SET OFF BY the offending pink and gold, which Xenia had once admired, Perry was admitted to the grand saloon belonging to his hostess where the small party expecting him at Cosgrave House was already in attendance.

Sir Samuel Wray and a gentleman introduced as Mr Danvers were playing cards in front of the fire, but Xenia waved Perry over from where she sat upon the sofa, hitherto deep in conversation with her friend.

'You kept us waiting, Perry,' she admonished him, tapping him playfully on the shoulder with her fan as he bowed before them. 'You remember my goddaughter, Mariah, don't you? She's been in a fever of anticipation to see you again.'

With mild surprise, he observed the blush that spread across Xenia's young companion's face before she averted her cheek with a stammered protest.

Good lord, another one, he thought, and knew he ought to feel sorry for her. Xenia had brought her along to humiliate her for her amusement, and the young woman was playing right into her hands. He almost felt like making up to Miss Morecombe if only to annoy Xenia, but he no longer had the palate for cruelty. Miss Rosington's refreshing innocence had tapped into some well of goodness he'd not known existed in his cold, black heart.

Ignoring Xenia's barb and Miss Morecombe's blush, he took a chair opposite the ladies. 'What titillating news had you two so absorbed when I was announced?'

He waited for the inevitable list of unfortunates Xenia would no doubt reel off. The greater the fall from grace, the more Xenia relished the tale.

Xenia was quick to oblige, and Perry listened with a sense of detachment as he studied the prurient gleam in her eye beneath her arched eyebrows, the pursing of the lips he once fancied he'd relish beneath his some day, and the tautness of her lushly rounded body which finally was to be his reward for more than a decade of patience. Now he felt not the slightest desire.

Beneath lowered lashes his old friend slanted him a knowing look as she prepared to deliver the *coup de grace* to her story of scandal and disgrace; perhaps she sensed his detachment, for she faltered for the merest moment before the ignominious ending tripped off her tongue.

'A salutary tale, would you not agree, Mariah? Perry?'

'Makes uncomplicated matrimony sound very appealing.' Perry sent both unmarried ladies a bland smile.

Miss Morecombe stammered something; Xenia merely ran a languid gaze from the floor up the length of his satin encased legs, lingering on his groin as she murmured, 'Widowhood is infinitely preferable.' She gave a gentle sigh, adding, 'A widow has far greater licence to sample life's possibilities without being shackled to them.'

'Marriage has done you no harm, Xenia.' Perry was able to sound more robust now. 'You have two fine boys at school and are considerably richer in assets than you were before you had a tiresome husband—or two—to consider.'

'Granted, they gave me wealth and my sons. I was fond of each of them in their way.' Xenia looked wistful and for a moment Perry imagined she was gripped by the poignancy of some distant memory. Then her mouth twisted and she said, 'But husbands are only for advancing one materially, and increasing one's status. One does not choose to marry one's lover. Is that not so, Perry?'

He thought of Miss Rosington. He'd wanted to make her his lover once. His uncle had conditioned him to believe that physical desire precluded marriage. A wife was to be an obedient brood mare. A man took a mistress so he could discard her the moment his wandering eye found some delectable morsel he preferred.

Certainly, he could think of few couples who'd married solely for love and those who had, he'd once thought rash.

He changed the subject. 'You are making Miss Morecombe blush. Perhaps she disagrees, yet does not feel in a position to contradict you, Xenia.' Rising, he indicated the recently vacated card table. 'Shall we play a game of whist, ladies?'

Obediently they rose, Xenia complaining mildly, 'And why should Miss Morecombe not feel confident to contradict me, Perry, if her thoughts run counter to mine? Robust argument is far more pleasing than insipid accord.' She looked severely at her goddaughter. 'Mariah must grow up able to hold her own in all company. Even dangerous company, like yours, Perry,' she added playfully.

'Dangerous? I am not dangerous.' He frowned as he held out his arm to Miss Morecombe, disliking the epithet he'd always relished when he had an eye for the ladies but a great caution when it came to becoming embroiled in anything that might propel him to the altar.

He'd not thought his roving eye would be content to

remain fixed. His uncle had done a good job persuading him it was not for men like them.

But he'd chosen well. He'd enjoy watching his own wife grow and blossom by his side, a loving helpmate.

Sir Samuel was rising from the fireplace, holding out Miss Morecombe's chair, requesting that Miss Morecombe take his place in the game that the others had chosen to continue.

'Ah, Perry, just you and I,' Xenia sighed after she'd dispatched her clearly nervous goddaughter to the company of the three card-playing gentlemen. 'I never see you alone these days.' She began to walk, indicating over her shoulder for him to follow her. The saloon was vast, with three clusters of seating, fine objects from around the world arrayed upon plinths and enormous oil paintings staring down from the walls. Cosgrave House was the family home of Xenia's late husband, and by virtue of the son Xenia had borne him, would be hers until the child came of age in fourteen years. Xenia had done well, but Perry knew she was rash with money and that she frequently lost great sums at gaming. Perhaps, in her usual style, she was considering her next ploy to shore up her future.

Perry's own fortune, perhaps?

Behind a large gilt-edged decoupage screen, which looked as if it had been brought back on his travels from the far east by Xenia's father, Xenia halted, and Perry's unchecked progress brought him into closer proximity than suddenly made him comfortable.

In this light she looked like a faery queen, the wax candle-light glinting on the jewels that adorned her high, powdered coiffure, her deep blue eyes sparkling with desire and mischief, her mouth pouting prettily. The instant image was in every way desirable but quickly displaced by the memory of what Perry knew her to be: venal, calculating and cruel.

Yes, cruel. And he'd been her ally. Disgust bubbled up inside at the thought that he'd agreed to her wager that night at the theatre.

But for now he must be careful not to offend Xenia, for she was unpredictable.

'I have been busy, Xenia.'

'Too busy to make time to see me, that's true.' She arched into him and raised her face from his chest, just like in the past, though she'd never allowed him to kiss her more than briefly. He remembered the many occasions when he'd left her company, churning with unsatisfied desire, breathless and determined to one day have this beautiful woman who'd made him her confidante and who teased and tantalised him so unmercifully. 'It's hard when old friends cannot make the time to strengthen the bonds of felicity so necessary to maintain mutual trust,' she murmured. 'I have missed your company. You've always been so dependable, Perry.'

'Between husbands and lovers?' He made sure his tone was light, not accusatory, and to his relief she responded in a bantering tone. The soft voices from the rest of the company at the far end of the room intruded faintly.

'I thought perhaps you were angry with me, Xenia.'

She sent him a look of surprise. 'Because you've not yet administered justice to that conniving wench Miss Rosington?' Xenia gave a little laugh. 'Perhaps we should all be grateful to her. Your sister is well rid of that low creature, Harry Carstairs; and if Miss Rosington and Mr Carstairs want to scandalise society and bring disgrace upon their families with their illicit liaison, what business is it of mine? Granted, their shabby behaviour inspired me with vengeance when I first heard of it, but now I think Charlotte has made a lucky escape.'

Perry kept himself as rigid and unresponsive, as he judged to be safe under the present circumstances. Xenia *would* lash out if he defended her offensive allegation against Miss Rosington or appeared to lack enthusiasm for her company.

Forcing a smile, Perry arrested Xenia's wandering hand, briefly brushing the back of it with his lips before giving her a bolstering and equally brief squeeze of the shoulders.

'The others will be getting ideas about us, Xenia, if we do not show ourselves.' He offered her his arm and she, after a hesitation and a suspicious look at him, took it.

With a dignified tilt to her chin as she walked with him, Xenia said, 'Perhaps you think that without your mission accomplished I will not reward you with what was promised?'

Perry chose his words carefully, and invested his look with something more suitable than the acute distaste he now felt at the prospect of sharing Xenia's bed. It was certainly not the time to reject her.

'We must choose our moment, Xenia. We must be careful. Shall we join the others?'

Chatting companionably, they reached the carpet in front of the fire as the door opened and the butler appeared, bearing what looked to be a hastily folded parchment upon a silver salver.

'For Lord Peregrine,' he said, when Xenia put her hand out to take it.

Surprised, Perry picked it up. Who would want to reach him at this hour? His first thought was that Miss Rosington needed him, but he quickly dismissed that for she'd not know his whereabouts. He certainly hoped she didn't.

'It's from Charlotte,' he said, in answer to Xenia's question, having scanned the few lines of the hastily scrawled note.

'And what does Charlotte want at this hour?'

Xenia indicated to Sir Samuel, who'd just risen from the card table, to refresh her drink.

Perry frowned and tapped the parchment with his fore-finger. 'Apparently,' he said with some bemusement, 'Harry has come home.'

Xenia clapped her hands. 'Why, that's marvellous news. So Charlotte has seen him then? Is he prepared to atone for his scandalous treatment of her and set a new wedding date? Forget my words of before. Charlotte is deeply in love and Harry is a marvellous catch. You must ensure he does the honourable thing, Perry.'

Peregrine frowned. The note suggested that achieving such an outcome would not be so straightforward.

Xenia quickly realised this, too, after snatching the note from his loose grip and reading the brief few lines.

'Why, he's not even seen her,' she said, handing it back with a gasp of outrage. 'Charlotte writes that he was observed arriving at his aunt's premises like a thief in the night, entering by the servant's door. You must go over directly, Perry, and hold him to account.' She swung round, the swish of her skirts causing the cards to stir and the players to look up in some angst.

Perry raised his hands, palms outward. 'I don't see what I can do.'

'You owe it to Charlotte, as her brother, to defend her honour.'

It was true, he conceded, that only Harry was in a position to tell them the truth behind his mysterious flight.

'You're *not* coming with me, Xenia,' he warned, turning at her soft tread behind him. 'You can't possibly leave Miss Morecombe alone, unchaperoned.'

She pouted. 'Very well then, leave me to make your apologies, though I'll expect a full reckoning the moment you're done with him.' In a change of tack, she put her head on one side, and was smiling at him when he turned at the door.

'Come back here afterwards, Perry.' Her tone was hushed and suggestive. 'I don't mind how late you are.'

'We'll see.'

By God, he was ready to have a woman to warm his bed again, but it wasn't Xenia he wanted.

An image of Celeste's pure face and sweet smile intruded. The idea of a marriage to a woman who embodied beauty, truth and purity was so very much more desirable than remaining unwed or chasing after experienced and jaded creatures like Xenia.

CHAPTER 11

*T*he night was dark with no moon, so the carriage had to travel slowly through the cobbled streets, which put Perry into a fever of frustrated irritation. Damn the wretched man for ruining his sister's life. He'd once liked Carstairs, a mild-mannered, almost shy fellow, he'd thought. Unremarkable in every respect, really, but for the fact he was an only son possessed of a sizeable fortune, thanks to his recent unexpected inheritance.

Peregrine supposed he was handsome enough in his way. Certainly Charlotte seemed to find his long white fingers, his slightly protuberant cow's eyes and his quiet intense manner to her satisfaction. She'd been overjoyed by his unexpected marriage proposal just before he'd set sail for Jamaica to attend to his business interests. During the five months she'd awaited his return she'd spoken of little other than the new life she was anticipating as Harry's wife, and as mistress of his country seat in Hampshire and Harry's Jamaican estates.

Then something dramatic had happened and Miss Rosington's virtue had been compromised in her quest to rescue Harry.

Well, now that Harry Carstairs had returned Perry needed to confront him, not least so that a satisfactory resolution that took account of Charlotte's feelings and her dignity, could be found.

Perry signalled to his coachman to stop a little distance away from the townhouse where Carstairs was reputed to be staying. Stealth and discretion were required, which meant a quiet arrival through the servants' quarters, not a loud and angry demand at the front door.

Perry was not unfamiliar with such clandestine operations. He'd once paid a series of similarly secretive visits to a young widow who put on a creditable show of mourning during the day and took a wildly passionate interest in Perry during the nights. Her lady's maid and the kitchen staff were well-paid accomplices who knew their continued employment relied upon their discretion.

The right coin could win anyone over, Perry knew, as he contemplated how much it would cost him to gain entry if Carstairs was in no mood to see him.

He checked himself. Carstairs certainly would not see him at this late hour and Perry was not particularly in the mood for confrontation.

However, without knowing the reasons behind the man's disappearance, he could not risk Harry eluding him again. He owed it to Charlotte, though it was Miss Rosington's need for the truth that motivated him more. Her reputation had been tarnished by the mystery surrounding Carstairs and the erroneous implication she and Carstairs were lovers.

After he'd negotiated entry to the dark and cavernous kitchen, Perry allowed himself a brief smile. Hadn't he reached the age when cloak-and-dagger antics belonged to greenhorns or fiery youth pulsing with the restless energy to prove themselves?

The gasp of a small, skinny kitchen skivvy brought him

back to the present. 'Hush, I won't hurt you,' he reassured the girl, pressing a coin into her palm as he slipped by, 'as long as you don't say a word.'

It was not very chivalrous, he reflected, to threaten violence he did not intend to helpless young women. Miss Rosington knew the rumours that swirled around him. She should have run at the first opportunity, and yet she'd been as intrigued by him as he was by her. That was sufficient for him. Already he felt himself being divested of the mantle of crusty irritability and world-weariness, ready to delight in indulging her girlish whims. What a refreshing change.

The scullery maid sleeping on her pallet by the kitchen range leapt up as he passed, bringing him back to the here and now. If he was to ensure that his dear Charlotte enjoy the same peace of mind and future of domestic felicity as he was intending with Miss Rosington, he must concentrate on gaining entry without anyone becoming aware. Peregrine must approach with the greatest of caution.

When the scullery maid beheld the shiny gold coin he'd given her, she offered him a lit taper after he'd told her that her master was expecting him for some secret business no one must know about. Clearly his expensive suit of clothes reassured her.

The reception rooms on ground level were in darkness but the taper Perry carried threw enough light for him to navigate his way to the stairs that led to the sleeping quarters.

It appeared the household had only recently retired to bed for he could hear servants still at their work in an adjoining room. To his surprise, several sconces of candles lit the passage along which the bedrooms were located. Snatching one up as he trod the stairs, Perry began his search for the chamber that contained Harry Carstairs.

The first was empty and obviously unused, but then it

was not well positioned. Seizing upon the most likely room for a single gentleman to occupy in terms of location and positioning, Perry quietly turned the doorknob and thrust open the door, holding his sconce of candles high to throw the light.

His patience and forethought were well rewarded, for with a cry of indignation the man who'd so cruelly abandoned Perry's sister at the altar leapt into a sitting position in the bed, his eyes wide in the glow.

Perry was surprised to see that Carstairs wore no nightshirt or nightcap and for a moment he was transfixed by the man's pale torso, lightly dusted with reddish hair. He looked weak and insignificant, prompting the fleeting wonder as to whether Carstairs really had the capability to satisfy his sister over a lifetime of intimacy.

'Lord Peregrine—!' began Carstairs in outraged tones, but Perry heard the puling fear behind them, and his lip curled as he advanced. By God but he was going to extract vengeance for dear Charlotte.

And then as he drew closer he saw that Carstairs was not alone.

Was this the reason for his defection? Another woman? Was Carstairs cuckolding his sister?

'Get out, my lord!' Carstairs shouted as the woman, apparently hitherto sleeping, raised herself onto her elbows and blinked at Perry with fright and confusion.

Perry opened his mouth to assure her that his argument was with her paramour. Her tumbled dark hair was not confined by a nightcap while her nakedness suggested she was not Carstairs' legal wife. Well, if Carstairs had a mistress, it did not preclude the man marrying Charlotte if that's what his sister wanted, and now it was Perry's duty to salvage Charlotte's honour, regardless of how he achieved that.

This reflection took a mere second to assimilate and it

was just as he opened his mouth to speak that a piercing shard of cognisance shattered his preconceptions as to what was before him.

He stilled, a poisonous disbelief turned dread permeating his bones.

Good God, what indeed *was* the demonic scene before him? Suddenly the entire ghastly miscellany of the devil's lair appeared to have conspired to make a mockery of every hope and dream Perry had entertained.

'Miss Rosington!' Her name was torn from his lips just as the kindness and the softness that had taken occupation of his heart—on account of *her*—was ripped out of his chest cavity; so that he stood, pulsing with pain and anger and no, not disbelief, for he could not disbelieve the hideousness of what was so plainly before his eyes.

The woman he'd fully intended to make his wife the very next day was lying naked in bed with the man who'd abandoned his sister at the altar; the man Miss Rosington had persistently claimed she'd been merely 'helping' the night they were apparently caught in a compromising situation.

By God, but Perry had been duped. Cursing himself for a credulous and lovesick fool, he advanced menacingly towards the bed and hauled back the bedcovers.

Violence had never been his immediate answer but he was ready to do violence to Harry Carstairs in this moment.

'Don't hurt him!'

Perry halted at Miss Rosington's distress and turned his fulminating stare upon her. Her mouth was open and her eyes wide with horror.

'I don't know what's happened. I don't know how I got here!' Her voice was faint and she looked terrified.

Well, Perry had no room for her play-acting now, though he did drop the covers with a contemptuous snort as he focused on Carstair's far from impressive manhood and his own pride writhed in agony.

It was painful even to breathe.

'Please my lord, I don't understand any of this.'

He cut her off with a snarl. 'And you were going to entertain *me*, later this week! You do have a busy schedule, Miss Rosington.' He turned on his heel and headed for the door. 'Carstairs, you may run and hide but I will know where to find you and I will have my revenge,' he flung over his shoulder.

He turned the doorknob as a fresh wave of anger rose in his chest. Or was it devastation? Either way, it was so painful it nearly felled him on the spot and his words sounded rasping as he felt compelled to add with pointed irony, if only to anoint his own grievous wounds, 'I hope you have great joy of her, Carstairs. A poisoned chalice is what she is.'

CHAPTER 12

*T*he slamming door reverberated through Celeste's head like a death knell. Her shock was so great she could barely formulate anything that made sense. Not that, in fact, anything *did* make sense. For one thing, what was she doing in this strange bed? Her breathing ratcheted up with each fresh realisation of her increasingly perilous situation. For perilous it was, indeed.

Who, for a start, was this strange man? Then she remembered that it was Harry Carstairs. He'd apologised before she passed into oblivion once again.

She'd woken to find Lord Peregrine standing at the foot of the bed, his face black with thunder, his scorn like a scalding lance.

What could she do except offer the truth?

'Please my lord, I don't understand any of this,' she'd managed, after pleading for the safety of the man beside her, who looked set to be plunged through with a rapier if the fulminating look in Lord Peregrine's eye was anything to go by.

She couldn't abide the idea of violence but that's exactly where this was going, she feared.

Her head felt woolly and she couldn't call on those reserves of clarity that usually came to her aid, even when woken from the deepest sleep.

She'd reached out her hand to Lord Peregrine to help her; tried to say the words to explain, to elicit his aid, for she was a captive and he did not know it. He had the power to whisk her away from here before anything worse happened to her. She ran her hands over her naked body, experimentally, in case there were some evidence that she'd been violated. She didn't think she had, but what about now? What about the rest of the night? What would become of her?

'Lord Peregine!' Though she felt as weak as a kitten, she managed to shriek the words which came from the depths of her soul as, disgusted, he turned on his heel to quit the room, his parting words knifing her to the bone.

But he did not come back. Instead she heard the soft, running footsteps of what turned out to be the older woman who'd been so kind to her earlier this evening.

And when Celeste looked up, Harry Carstairs was standing by the bed wearing his banyan, a nightcap upon his head and a worried look upon his face as he turned to the older woman. 'Aunt Clarice, I think she's taken another turn. I heard her shouting. Is there more of that calming elixir which so benefitted her last night?'

Protesting, Celeste was spoon-fed the strange tasting concoction by the woman while Harry Carstairs held her down. And soon her fear and horror melted away as the drowsiness that had earlier begun to recede resumed its insidious march upon her defences.

AN EVIL GNOME WAS WIELDING A PICKAXE IN THE RECESSES OF Celeste's brain. The consistency of each well-aimed stroke made her writhe in an impotent attempt to find peace and solace and her body was slippery with sweat.

She awoke with a pounding headache and a sob escaped her before she even opened her eyes, for she knew she was a captive and that she'd probably been ruined forever. Without a reputation she was a condemned woman, unable to marry.

And Lord Peregrine? He'd seen her but he'd not rescued her? No, he'd formed his own opinion. Or had she been dreaming when she imagined him staring with disgust from the end of the bed.

Perhaps everything from the moment she'd last spoken to Raphael had all been a dream, for the scent of bluebells and the warmth on her face did not accord with the musty cold of the chamber into which she'd believed she'd been thrust last night.

'Hush.' The voice that spoke was soothing, as was the gentle grip on her hand.

Tentatively Celeste opened her eyes, the sunlight that streamed through the window painful, though not as painful as her thoughts. What was truth and what was fiction?

What was Lord Peregrine thinking now?

What struck her most forcibly, however, glancing around the room, were the familiar comforting crimson curtains that surrounded her bed. She was in her own bedchamber and Raphael was sitting on a chair by her bedside, holding her hand.

She tried to speak but the words dissolved into sobs. It must have been a dream. Here she was in her own bed and, extraordinarily, Raphael was stroking her hair. Perhaps she'd been terribly ill.

'Dearest Celeste, do not cry.' She was aware of his awkwardness but that was hardly surprising. Where had he found her? What had happened to her? Or had she been here and delirious the entire time?

He cleared his throat. 'I blame myself but you're safe now. You're home and in your own bed and for the rest of our married life I'll make sure no one ever harms you again.'

No! She wanted to scream aloud. So it had *not* been a dream?

When she'd she mastered her emotions and kept at bay the sobs, she could only stare at him. Finally she forced out, 'Do you *know* what happened to me, Raphael? If you did, you'd never speak to me so kindly.' This time the shuddering sob wracked her whole body as she choked on the inability to articulate her shame. 'But how have I come to be here now? I remember so little, and yet I know I was a prisoner … And it was *not* a dream?'

Raphael tugged at his lace cuffs, clearly weighing up his words. He glanced at the door as footsteps passed, perhaps waiting to ensure they'd not be disturbed by servants or Aunt Branwell. 'You've been here a couple of days now, Celeste. I've been so worried. I'm glad to see you rallying.' He smiled, and even in her dazed condition she realised he'd not looked at her with such kindness in many years. It was extraordinary. 'My dearest Celeste, you have been badly used and I will forever blame myself. I just thank God we're leaving in three days for Jamaica, where you'll not have to encounter the cruel whispers and the blackballing that would be your lot were you to remain in England.'

So her reputation was in ruins, she realised dully. 'I don't understand,' she croaked. Her earlier words had been more taxing than she'd realised. 'I don't understand any of it. Have you seen Harry? Did you find me …' She shook her head, unable to complete the sentence: '*in Harry's bed?*'

Raphael averted his gaze. 'My love, you have been used as a pawn in a cruel and terrible hoax. Perhaps to punish me, though I don't know.' He stroked her hand, his expression sorrowful. 'I had no idea that when I requested that you get closer to Lord Peregrine he would use you so shamefully. That he would in every way live up to his reputation as a cruel and conscienceless philanderer.'

'Lord Peregrine?' Celeste closed her eyes against her memories of his anger, his look of derision before he'd flung out of Harry Carstairs' bedchamber.

She shook her head. 'This had nothing to do with Lord Peregrine,' she whispered. 'He … found us. He was furious … on his sister's account, no doubt,' she added hastily, confused and embarrassed.

Raphael shook his head sorrowfully. 'Yes, he witnessed your shame. Someone intended that you'd indeed be painted as the woman with whom Carstairs was consorting when he jilted Miss Paige.'

Celeste sat bolt upright. 'No!' she cried. 'That can't be true. Who would do such a thing? Who would wish to ruin me?' *Certainly not Lord Peregrine.* He'd asked her to marry him. It made no sense. He loved her. She knew it in the marrow of her bones.

'Hush,' Raphael said, rising. 'There is still much mystery surrounding why you were found in Harry's bed. I've merely voiced my suspicions based on the whispers I've heard surrounding Lord Peregrine's wager.'

'Wager?'

Raphael put up his hand to silence her. 'I won't say more, Celeste, until I've spoken to Harry personally, for clearly he'd never have been complicit unless he were forced. And why would he have been forced? That's what I need to find out.' A deep frown creased his forehead before he managed a clearly forced smile. 'Regardless, Celeste, you have saved Harry. Perhaps your ruin was required to secure Harry's release, but I do know Harry must have been as unwilling a participant as you. I have not seen him but I thank God to know he is safe and free and that as soon as you and I are married the three of us will set sail for Jamaica in three days. We can put this behind us. That is what sustains me.'

Confused and wracked with torment, Celeste pulled the covers to her chin. The tears began to flow but Raphael ignored them.

'You need to regain your strength for tomorrow night.' He was brisk now. 'I'll have Mary keep close watch on you so you're well enough to venture forth with your head held high tomorrow night. I shall get to the bottom of the terrible travesty of justice which has clearly imperilled Harry's life and tarnished your reputation.' He bent to stroke her face, ever so gently, his eyes pools of warmth and gratitude.

Tomorrow night? She tried to speak but the words would not come as her mind began to drift. Absently she ran her hands over her body which felt so alien to her in this strange, disembodied state, and yet unviolated she was sure, while she tried to summon words to detain him.

He seemed to know so much more than she, but Celeste was unable to ask further questions as she was soon reclaimed by the familiar, heavy drug-induced state from which she'd so briefly emerged.

The following afternoon Celeste felt better. Certainly well enough to rise from her bed, though she placed her feet tentatively on the floor to test her weight and her strength. She'd slept deeply, she'd been told, for nearly twenty-four hours.

Twenty-four hours? The sleep had indeed refreshed her but the knowledge that she'd been confined to her bed for so long sent fear coursing through her. Where was Lord Peregrine? He was to have come for her.

Then she remembered her last sighting of him: his face dark with anger and disgust and her stomach rose up in protest. She had to see him and explain.

Mary helped her onto the stool before her looking glass so she could attend to her hair. She'd not had it powdered this past week, and in her natural state she looked, to her own eyes, far younger than her years and far more vulnerable than a woman of her station ought to look. Raphael's ominous words regarding her duty to attend a society function tonight returned and she nearly sobbed aloud. She had no energy to go anywhere with Raphael and she'd certainly lost her confidence to return to society.

'What happened to me, Mary?' Celeste whispered, touching the shadows beneath her eyes, unable to believe she was the same young woman she'd been just days before. 'You were there.'

It was unsettling Mary couldn't meet her eye. 'I don't rightly recall, miss,' she muttered before seizing upon a lace tippet which had fallen behind the curtain as a chance to change the subject.

As Celeste stared at her reflection, she imagined how wonderful it would be if all her dreams of being in Harry Carstairs' bed and a furious Lord Peregrine looming over in the middle of the night were simply figments of a fevered imagination.

Her aunt's visit quickly disabused her of the notion that her true situation was remotely better than she feared. The older woman twisted her hands, her agitation clear. 'Dear Lord, Celeste, what is to be done? When you were conveyed here from the home of Mrs Carstairs I believed everything I was told: that you'd fallen ill and been nursed at her home. But now I find this is far from the *whole* truth.' She narrowed her eyes. 'You didn't tell me the rest, my girl, and now I fear I have no choice but to believe what hitherto I would have dismissed as scandalous rumours with utterly no basis in fact.'

Celeste put her hand to her lips while her head swam. A terrible agony rose up in her chest. 'What *are* people saying? I don't understand any of it, Aunt Branwell.' Her body felt heavy and unresponsive as she picked up a brush to run through her hair, then quickly gave up the idea. 'Raphael was evasive when I questioned him directly, though he seems to know more than I.' She put her face in her hands and moaned softly. 'I was drugged, Aunt Branwell. I don't know why, but I was.'

Her aunt hovered, unable or unwilling to catch her eye. She shook her head. 'What can I do but tell you the truth, Celeste?' She sounded angry rather than perplexed. 'You told me you were going to play cards with Miss Brownhill but you didn't go there, did you? You deliberately directed the coachman to take you to Harry Carstairs' aunt's house. Did you know that she was away in Cornwall, though she returned unexpectedly that evening? Still, that's of no comfort. The scandal that you were discovered in Harry's bed is spreading and I have no more idea of how to nip it in the bud than fly to the moon.'

Celeste's weakened constitution meant she succumbed easily to her tears and she leaned over her dressing table, weeping. Aunt Branwell said nothing, but after a few moments she put a hand on her shoulder to soothe her.

'How could you could be so naïve, Celeste? You went to consort with a gentleman ... *alone?*'

'I didn't go off to consort with a gentleman. I was sent a note.'

'A note?' Aunt Branwell cocked her head. 'Then show me

the note, Celeste. If you have been ill-used as you claim perhaps this may be all the evidence that's required.'

Celeste hung her head. 'I burned it,' she muttered.

Her aunt's opprobrium was no surprise. 'You burned the note? Well, who on earth would do such a thing unless they had something to hide?'

'Well, at least Raphael doesn't think ill of me,' Celeste returned hotly.

Her aunt shook her head. 'There's the wonder of it. He still intends escorting you to Lord Montague's ball tonight though I've counselled strongly against it, in view of all this vile chatter. I've had three visits from friends who cannot believe the stories they've heard.' She gave a despairing sigh, then summoned Mary with a peremptory wave of her hand before turning back to Celeste. 'Once your hair is done properly, Celeste, and the rabbit's paw has rendered its magic powder and rouge, you have no choice but to venture forth into the pubic arena and at least pretend to the world that you were tricked.' Then her aunt's shoulders slumped and she looked stricken as she added in a whisper, 'My dear Celeste, I really don't know what is to become of you. Thank God you'll soon be leaving the country.'

Celeste stared at them both in the looking glass. She looked as helpless and desperate as she felt. 'I'm still ill,' she whispered. 'I don't want to go.'

'Raphael insists.'

Celeste closed her eyes once again. 'And if Raphael insisted I rise from my death bed and don angel wings for his amusement, I'd have to do that, too,' she whispered.

After a short silence her aunt put her hand on her shoulder. 'We are women, Celeste, and we must obey. One day, I hope, you will be happy.'

At this thought, Celeste's previously dissipated spirits were soundly shaken back into life.

But then confusion set in. What *did* Raphael mean when he'd talked about Lord Peregrine's wager and the fact Celeste had saved Harry Carstairs' life? How? She'd been too drowsy to properly quiz her cousin.

And what of her plans with Lord Peregrine? What would happen now? A mantle of ice seemed to cloak her and she shivered as Mary began to fuss about her, readying her for this ball she had no wish to attend.

No! Surely Lord Peregrine couldn't believe the travesty of justice in which she'd been embroiled, despite what he'd seen.

And who was responsible? She cast around for her aunt to ask more questions but she'd gone, and when she once again demanded the same of Mary, her maid merely mumbled, 'I can't rightly tell you anything, miss, other than that the pound cake wot I was give'd in the servants hall at that strange house we went to was mighty tasty.'

Taking a few breaths to regulate her heartbeat, Celeste tried to reassure herself that once she told Lord Peregrine that she'd been tricked, he would become her ally in ascertaining who would do such a thing.

Surely she had the power to first erase his angry doubts and then to melt his heart?

CHAPTER 13

aphael was already in the saloon waiting for her when she made her appearance after a lengthy stint in front of her looking glass.

Tonight she'd been forced to do his bidding and after Mary had worked magic with her hair and dress, her aunt had walked in and declared that at least in looks, Celeste was everything Raphael could want in the woman he was soon to take as his wife. However, more urgent was Celeste's desire for this to be so for Lord Peregrine.

If he was going to judge her he must allow her to put her case to him. Not for a moment had she wavered in her desire to become his wife. He offered her everything she desired: passion, honesty and genuine regard. She'd have none of that with Raphael, that was certain.

If Lord Peregrine truly were the man she believed he was, then he would listen to her, believe her and try to help her.

'My dear Celeste, you are a vision.'

At least Raphael's admiration seemed genuine.

Nervously she smoothed the figured silk of her polonaise and forced a smile.

'Thank you, Raphael. I'm glad I was well enough to go out this evening.'

'I had the devil of a time persuading Aunt Branwell to allow it.' Was it her imagination, or did she see a flash of something akin to guilt cross his face?

Then it was gone and she realised she must have imagined it, for Raphael never felt guilt. Nor would a man of Raphael's pride have been a party to seeing his future wife put in an uncompromising position, she was sure of it.

But what did anything matter when he was being kind to her? Life was so much easier when Raphael was kindly disposed towards her. Tonight, of course, it was because Harry had been found alive. She wondered if he had seen him.

Shame and disgust swept over her as she remembered the feel of Harry's hairy legs against her own, but there was not much time to dwell on either past or future for the Mayfair townhouse to which they were being conveyed was only several blocks away. And in the melee of sedan chairs, carriages, and sumptuously dressed guests being ushered into Lord Montague's grand abode, Celeste could only think of responding to greetings with the requisite poise, and ensuring that she deport herself as Raphael would wish.

For a brief moment she thought she spied Lord Peregrine and her heart performed a strange contortion in her chest. Then she realised she must have been mistaken, for despite everything, she knew he would seek her out. He'd made her a marriage offer because he believed in her. He would have no choice but to listen to her side of this ghastly story.

Raphael seemed intent on proving the perfect escort. Celeste had never experienced such care and solicitude from him. But as the evening wore on his limpet-like attention became cloying. Though she smiled and inclined her head and laughed politely at all the right times, she never lost an opportunity to dart quick glances into all corners of the room. The desperation to unburden herself to Lord Peregrine was nearly as strong as her fear as she cast about for a sight of him. At such an illustrious event he had to be here somewhere.

With Raphael by her side, people addressed her with the usual respect, but Celeste was keenly aware of the curious and often suspicious glances slanted in her direction. Why had Raphael insisted she come? Surely it would have been better to simply have kept her hidden until their wedding. Not that Celeste would have meekly remained confined to her room. Lord Peregrine would make contact.

Her stomach contracted again. This time with fear.

While listening to Raphael and an elderly politician discuss terms of trade, Celeste's restless gaze at last alighted upon the gentleman she'd been seeking, and the shock was so great she could barely breathe. Lord Peregrine was shrouded in a dimly lit corner, deep in conversation with a woman whose back was to Celeste until, turning slightly, she saw it was Lady Busselton. Jealousy spiralled through her, for the pair's attitude towards one another seemed disconcertingly familiar.

'Where are you going?'

Raphael's question was sharp and Celeste blinked. 'The lady's mending room.'

She was surprised he seemed reluctant to relinquish her. Was it fear of what the mob might do to her without him by her side? What did he know that Celeste did not?

But now the freedom of not having to cling to Raphael's arm was overlaid with the deepest trepidation. Celeste was conscious of the way not only Raphael's eyes followed her, but the covert scrutiny of everyone else, it seemed.

Was this to be her future? A life of living in the public arena, her every movement dissected, and Raphael her gaoler? His possessiveness was not based on affection, that she well knew.

The closer she got to Lord Peregrine the quicker her heart raced, though she did her best to move with languid grace, taking comfort from the knowledge that he had to give her a hearing at which she was confident she'd make him understand she'd been used. Raphael had said it himself.

Stopping by a plinth supporting an enormous Sevres vase, Celeste bent down on the pretext of adjusting her shoe as she assessed Lady Busselton. The woman was uncommonly beautiful. Her flaxen hair was not powdered tonight and threaded through with tiny glittering stars. Her gown was of the richest brocade decorated with gold thread. Celeste wondered who funded her wardrobe, for such an ensemble was worth a king's ransom.

The knowledge that she and Lord Peregrine had known one another for a decade couldn't ameliorate the little stab of pain she felt when Lady Busselton tittered with laughter and tapped the viscount playfully on the nose with her fan.

Well, Lord Peregrine would soon hear Celeste's account of matters and then he'd understand she was still pure. He'd be enraged to learn of her terrible ordeal and then they'd be married. If he loved her as he'd sworn he did, he would champion her.

Yet as she brushed past the pair as she headed for the doorway that led into the back passage, she received no sense that he was as aware of her as she was of him.

She consoled herself with the knowledge that he'd not wish to give any hint to Lady Busselton his feelings as she sat heavily on the banquette in the mending room. Lord Peregrine was simply involved in a charade for Lady Busselton's benefit. Right now he must be seething with horror at Celeste's plight but unable to communicate safely with her for the moment.

Returning to the ballroom, she observed that Lord Peregrine was now in conversation with several older gentlemen, yet still he showed no signs of being aware of her. She set her course for Raphael's side but when suddenly the man with whom Lord Peregrine had been conversing bowed and stepped away, she could not lose her opportunity. 'Lord Peregrine.'

He raised an eyebrow, his look enquiring. Ironic. 'Miss Rosington.'

Where was the outrage? The concern for her?

Her throat was suddenly dry and her breath harder to summon as the truth came to her with all the force of a heavy blow to her head. Why, Lord Peregrine had been summoned to witness her shame ... and he *believed* what he'd seen.

She returned his greeting, dropping her little ivory fan with a feigned but impossible-to-ignore gasp, and within a moment Lord Peregrine was at her side, brandishing the article, and a smile that was far from friendly.

'I'm surprised you can look me in the eye,' he muttered, handing the fan back to her.

'You surely don't believe—?'

He snorted but before he could reply—if he even intended doing so—she whispered urgently, 'I was sent a message to go to that house. I was a prisoner in that room. Someone put something in my wine and then ensured you witnessed my... shame. If I am guilty of any wrongdoing it is because of ... loving you!'

There! She'd said it! All the doubts and fears that had besieged her during the past twenty-four hours burst from her in a tirade of fear. Fear that it was true and fear for what had become of her.

Her words had little effect on him, for the curl of his lip only grew more exaggerated.

'A strange way to show it. Do you really think me so credulous?'

He truly believed she could be so untrue after she'd pledged her heart to him on the day before she'd been so cruelly hoaxed? Curling her palms into fists to fight the pain, she whispered, 'I am the victim of someone's plan to make you think ill of me.' She wondered if her legs would buckle. Did he not have enough faith in her to at least look at her with mildly less disgust? 'I was tricked.'

'Tricked? A very elaborate trick, Miss Rosington. And to what purpose?'

'No!' He was passing on as if she were of no more interest than the old crone now speaking to his erstwhile companion. She swung round. 'You must believe me. Someone tricked me and I have no idea why.'

He hesitated and she waited, hope like a prisoner behind a door, ready to leap to life, to freedom given the chance. Then he turned, fixing her with a beady stare, his voice as smooth as treacle. 'So what *are* you to Harry Carstairs, Miss Rosington? I'm interested to know … and so is my sister Charlotte.'

'Nothing.' She shook her head wildly. 'He's Raphael's … friend.' She blushed as she stumbled over the word. 'I've met him only a few times.'

'The first time being when you were discovered with him, half clothed in his drawing room, the second when I discovered you both, naked in bed.'

'No!' She shook her head. 'I was a prisoner. When I woke to see you in the doorway of that room I could only think it a nightmare.'

Clearly, Lord Peregrine considered her response a charade. 'But—very inconveniently for you, it was not. Sorry, Miss Rosington, but I'm not quite so prepared to dismiss what I saw with my very own eyes. Good evening.'

PERRY HAD A HARD TIME KEEPING THE PAIN FROM HIS VOICE, though it was easy enough to make clear his disgust.

He wished Xenia hadn't been so near. Clearly she'd observed the short exchange for she was at his side within a few seconds, her hand upon his sleeve as she purred, 'Perry, darling, is that really Miss Rosington? I wonder how she dares to show her face—'

She never finished her sentence, for a sudden commotion near the entrance to the ballroom drew everyone's attention. Perry, who stood a head taller than many, was stunned when he saw the reason for the hush now descended upon the previously gregarious crowd.

He hurried over, torn, for much as he disliked admitting it, his first instinct was to defend the apparently hapless Miss Rosington. She stood in the centre of a cleared space staring at none other than Peregrine's own sister, whose apparent progress down the sweeping staircase had been arrested a few steps from the bottom.

Pity Miss Rosington or anyone else who earned Charlotte's ire. His sister could be terrifying when moved to anger. Quickly, though, he reminded himself that he'd been made to look a fool. Miss Rosington's contrived innocence and artless manner concealed a treachery that was difficult to fathom. Yes, he could believe she did not love her cousin, and that may well have accounted for her singling Perry out as a marital alternative. But her affair with Carstairs? What was that all about? It was impossible to say, but perhaps it was simply a convenient long-term arrangement and Carstairs had, after an inexplicable absence, returned—to Miss Rosington's great joy. If Perry wasn't so enraged, he'd demand she explain herself.

In three days she'd be sailing across the seas for a new life and he'd never have to see or think of her again.

That was what should sustain him.

Charlotte's voice was shrill. The entire assembly heard it. 'How have you the gall to deny what three others testify to having seen? You're the reason Mr Carstairs had to flee the country and you're the reason he came back.'

Revulsion at the public spectacle, as much as the painful words he was hearing, made Perry's skin crawl. He was ashamed of Charlotte for allowing her passions to rule her, and equally disgusted at Miss Rosington for her part in all this.

Making his way through the crowd to reach his sister's side, he took her elbow, murmuring into her ear that she deport herself with more decorum if people weren't to revile her as much as Miss Rosington.

His sister pulled away, protesting loudly. 'What does it matter what people think, when I'm to be hustled into holy orders. And why? Because I've been made to look the biggest fool and even my family can't bear the shame.'

'Holy orders was your idea, Charlotte, and you know it,' Perry muttered.

He caught Miss Rosington's eyes. She was pale and appeared shocked, staring about her as if she truly could not believe what was happening. If he didn't feel so badly used, he might have felt sorry for her. Clearly, she'd thought nothing of playing with *his* heart, so why she should look at him in such a plaintive way he had no idea.

'My friend Miss Robinson saw her, Perry. You know that? She saw her with Mr Carstairs.' She gulped convulsively. 'On several occasions, you must know.'

Charlotte was babbling now, on the verge of tears. Perry gripped her elbow more firmly and started to lead her away. He was unable to resist a glance over his shoulder but wished he hadn't for clearly he was still dangerously susceptible to Miss Rosington's allure, given the uncomfortable rush of sensation he experienced at the sight of Lord Ogilvy beside his betrothed. With a fierce glare at all those who remained goggle-eyed, the young man hissed, 'Miss Rosington retains *my* regard.'

'Then take her to Jamaica and keep her out of Harry's way!' Charlotte returned as she was led, weeping, towards the double doors by her brother, halting on the threshold to cry, 'She's ruined my life!'

TREMBLING, CELESTE ALLOWED HERSELF TO BE STEERED BY Raphael through the throng via a back entrance and into the street where, to her surprise, his carriage was waiting to whisk her away from the scene of her shame. She didn't understand any of it. It was like a sick nightmare, yet Raphael did not turn upon her vituperatively as she'd expected.

He didn't touch her either, once they were ensconced, but was quiet as he stared through the half-curtained windows at the moonlit sky. For a long time, the only sounds to be heard were the horses' hooves striking the cobbles and the distant shouts of those going about their business.

Finally Celeste whispered through lips that felt cold and thin, lips that would never know the heat of passion, 'I'm not guilty of any of those awful charges.' She felt disembodied from the girl she'd once been—the girl she'd once hoped to be—though she could feel herself shaking like one with the ague. She longed for the simple human contact of someone who understood her pain.

'I know.' Raphael did not touch her but the lack of opprobrium in his tone was both reassuring and unsettling.

She darted a look at him but he remained silent, staring

out of the window. *Was he angry? Disgusted?* Whatever he felt, he'd bottle the emotion until he unleashed it upon her at a more suitable moment. The thought was terrifying.

'What will become of me?' she finally asked. She'd been publicly branded an adulteress by Lord Peregrine's sister, and no one had rushed to her defence. At best, Raphael's had been half-hearted. Would she be blackballed by society, unable to hold her head up in polite company ever again?

'Soon we sail to Jamaica. It doesn't matter.' His tone was matter-of-fact. 'You must put this painful ordeal behind you, Celeste. Our wedding takes place in three days. Tonight changes nothing.'

Her mouth dropped open. Did he *really* believe that? Why, Celeste would not be able to show her face in respectable society without being the subject of whispers and innuendo —that's if she were admitted through *anyone's* front door from this evening onwards.

She began to cry softly. 'Raphael, what must *you* think? I am not guilty of the charges levelled upon me. I don't under-stand any of it. I was lured to—'

'And who do you think lured you, my dear?'

She jerked her head up at the caramel tones. Raphael shook his head. 'How many times do I have to imply the obvious? You were lured by someone who wished to see you destroyed, that is plain enough. But what might be their motivation?' He shrugged then answered his own question. 'Perhaps they believe you to be an unconscionable jezebel but lack the proof?'

'No!' Her hands flew to cover her ears. She refused to believe his insinuations but Raphael went on, 'Why, it's someone who already believes you guilty of involvement with Harry Carstairs, of course. Someone who despises you, my dear, though it pains me to say it. Someone who despises you *enough* to go to these elaborate lengths, so as to ensure you are blackened for the crime they couldn't pin on you after you were first found consorting with Harry Carstairs.'

'Lord Peregrine?' His name scorched her throat, its sound bitter on her tongue. 'I won't believe it!' He couldn't … wouldn't … have done such a thing!' The connection between them had been so intense, so honest.

'Yes, you were lured, Celeste, we both agree on that. But lured by whom? I wish you would accept the truth.' He sighed, as if he were weary of the topic, his expression shuttered as he examined the half moons on his right hand. Raphael was as particular with his grooming as he was with surrounding himself with order. Right now Celeste was disturbing the precision of his life.

She digested his painful allegation while she tried to read his face. But then, she'd never been able to read Raphael. Except when he was joyful. During the games they'd played as children she'd tried hard to make sure things went Raphael's way, for life was so much more pleasant when Raphael didn't lose. He'd take great risks—and deal out harsh consequences—to ensure his self-respect was not at risk; suffered no damage.

Finally she broke the silence. 'So you truly believe Lord Peregrine is behind this? That he believed his sister over me?'

A nerve twitched at the corner of his mouth but he didn't speak; didn't look at her. Celeste was used to Raphael ignoring her when he was irked. Anger rose up in her breast. He *would* speak to her.

She raised her chin defiantly. 'You know I loved Lord Peregrine.'

'Well, clearly Lord Peregrine loves his sister more.' His mouth quirked. She could almost imagine her outburst amused him.

However, the pain caused by Raphael's assertion was eclipsed by his reaction. The man she was to spend the rest of her life with was not the slightest bit jealous that she had feelings for another. It gave her the strength to move beyond her inertia.

The carriage took a sharp bend and she had to grip his arm to keep her balance. 'Tell me you're enraged that I could lose my heart to someone other than my intended—just as *you've* done, Raphael!' she hissed.

He sighed and pulled away. 'A woman's passions are easily excited. I do not condemn you for it, Celeste—certainly not after I pushed you in his direction for my own ends, granted.' He looked unperturbed. 'To be honest, it is much as I expected. I have little faith in the constancy of a woman's heart, therefore it is no surprise that yours was snared by the first tolerably handsome stranger to glance in your direction. I'm sorry he proved so unworthy.'

If possible her heart dislodged, pulled by gravity and devastation to slide even further downwards. She wanted to claw her fingers across Raphael's marble-like cheeks. Anything, if it would draw some emotion from him. Heaving in a breath she gasped, 'Unworthy? I at least have a greater understanding of human nature than you, for I won't condemn him for what was put before his eyes.'

Raphael shrugged. 'I am hurt by your insinuations that I am unfeeling. Surely I'm being remarkably forgiving given that you were—as you've just corroborated—obviously enticed into a compromising situation by the man with whom, I surmise, you intended to have a secret affair behind my back.'

Celeste winced, for Raphael spoke a truth which hardly reflected well on her. She began to speak but was halted as a great illuminating truth descended upon her, joy surging through her as she cried, 'Why, it was you, wasn't it, Raphael? *You* are behind this?' Why had she dismissed her vague doubts of earlier? The conclusion was obvious.

Despite the horror in which she was embroiled, she felt joyful. Yes, joyful; for now she was sure that Lord Peregrine had been as duped as she. Feverishly, she went over the implications. First she must make clear to Lord Peregrine that Raphael had set her up and then enticed His Lordship to see what would only disgust him. Oh, how she loathed Raphael in that moment, but what did it matter when she had only to tell Lord Peregrine the truth and he'd …

She stopped, biting her lip and looking, shocked, at the little fan she'd snapped when common sense intruded. What *would* Lord Peregrine do? Even if he could be made to believe she wasn't guilty, what would he do? Celeste pocketed the damaged fan, staring at her embroidered shoes peeping from beneath the hem of her pink and blue brocade dress. She refused to abandon hope. If Lord Peregrine were the honourable man she believed him, he would do all he could to salvage her reputation.

Might he even marry her still?

She was unprepared for Raphael's crushing response; his soft sigh followed by the tone of regret. 'My dear Celeste, I believe that in this moment I actually feel sorry for you.' His expression was implacable, his blue eyes cold, his mouth thin, transporting her to her childhood when Celeste was nothing but an empty-headed girl trying to keep up with her superior cousin.

'Why would I wish to see my own intended wife tarnished in the eyes of the world, even if we are to leave the country?' He shook his head. 'Anger that you should go so far to follow your passions might motivate me to exact a more private revenge, but why would I elicit Harry Carstairs as the instrument of your shame, and do so publicly? Just think on it, my dear … Who has greatest to gain from seeing you shamed? *Me*? Lord no, not when I am to wed you within the week. Or Lord Peregrine, who believes you guilty of shameless conduct and was clearly frustrated at being unable to prove it?' He touched her shoulder briefly. 'Let's not waste time worrying over what's done already. Later, after you have slept, Harry can tell you what he knows of all this.'

Celeste ran a hand across her pallid forehead. Dully she asked, 'Have you seen Harry?' *The man I woke to find in my bed? The man who was complicit in ruining me after I saved his skin at your request all those weeks ago?* Of course, it served no purpose to say this. It would only whip up Raphael's ire, and her life would be a good deal easier if she kept her head down and accepted everything that suited Raphael.

'I have made arrangements to see him tomorrow.'

Tears pricked at her eyelids. 'Won't *you* tell me how it was that he …?'

'Your chastity is preserved, even if your reputation is not. However, that will not matter once we're in Jamaica. I'm sorry, Celeste, but let us consider the matter closed.'

Silently she digested this. 'Why are you keeping secrets from me, Raphael? I have been ill-used, and I accept that I can't change what's happened. But surely I deserve to know why.'

Raphael looked at her with pity. 'It's true that I do not love you, Celeste. But nor will I deliver you a truth which puts your life in jeopardy.'

A PLETHORA OF EMOTIONS STORMED THROUGH PEREGRINE AS he'd watched Miss Rosington escorted from the ballroom on the arm of her betrothed. Righteous anger, though, was quickly succeeded by simple pain at the depth of her betrayal.

All the time she'd pretended she was in love with Perry she'd been consorting secretly with Harry Carstairs.

Why?

His grief in that moment was almost debilitating, though why he should feel it so keenly, he couldn't explain. It wasn't as if he'd done more than kiss her several times. She should not have got under his skin in so short a time.

Xenia glided up to him, Charlotte clinging to her arm. His sister had pulled away earlier as he'd exhorted her to leave but now she was back with Xenia, his old friend saying crisply, 'I think it's time your poor sister should be escorted home. She's been through a great deal tonight and it appears you can do more for her, Perry, than I can.'

Guiltily Perry acknowledged he'd shirked is filial responsibilities in the weeks since Charlotte had been jilted by Harry Carstairs. Observing that his sleeve was quite damp from the girl's tears, he tried to put aside his own misery. Charlotte was to have married Harry Carstairs; Perry's disappointment was not on such a scale.

He checked himself. Yes, it was. With each meeting, Miss Rosington had occupied an increasing proportion of his mental energy. What had begun as a wager had quickly turned into a delightful diversion. Yet the connection between them had been instant and the strength of it had made him reassess his views on matrimony.

And he'd offered for her. With his heart in his mouth he had asked the most important question a man could ask and his joy had known no bounds when she'd accepted.

Peregrine had never seriously considered marriage before. Now he was convinced he'd never entertain the idea again.

Not after having been betrayed in such a manner.

Yes, betrayed, just as Charlotte had been, and had he not taken it upon himself to avenge Charlotte's shame—only to be duped by the very woman who claimed, herself, to have been duped—he would be happily enjoying his bachelor-hood, as before.

'You know Miss Rosington and Mr Carstairs planned to elope tomorrow night.' Xenia's eyes danced as she waited for Perry's reaction while they crossed the ballroom. 'Yes, Perry, she planned to elope the very night you'd intended inviting her into your bedchamber. Oh, don't pretend that wasn't your plan.' Xenia tapped his shoulder playfully with her fan. 'Not that she was going to sleep with you. You should know that, for her maid reported to my good Annie that Miss Rosington was overheard hatching the plan with Harry Carstairs to do what she had to in order to gain access to your bedchamber and reclaim that which Harry needed in order to make good his escape.'

'I don't believe it.' He spoke woodenly, as if he felt no emotion while inside, his heart was an emasculated wreck. 'What do I possess that would be sufficient to drive Miss Rosington to such extremes?'

Charlotte had strayed a little distance away and Xenia put out her hand to draw her back. His sister looked as if she might collapse upon the spot. 'As you're not attending to me, Perry, I shall take your sister home. She needs more than you can offer her right now.'

Absently he agreed with this, while in his mind he went over the similarities between his situation and Charlotte's. What an elaborate plan, though the truth had been so simple. It had been just as he had thought from the first: Miss Rosington and Harry were lovers.

He was the one who'd agreed to a wager to expose her yet he was the one who'd lost his heart. He'd been well and truly hoist on his own petard; duped by Miss Rosington as his sister had been by Mr Carstairs.

For a short moment he envied the strength of such single-minded passion, before a rush of pain coursed through him. It took all his willpower not to raise his head and bellow like a crazed beast across the ballroom before collapsing to his knees.

Instead he merely looked Xenia in the eye, trying to pay her the attention politeness required in the circumstances, for she clearly had more to say.

'I'm sure Miss Rosington was very fond of you, Perry, for who could not be, but this was not about love. Before I go, I have to tell you that Miss Rosington was sent by Mr Carstairs to retrieve the locket Charlotte had taken before giving to you.'

'Nonsense!'

'My dear Perry, why would Miss Rosington pretend to be interested in you when she was carrying on with Harry Carstairs? Of course she had an ulterior motive.'

Xenia had a point.

He clarified, 'The locket containing Charlotte's likeness, which Charlotte hurled at me in disgust the morning after Harry disappeared?'

'That's right, though it contained more than Charlotte's likeness. The locket had six numbers engraved behind the miniature.' They were near the entrance now and Xenia spoke more quickly. 'The locket was given to Harry Carstairs with a letter outlining how to use it to claim his inheritance. Carstairs was to marry Charlotte that week; only he didn't love Charlotte, he loved Miss Rosington whose dowry, alas, was too meagre to fund the high life they both required. So when Mr Carstairs realised just how great his inheritance would be, he tossed Charlotte over. Ah, but how can we forget *that* night. However, in his haste Harry lost the locket. He was lost without it for he had no record of the numbers required to open the safety deposit box which contained his handsome reward.' She brushed Perry's cheek with her fingertips as though to soften the blow. 'When Miss

Rosington learned you, Perry, had the locket, Carstairs sent her to entice you into her lair. And very susceptible you proved, too.'

Perry blinked and shook his head. 'It's all nonsense. Miss Rosington is marrying her cousin. Not Carstairs.'

'Lord Ogilvy always has been her intended, but she does not love him. You know that. No, she intended running away with Carstairs just as soon as she'd retrieved that locket. Since she prevailed upon you to hand it over without her being required to actually sleep with you, or visit your bedchamber, Perry, she had no more need of you.' She clicked her tongue. 'I'm sorry, Perry. It's hard for a man to hear a truth like that. I know you'd grown fond of her and you feel cheated of the means by which were to have won our wager.' Flicking open her little ivory fan, she regarded him over the top. 'And now, if you won't, I shall see Charlotte home. She looks half dazed, the poor child. Your Miss Rosington has a lot to answer for.'

His Miss Rosington? The trouble was, that even after all that had happened, he still wished she could be his.

CHAPTER 14

$\mathcal{A}$t midday two days following the terrible event that had changed Celeste's life forever, Mary announced that Raphael was waiting in the drawing room and that he intended taking her to see the animals in the Tower.

'He says he'll not have your ill health on his conscience, and that as you're so soon to be wed you must go out at least today to take the air,' Mary reported.

Celeste, who was still in bed, pulled the covers over her head and declared she had no intention of ever seeing another human being ever again, much less any mangy, half-starved performing animals.

Then Raphael came marching up the stairs, throwing the door open and saying in unusually jovial tones, 'Enough of your moping. Get dressed, Celeste, and let me prove that you'll not be consumed by fire and brimstone for showing your face in public. I intend showing the world I'm not ashamed of you. Isn't that what you want?'

There was very little she could do to resist his single-minded determination to venture out with him, though once they were at the Tower Celeste was nevertheless conscious of the interested stares and obvious whispers of more than a few patrons. And she knew it wasn't her imagination.

Raphael had selected her gown: a bold and lavish confection of blue brocade adorned with scarlet bows. It did not match her mood by any means and she refused to be drawn by her betrothed's uncharacteristic banter as he sauntered over the cobblestones, drawing her so fast in his wake she had to cling to her flat-topped straw hat to stop it blowing away, despite the ribbons beneath her chin. They were cousins and they were betrothed; she had no need of a chaperone yet she'd never felt so vulnerable or in need of one.

Really, she wanted to retreat back into her safe bedchamber and hide. She was glad she'd soon set sail for Jamaica. It was too painful to be confronted with all she'd lost, here in England.

When they were on the battlements of the South Tower, Raphael seemed disposed to pointing out the many views of note, and the barges upon the river. Celeste couldn't care in the slightest about the view. Her heart was breaking.

Yet she'd never seen Raphael more carefree.

An enormous raven alighted on the crenelated battlement against which they rested and she moved away, stumbling into Raphael's embrace. She didn't miss the slight shudder he gave at the contact before he put her away from him.

Yet when an old beggar shuffled by and boldly put out his hand, she was surprised that instead of disgust for its shambling appearance and its rags, Raphael rummaged in his purse for a coin. She closed her eyes against the pain of knowing he had as much love for her as any beggar that crossed his path, blinking with surprise to see the glint of gold as the beggar's palm closed over not a coin, but the locket Raphael had gone to such pains to have Celeste reclaim.

Sweat prickled her scalp as she caught a glimpse of the

ragged creature's familiar eyes, which darted guiltily away from her gaze before he pulled down his cowl and shuffled away.

A quick intake of breath made Raphael turn in her direction, but his expression was guileless and his tone almost careless as he said, 'Yes, I know more than you, Celeste, but don't look at me with such opprobrium. I am not behind your fall from grace.'

She didn't know what to say, stammering as she pointed to the disappearing shambling creature. 'You gave him the locket.'

'The truth is, I've been shielding you since that shameful night, for you've had enough to bear, my dear.'

'Shielding me?' She stared. 'You've not shielded me from anything, Raphael.' Tears rose close to the surface. *'You've* thrust me into the thick of it. You forced me to attend Lady Montague's ball when you must have known I'd become a target. I was publicly shamed!'

Raphael considered her a moment. 'Ah Celeste,' he said softly. 'If only they were the *worst* of the rumours swirling around. If it were possible to whisk you off to Jamaica right now in order to protect you from what I fear would truly break your heart, I would.'

'Don't you dare speak to me of protection, Raphael,' she muttered. 'You care nothing for me! You'd sacrifice me to the wolves if it furthered your happiness. Tell me, why did you give the locket to that *beggar*? Only it wasn't a beggar, it was Harry, wasn't it?'

Raphael rested his hand on the battlement and shook his head. 'My dearest Celeste, do not look at me as if I'm the devil incarnate. Reserve your anger for your erstwhile admirer Lord Peregrine, who agreed to his lover Lady Busselton's wager in which you were the spoils. Little did I know I was playing right into his hands by begging you to discover from him whatever you could.' He reached across to touch her cheek, his expression aggrieved, but she drew back. Unperturbed he went on, 'Only when the news was about town that Lord Peregrine and Lady Busselton's wager was even listed in the Betting Book at White's was I forced to act in a manner that would protect you as best I could.'

Celeste clutched her hand to her heart. 'No!' she whispered. 'It cannot be true.' He'd made mention of a wager in the vaguest of terms when she was still recovering, physically, from her ordeal. When he'd not elaborated she'd dismissed the idea. Forgotten it, even.

She shook her head wildly as she stepped back, stumbling on the flagstones. 'Lord Peregrine would never have done such a thing! He may be a libertine but his regard for me was real!'

She had to believe it or her entire perception was off kilter. Seizing for crumbs she cried, 'But he didn't ruin me, did he, Raphael?' Her breath came quick and fast now. 'Harry did! Your beloved Harry! Someone coerced him and he played along. What do you think of him now? Of the man who would be part of someone's twisted plot to see me ruined. For that's what it was, wasn't it? I was an innocent pawn, nothing more.'

Raphael glanced at her before gazing into the distance. 'Lord Peregrine only had to see you ruined, my dear,' he murmured. 'Not be personally responsible. Was it his abhorrence of innocence that was at the root of that? Or his devotion to Lady Busselton?'

Anger gave her backbone. 'Well, Raphael, Harry may have used me and you may not love me, and but Lord Peregrine *did*. I know it. We were running away together. Eloping! I was responding to a message supposedly from him, only I was tricked into going to Harry's residence.'

Peregrine raised an eyebrow. 'Why, my dear, you are a

dark horse. I think you'd have been wiser to have withheld that. Still, it does not change the fact that Lord Peregrine only sought you out after Lady Busselton proposed your ruin as the means by which he could win her wager. Ask anyone, though they might blush to tell you the truth.'

Celeste shook her head. 'I don't believe it,' she whispered.

Raphael sighed. 'My dear Celeste, you can imagine how hard it is for me to forgive you for your own treachery in view of what you've told me. Do not look at me as if you're the only one wronged here.'

Celeste blinked. His every word was like a shard of pain being driven through her soul. Ignoring his remark, she whispered, 'What was his reward?'

Raphael raised his eyebrows as if the question surprised him. 'Why, Lady Busselton's favours, of course. I told you they were lovers. Well, after the terms of the wager were satisfied they quickly *became* lovers. Lord Peregrine's been dangling after her more than a decade before, and since her two husbands. All society knows it.'

Celeste could barely breathe. Each shallow intake was almost more than she could manage. She took a step backwards.

'But why Harry? Harry doesn't even like ...'

'Women? No, my dear, he does not. But Harry had little choice in the matter. Not when he owed Lord Peregrine such a large sum. Apparently Harry owed a lot of people money and when he returned to town, Lord Peregrine was the first to claim what he was owed. However, after some discussion the men came to the arrangement involving you. And no, I had no idea at the time, I assure you, but what could I do? Harry feared for his life. His creditors were baying for his blood and even after Harry had done his lordship's bidding and enticed you into his bed, he still feared for his life. He wanted to take no chances so immediately slipped back into hiding. Lord Peregrine is a dangerous man.' He indicated the corner of the battlement where Harry in disguise had last made an appearance. 'I therefore needed to secure his freedom and that meant retrieving the locket on Harry's behalf and returning it to Harry, who will remain in hiding until our return to Jamaica.'

All Celeste's anguished churnings over who was in fact behind her devastating fall from grace seemed to scream through her mind like a terrible wind storm until she was blinded and deafened by the sight of her cousin, her betrothed, the man into whose care she was entrusting her life, smiling guiltlessly at her.

'How can you tell me all this and look as if you don't even care?' she cried, backing away. 'You care nothing for me, Raphael. You never have! I hate you and I will *never* marry you!'

'You have no choice, Celeste.' Raphael spoke calmly. 'Who would have you now? You are disgraced. You have no dowry. Unless you choose to take Holy orders, you have nowhere to go.'

'Perhaps I shall join Charlotte and we'll both find peace and solace in a nunnery, for by God there's little peace for me on this earth!' Celeste positively screamed the words before picking up her skirts and rushing along the walkway to the staircase at the far end of the battlements. The descent was steep and narrow and ill lit but she couldn't remain with Raphael another moment.

Lord Peregrine had agreed to a wager in which she was the spoils? She'd given him her heart. She'd nearly given him her body and it wasn't even consolation that he may have found scruples. Was he in truth disgusted by her? That was not a concept with which she was unfamiliar, having been betrothed to Raphael so long and learning his views on women.

Her world was in tatters and she needed to escape, if she could find somewhere that offered her refuge.

The treads of the narrow winding staircase were uneven. Twice she lost her footing but she kept on running. If Raphael could do this to her, then what other horrors had he in store? Blind terror spurred her on, fuelling her speed though she had no idea where she was going, her feet transporting her as if on wings—until she stumbled on a chipped step.

With a scream she spiralled into space, that disembodied feeling a precursor, she knew, of the pain to come. Well, so be it. Nothing could be more painful than knowing the man she was to marry would sacrifice her on the altar of his own twisted pursuit of happiness.

And then a pair of strong arms swept her up and bound her tight. Peering into the gloom, she gasped as she recognised her rescuer.

'Lord Peregrine!'

Her heart, already in a state of upheaval, felt as if it were in danger of bursting out of her chest; ripping her in two in the process.

Here was the man who'd tricked her most cruelly. This villain had pursued her from the outset, wooing her with his pretence of growing regard, winning her trust only to sacrifice her to his own lustful desires.

For another woman!

Yet when once she was again in his strong embrace, she felt the connection between them as strong as ever. He'd followed her and now he'd saved her from breaking her neck, and although she could not tell what he felt right now, at least he didn't withdraw at her touch as Raphael had. Yet he had wronged her. So cruelly!

'Lord Peregrine?' she managed, her breath coming in short, difficult bursts as she registered his arms tighten about her. 'Let me go!' She began to struggle. She hated him yet she could not rid herself of that compelling need to draw closer. He'd always been dangerous, even when she'd thought he desired her, admired her. Now he was even more dangerous for the feelings of desire were all on her side, despite what he'd done to her.

'Are you so cruel that you'd *gloat* over my painful situation? Let me go, I say!'

'Painful?' She felt the tightness in him and the angry timbre of his tone as he went on, 'Or would that be conflicted? Well, it was your choice, my dear. You made your bed and you chose to lie in it. Don't blame me if you have regrets.'

She squeezed shut her eyes, deeply conscious of the heat from his body.

'I was drugged, my lord, as you well know.' She glared at him through the gloom. 'And now I am ruined, you have won your wager with Lady Busselton.' Her voice broke. 'May you have much joy of her. I hope that destroying my life was worth it!'

'You destroyed your life with no help from me, Miss Rosington,' he ground out. 'Don't blame me, for as God is my witness this was one unfortunate wager I had no intention of claiming on.'

'But you have, my lord,' she sobbed, 'and as I daresay you take the Lord's name in vain with as little compunction as you were going to take me, there's no comfort to be gained from your cheap words.'

'By God, but you've possessed me, Miss Rosington,' he ground out as he drew her closer against his chest. 'You have wronged me, cruelly. You swore there was nothing between you and Carstairs but you lied to me, yet still I cannot rid my mind of you. You torment me!'

Eyes like those belonging to the dangerous wild cats she'd

seen incarcerated in the dark dungeons blazed out from beneath his disdainfully arched eyebrows. Celeste shrank back from their malevolence but still he didn't release her. He put his face closer to hers, his dark searching look boring into her very soul, it seemed.

She needed no greater proof that he was determined to destroy her. He really *did* hold her responsible for his sister's shame and unhappiness.

'You truly believe I was guilty of more than furnishing Harry with the petticoats to escape when I explained *everything?*' It was indeed a terrible blow to know his vengeance could cut so deep. 'It is my fervent wish that the truth will somehow be revealed to you, Lord Peregrine!' she whispered harshly, for now that seemed about as likely as Celeste managing to avoid marriage with Raphael.

He paused for only a second to communicate what he thought of her remark through blazing eyes and curled lip, and then suddenly his lips were no longer full of hate, but of passion as they took possession of Celeste's.

Caught by surprise, she struggled momentarily before the energy that surged through her came from a different source: the determination to feel something from him that was not anger or indifference.

Passion. Whatever he'd done to her, whatever humiliation he might have engineered for her, there was no denying his passion was real as he held her pressed against his hard chest, still in his arms with the wall at her back. Perhaps he wanted to punish her for the fact that he desired her after yet tasting the fruits of his lust with Lady Busselton. His was the greed of a man who was never satisfied.

Yet as his mouth bore down hungrily upon hers and her initial resistance weakened, turning her instead into a pool of heated longing, all reason deserted her.

So this was passion? These heady sensations were what

caused men and women to risk everything in exchange for the fleeting sensation of desiring and being desired. Her nipples ached and her body cried out for something more she couldn't define as Lord Peregrine held her hard against him, only releasing her when Raphael's disembodied voice floated down from the battlements above: 'Celeste, I know you're down there. There's no point in running away when you have no choice in the matter.'

Lord Peregrine arched his eyebrow. 'Don't tell me you had no choice, Miss Rosington,' he said under his breath.

Despairingly Celeste swung out of his orbit, held up by a different kind of passion. 'I have no choice, now, when it comes to marrying my cousin,' she hissed, turning to run lightly back up the stairs, stopping near the top to add over her shoulder, 'Don't blame *me* for the fact you still want me, even if you can't believe the truth from my own lips—though I don't understand how any decent human being could pretend kindness while engineering the ruin of the woman he professes to love. I rue the day I ever met you!'

WELL, DIDN'T HE JUST WISH THE SAME?

Yet for the first time her impassioned denial of culpability hit a nerve. Xenia and Charlotte had been convincing in their condemnation while he had exhausted every counter argument. Yet *could* there be a kernel of truth in her fiery protestations?

Weary now with spent passion, Perry returned to his carriage where he rested his head against the window while the coachman awaited orders.

How could he distinguish truth from fiction, when on the one hand all he had were Miss Rosington's denials of wrong-doing counterbalanced with the irrefutable evidence of finding her in bed with Harry Carstairs, an illicit relationship backed up by a mountain of hearsay, rumours and innuendo that Carstairs and Miss Rosington were long-time lovers?

'Where to, my lord?' The coachman's impatient, yet respectful tones floated down from the box.

Perry rubbed a weary hand over his face. He should call on Charlotte and see how she fared if he were the loyal brother he professed to be. Last night he'd assured her he believed her assertions against Miss Rosington if only to stop her taking a knife to her wrists.

Nevertheless, the thought of spending a gloomy fifteen minutes in his sister's company was the last thing he felt like. He hoped Charlotte would be sufficiently satisfied by the social ruin of the woman who'd caused Harry Carstairs to abandon her at the altar to stop harping on about it.

To his dismay he found Charlotte in a listless mood, staring out of the drawing room window when he was announced.

'Should I order refreshment, Perry?' she asked, languidly waving him over. 'Or is this a bolting visit to satisfy your conscience that I've not tried to slice my wrists again?' She held up her hands and contemplated the lace ruffles that festooned from the elbows of her polonaise. 'Well, I haven't, but nor have I ruled it out.'

Perry rolled his eyes as he took up position at the window beside her. 'Harry Carstairs was clearly not for you, Charlotte, so now that your nemesis has received her just desserts, don't you think the time has come to move forward? You're beautiful with a sizeable dowry and the season is only half over. Consider it a wonderful opportunity.'

'My nemesis?' She turned and blinked at him. 'You mean Miss Rosington?' With another sigh she dropped her head to study the half moon of her nails. 'Oh, I don't think she's my nemesis,' she said vaguely.

Startled, Perry cocked his head. 'I don't understand you, Charlotte. Are you sure you're all right? Last night your angry assertion that Miss Rosington was the devil incarnate had you ready to take your own life. Why, you came dangerously close to ruining *yourself* with your public diatribe against her at Lady Montague's ball.'

Charlotte shrugged. 'Whatever happened between Harry and Miss Rosington the night Harry fled, I don't think Harry was interested in her. Not romantically—though it would be preferable.'

'Good God, now you are talking in riddles!' Perry exclaimed, gripping Charlotte's shoulders and forcing her chin up so that she had to look at him. 'You swore it was so. That the two were long-term lovers. And pray what do you mean. Preferable to what?'

Charlotte focused her troubled gaze upon her brother while he searched her face, wondering if Miss Rosington's actions accounted for the fact that his sister was now losing her wits.

Charlotte shrugged herself out of his grasp and put the gold velvet curtain between them, her look uncertain as she returned her gaze to the street.

In the silence he waited while his own thoughts churned over all the conflicting doubts and emotions he'd entertained regarding Miss Rosington and her seemingly inexplicable actions.

Her own anger at the Tower seemed more than just the expected defensiveness of a woman caught in the wrong.

'Perry, you remember when Harry offered for me, just before he went to Jamaica all those months ago? I was the happiest woman in the world, for I truly believed he loved me and not only because of my dowry.'

Perry forced his thoughts away from Miss Rosington's complex counterattack. Of course she'd lashed out and wanted to blame him. She was guilty and, having been discovered in the wrong, she was ashamed.

Well, a little too late, he thought, choking down his disgust.

He returned his attention to Charlotte's words. What she said was true. Charlotte had been like an uncontrollable puppy. He'd wanted to suggest to her back then that she tone down her high spirits, for she'd been wont to surprise her husband-to-be with tokens of her regard when he might least expect it. Still, Perry, too, had thought Harry Carstairs had been smitten with Charlotte for, at a little over thirty he'd never been linked with another female to the best of Perry's recollection.

'But I was wrong.' She turned soulful eyes upon him while her agitation grew. She twisted her hands and the tiny rose buds adorning her stomacher rose and fell as her bosom strained against her bodice. 'As you know, Harry went away to Jamaica not long after his proposal.' For a moment her eyes shone as if she were once again reliving those heady days of infatuation. Then the sorrow returned to her voice and shoulders slumped. 'After five months the anticipation of seeing him again was almost more than I could bear so I decided to surprise him, calling unannounced at his house. He wasn't expecting me—clearly.' She swallowed and dropped her eyes, saying finally at her brother's prompting, 'He was with Lord Ogilvy. They were in a window embrasure at the far end of the room and they both swung round when I was announced.' Charlotte looked increasingly distressed. 'There was something about their attitude that seemed ... out of place. I couldn't put my finger on it, and I was uncomfortable but I put on a bright show, saying when I observed the gold locket Harry was holding, 'Why, is it a gift for me?' and pretending to seize it from him. He grew quite angry then and it was Lord Ogilvy who said in genial tones,

'Why, it is for Harry to contain the miniature he's commissioned of you and which is now done. See. Do you not like it?'

Perry cocked his head and frowned. 'I don't know why he couldn't have been truthful.' He hesitated, unsure whether to tell Charlotte what he knew. She was highly excitable, but then, she also deserved the facts. Slowly he went on. 'In fact the locket had been left to him by his great-aunt and was engraved with the numbers of the security box that held his inheritance. He'd just visited his lawyer who'd given it to him. Of course he would not gift it to you-at least not then.' His tone changed and he was unable to conceal his pain which he wrapped up in irony. 'Retrieving this locket was the reason Miss Rosington was so keen to make my acquaintance after she learned you'd handed it over to me. Obviously Miss Rosington was directed by Carstairs to do whatever it took to reclaim it.'

There! How could he dismiss that fact? It was all but irrefutable proof that Miss Rosington saw him as nothing more than a means for her and Harry Carstairs to be together.

Charlotte shrugged. 'I think you're wrong. However, the locket did not concern me. Harry's agitation when I walked in, did. You see, Perry, now I think upon it, I do not believe Harry was ever interested in me as a woman. I do not believe Harry *could* ever be interested in a woman.' Her mouth worked and her voice dropped to a whisper. Rubbing agitatedly at a spot on her hand she said faintly, 'I've had a long time to come to this conclusion but … I believe Harry only ever wanted to be with Lord Ogilvy.'

Perry, who'd been about to say something, was struck dumb. For a second he could only stare as he tried to imagine the notion his sister suggested. The idea was shocking, disgusting and preposterous. He shook his head. 'No, Charlotte. Harry and *Miss Rosington* are lovers and have been for a long time. Their illicit liaison is the entire reason you've landed in such an appalling situation. You said it, yourself. At the ball on Friday. To the whole world, I might add.' Whatever doubts or confusion he entertained, he had to say it to Charlotte.

Sighing, Charlotte trailed her hand across the windowsill. She bit her lip as she raised her head to look at her brother. 'Xenia persuaded me it was true the night Harry left me and I found the note. That Miss Rosington and Harry were lovers, I mean. At the time I was filled with fury and vengeance. Xenia told me Miss Rosington had been seen not once, but twice, in compromising circumstances with Harry. By the time she'd finished talking to me I believed it to be the truth, myself, even though I'd long harboured other suspicions.'

'But how could you have other suspicions?' Perry shook his head. What Charlotte suggested made no sense as far as Miss Rosington was concerned. 'The scrap of note in the locket contained the last four letters of Miss Rosington's Christian name. It's what determined you, Charlotte, upon Miss Rosington's guilt.'

Charlotte's brow creased. 'There was more,' she admitted haltingly. 'I haven't told you this but in fact I found the rest of the note in the half seam of one of the discarded petticoats signed by Harry.' She swallowed. 'It was addressed to "My Dearheart—'

'Referring obviously to Miss Rosington.'

Charlotte reddened. 'It couldn't have been, for the note referred to Miss Rosington later, saying "send Celeste immediately", however, as you say, a few letters were torn and left with the glue.' She looked searchingly at her brother. 'I showed Xenia the letter and told her of my suspicions and that I couldn't understand why Harry would address a letter to Lord Ogilvy with the salutation, "My Dearheart", only she said I must be mistaken and that clearly Miss Rosington was the woman Harry was consorting with.'

'Xenia had no right to meddle,' Peregrine said, uncomfortably aware of his own willingness all those weeks ago to proceed with Xenia's plan to ruin Miss Rosington. 'What would Xenia know, anyway?'

Charlotte shrugged. 'Xenia has been a good friend to me. She understands what it's like to feel society's scorn and she's done everything she can to protect me from the scandal.' She put her hand on her brother's wrist, her look plaintive. 'I know she admires you very much, Peregrine, so even if she has confused matters, her motives were pure.'

WHEN PERRY FINALLY EXTRICATED HIMSELF TO RETURN HOME and prepare himself for a rout that evening, his thoughts were in turmoil.

If his own sister did not believe Harry Carstairs capable of desiring a woman, then why had the wretched man been discovered in bed with Miss Rosington?

Again the doubts loyalty had forced him to dismiss returned. Miss Rosington swore she'd been tricked. She even insinuated *he* were behind her fall from grace, but then what did a cornered animal do? Lash out, of course.

Wretchedly he shook his head. In whose interest was it to trick Miss Rosington into sharing a bed with Harry?

With an hour before he was to go out again, Perry stood in his dressing room and submitted himself to the ministrations of his manservant.

Tonight was a long-standing engagement and Perry had promised to escort Xenia, but as was increasingly the case he had little enthusiasm for it.

Little enthusiasm for anything, really. Not the gaming

that once fired his blood, or the hunting party he was to join five days hence.

'My lord is not in a good frame,' Nelson observed drily as Perry flicked a piece of lint from his lace sleeve with a gesture of irritation.

'A good frame?' Perry repeated, before understanding his valet's meaning and mimicking his choice of words in his plummy accent. 'No, my lord is indeed *not* in a good frame, a good mood or a good mind to do anything except thrash a certain gentlemen out of London town if he hadn't already disappeared again.'

'And which certain gentleman might that be?'

'No gentlemen that concerns you, Nelson.' He frowned at his reflection, thinking how bad-tempered he appeared, and only looking considerably more bad-tempered. He and Xenia were well suited, he thought cynically. Neither of them had morals or a heart. Loathing for mankind in general, and himself in particular, welled up in his breast. He was no better than any of them, yet it was Miss Rosington with her particular talent for appearing the innocent ingénue for whom he reserved most of his spleen.

He *had* to dismiss Charlotte's ramblings and his own doubts or he'd drive himself mad. The proof was irrefutable and Miss Rosington's unbelievable denials only to be expected. Charlotte had been present when Carstairs and Miss Rosington were caught *déshabillé* the first time, and Perry had been on hand the second to discover them naked and in bed together.

For no good reason other than Nelson's silence was the prompt to expand on his theme. He muttered, 'This gentleman who shall remain nameless has caused my sister great heartache, but it is not only for that reason I would be avenged.

'Avenged? Vengeance is a very serious business, my lord.'

Perry raised an eyebrow. 'I was asked the other night how I could sleep at night with you so close, Nelson. A slave. I have bought you. I own you yet I allow you great freedom as a slave. Why have you never tried to escape? Should I fear for my life? There. Answer that if you will. It will take my mind off my current troubles.'

'To discuss, instead of your wish for vengeance, my lord —mine?'

'If that is how you like to look at it.'

Perry watched Nelson's smile as the black man brushed Perry's fine brocade coat. During the years he'd owned him, Nelson had grown from a young stripling he'd admired for his developing physical prowess into an intellectual Perry admired now for his deep thinking.

'You have nothing to fear, my lord, if it's worrying about your throat being slit.' Nelson paused, the brush suspended an inch from Perry's coat sleeve, as if weighing up something of great gravity. Quietly he added, 'You have friends who might be well to guard their backs, however.'

Startled, Perry shot him a look in the cheval glass. His slave looked as if he were caught in the middle of a moral dilemma, and for the first time Perry felt a frisson of alarm. 'Are you giving me notice of an insurrection, Nelson?' he asked. 'I hope you realise I cannot dismiss your words without demanding greater explanation, which may well lead to outcomes you can not foresee.' His alarm only grew as he observed the deepening of his manservant's frown. 'I insist you tell me what you know, Nelson, so I may warn these so-called friends of mine.'

'Oh, they know who they are, and if they were human beings with true consciences they would understand that what they have done is so terrible that they invite murder and insurrection. But I think, my lord, their arrogance blinds them to the real danger they face.'

Perry turned slowly so that he faced Nelson, eye to eye. His servant lowered the arm that held the clothes brush, and his look contained none of the deference Perry would expect or should demand.

He swallowed. 'You cannot remain silent, Nelson, you do know that.'

'With all due respect, my lord, I would be obliged if you allowed me to tell you my tale without this ... what do you call it? Cross-examination.'

The bluster left Perry as he acknowledged that Nelson had been the one to initiate the topic and, for all Perry knew, may have been looking for an avenue for some time.

In a rare act of contrition, he actually apologised. Then he added more calmly, 'Pray tell, Nelson, what are the details of this planned attack you speak of?'

'I speak of no planned attack. I merely point out that recent certain happenings to my fellow black man might well justify—in their eyes—thoughts of vengeance.'

'Indeed. And what happenings do you refer to?'

'The loss of one hundred and thirty-four slaves aboard the *Batavia* last month, sir.'

With a mixture of relief and unrealised fear, Perry released the pressure of air that had built up in his lungs. The heat had been taken out of the topic, though it remained one that concerned him deeply. 'Alas, slavery is an abomination and I would fight to have it outlawed. I regret the loss of these poor creatures from Africa as much as you do, believe me.' His words were heartfelt. 'Their conditions are inhumane. It is small wonder so many die. And I now realise to whom you refer. Nevertheless, Captain Higgins operates within the law. He's made it a common practice to transport slaves aboard his vessels and has done so for many years. It is how he has become so wealthy. He has no fear and he is well protected, I've no doubt. So just make sure your black friends know that any hint of violence is likely to see *them* at the end of a noose.'

For a long moment Nelson said nothing. Perry frowned as he watched him, a vague uneasiness beginning to grow from the roots of his former relief.

Finally Nelson looked up, wearing an expression of great sorrow. 'Ah, but my lord, I am afraid the slaves did not die from disease.' He shook his head slowly. 'And Captain Higgins did not act within the law.'

A strange tingling in the tips of Perry's fingers was a portent of something truly ominous to come, he feared. He took a breath. 'Explain yourself, Nelson.'

Nelson ran the clothes brush over the arm of his own livery, clearly lost in thought. Finally he raised his head, and his mouth worked with a deep emotion he was quick to master as he drew himself up to say stolidly, 'These slaves were thrown overboard, my lord. Thrown overboard so the captain could make an insurance claim as he saw greater profit in that than bringing the poor half-starved souls, weakened as they were by disease, back to port.'

Horrified, Peregrine stared at him, the notion of such barbarism impossible to comprehend, before his natural defence of Xenia's father sprang to his lips. 'Captain Higgins would not countenance such an act. Where have you heard this, Nelson? This is all hearsay. Of course your fellow slaves would be quick to invent a tale like this, but as no slaves survived the voyage there are no witnesses and therefore no one to refute or support what you're telling me.'

Nelson's compelling gaze bored into Peregrine's as he waited for his master to finish speaking.

With commendable deference he inclined his head in acknowledgement, before fixing Peregrine once more with a level look.

The sound of a passing wagon in the street below punctu-

ated the tense silence as Peregrine waited, alarm and anticipation building in his chest.

'With all due respect, my lord, there was one witness.'

Perry shook his head. 'There were no survivors, Nelson.'

'No *slaves* who survived, my lord, that is true.'

A curse in the street drifted through the half-open
window. Peregrine studied the set jaw of his manservant as
he teased out the insinuation. Nor did he lose concentration
at the jingling of harness and the clatter of what sounded like
a barrel falling to the cobbles.

'Go on, Nelson,' he said softly.

'Mr Carstairs travelled as a passenger from Jamaica
aboard the *Batavia* with a cargo load of slaves.'

The air inside Perry's chamber seemed suddenly dense.
Fragments of truths and half-truths danced on the periphery
of his brain. Words that had blithely tripped off Xenia's lips
with relation to her father's business. His sister's new revelations, which had muddied the waters. But above all, Miss
Rosington's tearful rebuttals. All of these fragments began to
coalesce into some still as yet undefined truth, damnably out
of reach but all pointing to one irrefutable fact: that all layers
were connected to Harry Carstairs. Was *this* the reason he'd
taken flight?

Perry ran his finger around the inside of his stock to give
himself more air. Sweat needled him and he swallowed as he
asked, 'Whom did Mr Carstairs tell?' He could not pretend to
understand the half of it but he had to find out what he
could.

'After Mr Carstairs disembarked the *Batavia*, he attended
his lawyer then returned to his house where Lord Ogilvy
visited him. He was overheard by one of the servants telling
Lord Ogilvy he'd witnessed all one hundred and thirty-four
slaves thrown into the sea.' Nelson's lip curled as he added,
'For the sharks.'

Perry stared at him as he tried to comprehend the ramifications of such a crime—and the ramifications for Carstairs should it be discovered by Captain Higgins that his passenger had seen what he ought not and, moreover, that he was talking about it. He grunted. 'I take it word got back to the captain of the *Batavia* and that's why Mr Carstairs fled for his life?'

Nelson nodded. 'Captain Higgins is guilty of murder, my lord, *even* if it was the killing of a number of black so-called savages from Africa by a white man from England.' His chest rose with emotion. 'But even if throwing one hundred and thirty-four slaves overboard for the sharks is not considered murder in this country, the captain is still guilty of claiming his funds illegally. And insurance fraud is a very serious business in the eyes of the law, my lord.'

'*P*erry darling, you have not yet complimented me on my new polonaise? Lord William says the silver thread embroidery sets off my eyes magnificently while wicked Sir Samuel declares he shall compose an ode to my creamy shoulders.' Xenia's coy look only highlighted the sexual animal cunning that had always been such a successful ploy in drawing him to her.

Tonight it left Peregrine more than simply cold. Beneath the chandelier of a hundred beeswax candles Xenia looked an exquisite figure, cast in gold and ivory. Nestled amongst the curls of her pomaded hair, styled a foot high, was the ubiquitous galleon, symbol of her father's wealth and the source of her own extravagant lifestyle.

That she would remain a beauty as she grew old was not in doubt. Her mother's aristocratic legacy could be seen in her finely chiselled nose, high cheekbones and the hauteur that would inflame some with respect and desire, and others with deference.

Where once Perry had hardened each time Xenia sent

him one of her suggestive looks, he now felt positively repelled. Xenia's allure was like a brittle casing of the rotting being within. She had no softness, he realised. Her motives were entirely self-serving. Oh yes, she might desire Perry for the fleeting moments their naked limbs were entwined and she might use her body as enticement for some service rendered. But she would never give her heart.

'Your beauty is exalted by your liveliness tonight, Xenia,' Perry remarked truthfully, while his thoughts ran wild with regard to how much she knew of her father's unlawful dealings. For now, though, it was incumbent upon him to retain the careful veneer of polite interest as a foil for his turbulent thoughts. 'Pray tell, what is your secret. Something has excited you.'

She halted her progress from the mantelpiece to the clustered seating where he loitered, drink in hand, awaiting the moment their carriage was announced.

'Why Perry, surely you are only teasing me.' She tapped him playfully on the shoulder, her lips forming a *moué* while her eyes sparkled. 'Tonight I am a happy woman. Justice has been served and I am now in a position to enjoy the fruits of my efforts to achieve it. Charlotte has been avenged and you may now claim your reward.'

She drew a deep breath and her bosom swelled. But the effect was not enticing, as Perry would once have found it. The tiny love-heart shaped patch she'd placed just above the nipple of her right breast didn't send the heat to his loins, as it once would have.

And he could no longer pretend what he did not feel.

He turned away from her and took a step towards the fireplace. What evil had Xenia perpetrated in her quest for self-fulfilment or aggrandisement? Clearly she wanted Perry. But what else would inspire her to go to such lengths?

He took a difficult breath. *The need to protect her father's fortune?*

Though he said nothing she must have sensed his reserve, for her voice held a brittle edge. 'You have desired me throughout two husbands, Perry. You have gone to great lengths to win the reward I promised you all those weeks ago. And although it wasn't you, directly, who exposed Miss Rosington for the jezebel she is, I consider it even more effective that she did that herself.'

'So we are to celebrate the destruction of Miss Rosington by indulging our carnal desires?' His lips twisted into a semblance of a smile. 'Now that Charlotte is avenged?'

She inclined her head. 'Miss Rosington will never recover from the slur that Charlotte herself has levelled upon her. And if for some reason you pity Miss Rosington, then don't. She is soon to set sail for Jamaica and her marriage to Lord Ogilvy takes place, as you know, two days hence.'

If her words had been calculated to alter his disposition towards Xenia, they missed their mark. Xenia had desired the destruction of Miss Rosington for reasons other than avenging Charlotte, of that he was sure. Had Miss Rosington played into her hands without Xenia having to lift a finger?

And how much did Xenia know of her father's dealings?

Tonight he planned to find out.

Despite all that he had seen, the ravaging desire he felt for Miss Rosington would not be quelled; even when he conjured up hideous visions of Miss Rosington's creamy limbs curled around Carstairs' naked body.

Wincing, he shook his head. He no longer believed she had entered the man's bed of her own volition. But had she been manipulated by others and reluctantly agreed? Tacit involvement would not exonerate her but if, as she claimed, she *had* in fact been tricked …

'Yes, Xenia, my sister has assuredly had her revenge.'

Perry agreed to this with more thoughtfulness than spleen, which obviously interested Xenia.

'You can't really be sorry for Miss Rosington?'

He did not miss the deathly challenge in her question, though her tone would appear almost bland to anyone who did not know her.

Perry knew her only too well; Xenia was at her most dangerous when she appeared most benign.

'Granted, she betrayed my sister with the man Charlotte was to marry. I saw it with my own eyes.' He studied the intricate enamelwork of his snuffbox while he chose his words carefully. It was too dangerous to look Xenia in the eye. He suspected she could read him as well as he could read her. 'But she has been exposed now to the world for what she is.'

'I asked if you were sorry for her. Your manner does not suggest exultation. I was curious.'

Perry exhaled on a sigh of frustration. 'Is it not enough for you, Xenia, that Miss Rosington will never be received in polite society again? Is my round condemnation required? Perhaps I'm more concerned about Charlotte and what happens to her now than I am about Miss Rosington. Miss Rosington will, as you have just pointed out, be leaving for Jamaica before the week is out. Meanwhile Charlotte is still talking about joining a nunnery. But what of Carstairs? What's he doing in all this? Has he been roundly condemned for his behaviour? I hardly think he's about to beg my sister for forgiveness.'

'He is travelling to Jamaica on board the *Veronique* in the company of Lord Ogilvy and Miss Rosington, or rather Lady Ogilvy as she then will be,' Xenia said smoothly. 'Meanwhile I shall dissuade Charlotte from her life of celibacy, I promise you, Perry.'

She'd crossed the carpeted expanse as she spoke and now

her body was but an inch from his. Perry could see the lust in her eyes as her bosom rose and fell with each breath.

'Celibacy is so overrated,' she whispered, tucking a lock of Perry's hair back into his queue as she rested her cheek against his, angling her head so she could look into his eyes. 'And you've been chafing against it for too long. But tonight …'

Her suggestive promise was accompanied by a raising of one eyebrow and the curl of her painted lips, but Perry felt no answering desire. He would have recoiled had he not been aware of the dangers in denting Xenia's pride. No, he'd have to tread carefully, but at the same time he couldn't bring himself to melt into her embrace as she so clearly expected.

A falling log in the fireplace provided the excuse he needed to push her away, feigning concern at the possible singeing of her skirts. He looked out of the window towards the moon for a hint of the time. 'All good things worth waiting for are made the sweeter for not rushing into them, Xenia. Come.' He offered her his arm as he turned for the door. 'We are expected at Lady Milton's, but when we've made our excuses the night will be ours.'

He wasn't quite sure how he was going to extricate himself from being the recipient of Xenia's promised affection without inciting her fury, but that was a problem for later. In the meantime the thought occurred to him that if Nelson knew so much of the affairs of Captain Higgins and Carstairs, his manservant's below-stairs connections might well prove useful in the search for the truth regarding Miss Rosington's involvement in all this. For what he'd taken as irrefutable proof of her guilt now seemed completely at odds with the abundance of conflicting evidence and motives surrounding the Carstairs mystery.

'Do try to look a little cheerful, Celeste.'

Although her aunt's rebuke was not harsh as she surveyed Celeste in her wedding finery, tears still pricked Celeste's eyes. She dropped her hands to her sides as Mary began to unlace her, now that the final fitting had been approved by the small company who surrounded her.

'Perhaps I shall miss England. That warrants tears, doesn't it?' She sniffed, rummaging in her pockets for her linen handkerchief. 'I've been affianced to Raphael for seven years but neither of us had heard of Jamaica when the marriage contract was signed. Now I'm condemned to live there for the rest of my life.'

Aunt Branwell sent her a tired smile from her seat upon the gilt settee. 'It is hard, I grant you that, child,' she agreed. 'But you will not lack comfort. Raphael will keep you in great style, there's no doubting that.'

But there'll be no love in my life, Celeste thought with a pang. Years of emptiness stretched before her in a land that was hot and frightening. She felt like a sailor about to venture into unchartered waters where sea serpents and the edge of the world were frightening realities.

'And Harry will be accompanying us on the same boat. How does that help my reputation in view of the whispers that have all but blown London off its foundations? I don't understand Raphael.'

Well, she did and that was part of the problem. He'd chosen to sacrifice Celeste when Lord Peregrine gave him the choice. Surely Raphael could have chosen to bail Harry out financially rather than allow Celeste's ruin?

She clutched her stomach, for the pain was physical. Lord Peregrine had accepted Lady Busselton's wager and then offered to waive Harry's debt by ensuring Celeste's ruin.

Harry and Raphael had kept close company for some

time, but of course the situation would have been misread as Harry having an interest in Celeste—not Raphael.

Yes, she'd been the spoils of a wicked wager between Lady Busselton and Lord Peregrine, just as she'd been assigned the role of scapegoat so that Raphael and Harry could enjoy their blissful union in another country, leaving England where their kind of love was against the law.

Soon Raphael would have achieved his heart's desire.

But what of Celeste's heart's desire? That was of no account to be sure, though assuredly the state of her heart was something she was entirely unable to put into words were she granted the chance.

Now Raphael had Harry while Lord Peregrine was enjoying Xenia's favours. Oh, hadn't Raphael laughed at that just before Celeste's fitting, knowing as he did the feelings Celeste had developed for the wicked viscount.

She'd wanted to flee from the room, shrieking, 'Run away with Harry, but I beg you, don't shackle me to your side as your whipping boy so you can enjoy a love I will *never* know.'

She hadn't said that, of course. She'd simply remained silent and he had done the speaking.

'Imagine the irony!' he'd marvelled in that measured, pleasant, condescending tone he liked to used when talking to her. 'You've been ill-used, I grant you, Celeste, and I will concede that you deserve sympathy when all is said and done. But you would have humiliated me, had you been given the chance. Still, as you shall enjoy all the riches and comfort you could ever want in Jamaica, I don't think you can complain.'

And while there was a painful truth in his words, Celeste still could not erase the last trace of feeling she felt for Lord Peregrine.

Her mind constantly replayed their stolen moments, while she was filled with an overwhelming confusion. There was no doubt his motives were evil from the start. He'd set out to ruin her to avenge his sister, but surely it was not possible to manufacture such intensity of affection? She had to believe he'd once loved her, otherwise she could never trust her perceptions again.

Not only that, she'd have nothing with which to sustain her during the long empty years ahead.

Stepping out of her gown and adjusting her panniers, she said, 'It will be the strangest wedding anyone has been to for a long time. There! That's made me smile. I'll be surprised if we have any guests at all.'

'Prurient curiosity is a great motivator for overcoming one's moral scruples,' Aunt Branwell observed. 'You know, of course, that I, for one, do not believe in this nonsense that connects you with Harry Carstairs.'

Celeste smiled gratefully as she ran her hands down her stays, half boned and rigid enough to give her the inverted V shape required to achieve the fashion of the day. Mary was holding out her petticoat, a pale cream silk box-pleated confection, before the polonaise went over her head, transforming her into exactly what Raphael required: a well-packaged lady of fashion, constricted and restricted in every way, constrained by clothes, duty, upbringing, expectations and the ever-present threat of losing everything were she to abrogate any of the heavy expectations that weighed upon her shoulders.

'I shall need new clothes in Jamaica,' she whispered. She could not inject any more strength into her voice. 'Raphael told me this some time ago but ...' She swallowed painfully and closed her eyes before finishing the sentence. 'I couldn't believe I would really go.'

Aunt Branwell darted her a sharp look. 'I pity you, Celeste, but you were naïve to allow sway to improbable daydreams. Women like you—like us—only make life harder for ourselves if we indulge in foolish fancies.'

'Then I was more than the common fool, for not only did I indulge in foolish daydreams but I was duped by the very man I thought would transport me to my fantasy land.' She sucked in a quavering breath. 'I loved Lord Peregrine but he betrayed me most cruelly.' Celeste was reasonably certain Aunt Branwell suspected the truth, and what did it matter if she did? There was no one else to whom she could unburden herself, and that's what she needed right now. In just a few days she'd be wrenched from her homeland and everything that was familiar.

'You believe Lord Peregrine wrote the note that sent you to the location where you were compromised by Harry Carstairs?' Aunt Branwell spoke plainly as she moved her brown-silk brocaded and upholstered body forward in her seat, her eyes full of sympathy in her wrinkled face. 'Mary told me everything but I don't believe Lord Peregrine is guilty of more than agreeing to a wicked wager proposed weeks ago by Lady Busselton.' She put up her hand to stay Celeste's protest. 'Bad enough though that is, I think it's possible he changed his mind and had no intention of following through with the plan to see you ruined.'

Celeste shook her head. 'He admitted it, Aunt Branwell.'

'He admitted accepting a wager that would see your reputation besmirched, granted.' She looked pointedly at Celeste. 'You are a beautiful young woman and he was clearly taken, therefore it makes no sense he'd pass the "spoils"—to speak bluntly—to the very man he despises, when he could both enjoy you and ruin you himself.'

Aunt Branwell did not exhibit the distaste and horror Celeste felt was justified by such talk.

'Such cruelty is bred of the boredom that comes from

having nothing meaningful to do with one's life,' her aunt went on. 'Lord Peregrine has had his every whim granted since the cradle. Both his parents were dead by the time he was nine. He was made the ward of a wastrel of an uncle who managed the estate and who creamed off a considerable proportion, I might add, before he died of his excesses. Meanwhile Lord Peregrine was brought up by nurses and nannies and encouraged to indulge his appetite for whatever he chose as soon as he was old enough.' She seemed to be gaining animation from her talk. 'He's known no civilising influences since his father—a reformed reprobate himself —drowned in the river accident that took Lord Peregrine's mother. Nevertheless, I do not believe Lord Peregrine is a bad man. And certainly not the kind who would set out to ruin an *innocent* young woman for a wager. Or at least, to follow through on such a wicked wager and *that*, I would argue, is an important distinction.'

'I believed he loved me.' Celeste fingered one of the cream rosettes that adorned her gown. She didn't care that Mary, who was fastening her into her wedding finery could hear. In the eyes of the world Celeste was more than damned and now she was being banished. She could sink no lower.

'And he may well have.' Aunt Branwell twisted her hands in her lap, her look thoughtful. Briskly she added, 'But sometimes that's not enough, my dear. Now, Mary, more rouge for my niece. Let no one tonight assume she's the dispirited creature she has every right to be.' She chuckled. 'My goodness, Celeste, suddenly I'm starting to look forward to this ball assembly. At least, I'm looking forward to testing whether my theory is true.'

'But I'm not going to the ball assembly, Aunt Branwell.' Celeste threw her a stricken look. 'I'm to be married in the morning.'

Aunt Branwell seemed to come to a sudden decision. Clasping Celeste's wrist as she rose, she asked with quirked lips, 'Are you afraid that people will talk?' She stared at their twin reflections in the looking glass. 'Of course they will, but they're talking already. Celeste, you have one final chance to speak to Lord Peregrine before you are forever condemned to a life that you know offers you nothing but the greatest unhappiness.' She sobered as she turned to look at her niece. 'Tonight you're still under my care: I would desire that you accompany me to Lady Belcher's ball.'

'I don't think I have the fortitude to go out tonight, Aunt,' Celeste whispered as she moved away from Mary who was holding the rabbit's foot loaded with rouge.

Her aunt seemed not to hear her. 'You'll have to change your dress, too, of course. I think the cloth of embroidered gold would be just the thing.'

'No, aunt. I can't! I had that made especially for my first public engagement with Raphael.'

'Humour an old woman. I would like to see you wear it tonight.' Her smile was grim and determined. 'Unless, of course, you really do want to spend the rest of your life as Raphael's slave.'

While Celeste was quaking with terror at the mere idea of going out in public at all, her aunt looked as excited as if she were contemplating her first ball. Once a highly reluctant Celeste was dressed, she raked her niece's finery with a frown.

'Celeste, you are a far more enticing prospect than Lady Busselton. Tonight I grant you licence to try one last gambit to make him see the truth. Charge his lordship with the fact he was a calculated cad in setting out to ruin you and hear him out when he denies it, or at least tries to excuse himself. My belief is that he truly accepts that what he saw with his own eyes was simple evidence you and Harry Carstairs have been enjoying a dangerous liaison behind everyone's backs.' She clicked her tongue. 'Except that everything we both know about Harry Carstairs refutes the possibility of such a thing. Somebody had a very different motive for engineering your ruin, Celeste, and I don't believe it was Lord Peregrine. Tonight is your last chance to discover who wanted to discredit you, and why.'

CHAPTER 16

*W*as her heart black with sin or was she a blameless angel?

Lord Peregrine had never felt so conflicted in his life as he sat opposite Xenia on their short ride to their evening's entertainment. No, he was not thinking about Xenia. As ever, his thoughts centred upon Miss Rosington.

He glanced at his well-turned calves in his white silk stockings above silver buckled shoes and below his black pantaloons. Carstairs used false padding to create what Perry had been granted in a generous allocation of physical attributes at birth. What would prompt Miss Rosington to choose that puny physical specimen Carstairs over himself?

Then there was the opposite conundrum. If she spoke the truth when she declared she'd been the one deceived, could she *truly* believe Perry was behind her fall from grace? And if Miss Rosington had indeed been set up to appear a jezebel with Carstairs, then who stood to profit by her ruin?

He directed a suspicious look at Xenia. She wanted Perry, there was no doubt about that.

And yet …? Xenia was devious. Could she have had a

hand in orchestrating something that appeared quite unrelated to her real motivations?

With a sigh he returned to the night at hand. The ball was being held at a beautiful estate by the river. It would provide many an opportunity for secret trysts behind spreading elms along meandering walks. Perry knew Xenia well enough to know it was what she planned.

Dalliance, however, was the last thing on his mind. No, he needed answers. Answers as to why Miss Rosington was in that bed, naked, with Harry Carstairs. It could *not* be because she preferred him to Perry.

He glanced down and noticed his foot beat an agitated tattoo. Xenia's secretive smile and raised eyebrow suggested she'd made her own interpretations as to Perry's impatience. Fanning herself, she reached across and ran her fingers gently down his cheek.

'How much greater the reward when patience has been exercised,' she purred. 'You shall get all that you deserve—and more—my darling Perry, when we have performed this evening.

'You make it sounds as if we'd been engaged to do tricks for the crowd.' He didn't mean to sound so terse but he couldn't help himself. All pleasure had been sucked out of his existence since Miss Rosington was no longer part of it.

Tomorrow she'd be married. But God, *he* wanted her.

He'd grown up indulged, moulded into believing that whatever he wished could be bought. He'd never done anything remotely noble or courageous in his life.

Perhaps if Miss Rosington were not due to set sail for Jamaica, putting her forever out of his reach, he'd feel differently.

No. He rejected this. He had loved her.

He still did.

'My dear, the crowd will be vastly interested in us, I

assure you. We are London Town's greatest celebrities, surely you know that?' Xenia moved a little closer, releasing a waft of gardenia perfume mixed with desire as she rested her head on his shoulder. 'I am known to go to great lengths to get what I want—when the prize is worth it.' She touched her lips to his jawline, whispering, 'And after ten years I've finally decided, my darling, you're worth it.'

'Two husbands ago you were not of the same mind.'

'Are you still smarting over that, Perry? Surely you understand the vulnerability of youth? Of an unmarried woman?' She straightened and looked him in the eye. 'My wishes counted for nothing when my papa had secured a rich, older man, with far greater prospects for aiding a sea captain in his enterprises.'

'So you loved me then?'

Xenia contemplated the ivory points of her fan. 'I loved you, but I also knew it was more expedient to marry Sir Edward. And so it proved. My first husband paved the way for papa to become the biggest slaver now in this country.'

Perry was conscious of a churning in his stomach at the mention of slaves. 'Nelson, my valet, came over in your father's first shipment ten years ago,' he said. 'He was stolen from a coastal village when he was a young man, hunting to feed his family who are now, of course, all but dead to him.'

'Perry darling, you speak as if your Nelson has feelings. Why, you have transformed him from a savage into a gentleman since you won him. He should be eternally grateful to you—and to papa, for that matter. Now, kiss me.'

He looked down at her with dispassion, glad she could not see his expression for her eyes were closed in anticipation of the prelude to the lovemaking she had planned for later that evening.

His stomach churned even more at the prospect. No, not with desire. Xenia, like a beautiful effigy and his for the taking, was a poisoned chalice. He'd done her bidding as eagerly as the drooling puppy dog he'd been when he was barely in his majority, and now he was filled with self-loathing. And loathing for everything she represented.

'Tell me, Xenia, did you know the reason your father was so desperate to find Harry Carstairs?'

She shrugged. 'Papa said we'd be ruined if the man was *not* found. That was good enough for me.'

Yet she was evasive. He did not believe her.

'If all eyes will be on us, Xenia, then for the sake of your dignity I am reluctant to make inroads into the vermillion which colours your lips. We are nearly there. A little more patience will sweeten our reward.'

He was relieved the carriage lurched to a halt at this point, even though it was to give way to a passing cooper's wagon, before it rumbled towards its destination.

With a grumble, Xenia straightened and Perry noticed by the light of the full moon, which drenched the interior of their carriage, the fine lines etched into her porcelain skin. He could see no evidence of smile lines. Not the tiny lines that were in evidence on Miss Rosington's face and which indicated a sunny temperament, but lines of dissatisfaction at the corner of Xenia's pouting mouth.

'We have arrived,' he murmured, and was never more glad to make his escape. Already he was conscious of the interest of the small group of guests who'd gathered at the top of the staircase to the front doors in preparation of being announced. With an enquiring look at Xenia, he whispered, 'Pray enlarge upon the actual reason we may be of particular interest this evening.'

Xenia's gurgle of laughter was genuine. 'Why, Perry darling, when you championed your sister last week before escorting me home and endorsed society's general disgust over Miss Rosington's conduct, you were signalling that the terms of the wager had been satisfied.'

'There was no wager, Xenia, beyond your chivvying me to do what any good brother would do to honour his sister, then suggesting that you might like to reward me since you were at a loose end.'

Xenia raised an eyebrow as they mounted the steps, though she was careful, he noted, to rein in her temper. He could see the tiny muscles working at the corner of her mouth and knew that were they in private she may well at this moment be looking for a convenient urn to hurl at him.

'That was not how it was, and you know it,' she hissed. 'Why, all London knows that you and I wagered whether you could bring down the evil creature who destroyed your sister's life by proving to the world that she's not the innocent ingénue she pretended to the world.' She slowed her steps as she brought home her point, which only increased Perry's shame for he knew it to be the truth. 'It's in the betting books. Good lord, it was in White's Betting Book and you're a member.' Her eyes, which had flashed fire, took on a softer glow as they were ushered into the warmth. 'Everyone assumes we're already lovers. Why, Peregrine, for a man with no conscience, you're doing a remarkably good job of trying to appear as pure as the driven snow.'

It was as well they were now at the front doors, stepping into the lobby, the butler announcing in stentorian tones first Xenia and then, "The Right Honourable, the Viscount Peregrine," otherwise it might have been Perry who lost control of his temper. Nor would it have been solely directed at Xenia, for undeniably there was a good deal of self-recrimination there also.

He'd acted a cad from the start and now he was being feted as if he'd somehow engineered something very cunning. For there was Miss Fotheringay and her aunt, Lady Louisa, fawning over Xenia and purring, 'At least poor Charlotte can hold her head up high. But can you believe it? I hear whispers that little trollop Miss Rosington has dared to show her face. She's with her aunt, which is why I suppose the butler didn't turn her away.'

A most extraordinary jolt passed through Perry at this news, though he hid the turbulence in his heart behind an implacable stare, allowing Xenia to voice her moral outrage.

'Come, my dear, we are holding others up,' he murmured when she'd said her piece, taking her elbow to lead her through the crowd, and determining he'd hunt down Miss Rosington. He wanted to hear from her own lips an expanded account of what he'd been so quick to deride the last time she tried to voice her innocence.

He was aware of Xenia's sharp eyes on him as he looked over the crowd. Well, let her see what he really felt, for once.

On every side they were feted and complimented, as if they were the reigning couple of the day, he noted drily. Undoubtedly, Xenia shone in her gown of blue and silver thread intricately patterned on cream silk. It matched her powdered hair, which was naturally blonde, and cleverly supplemented where needed to achieve the extreme fashions of the day.

For some reason it brought to mind the occasion he'd chanced upon Miss Rosington with her naturally dark tresses cascading down her back, a reflection which occasioned the most intense surge of desire for her.

Soon he was collared by a couple of gentleman with opposing political views, which made for some diverting conversation. He was relieved when Xenia found her own coterie of admirers, including Sir Samuel Wray, but once he'd seen she was happily occupied he could not be still. Where was Miss Rosington? Though he might do well to ensure he didn't stand within throwing distance of a convenient urn.

So when he was in the midst of discussing his latest piece of horseflesh with Sir Beadnall and a soft, familiar voice enquired, 'Satisfied, I trust, Sir Peregrine?' he could not conceal his astonishment. Nor could his companion, whose hooded eyes literally bulged out of his bullet-shaped head.

'I take no satisfaction in the ill fortune of others, Miss Rosington.' He would have said more, but Xenia was parting the crowd, gliding between them and swinging round with a rustle of skirts, the beeswax candles glinting on her small pearly teeth, bared in a threatening smile.

'Gloating in public, Miss Rosington? How dare you show your face when you have destroyed the happiness of my friend, Miss Paige? Now go!'

Her words cut through the chatter of those nearby. Miss Rosington raised her chin and Peregrine saw the tears gathered in her eyes. He stepped forward to challenge Xenia. But then Miss Rosington's aunt was there, her arm upon her shoulder, leading the girl away. He stared after her. Her head was bowed and the forlorn sweep of her shoulders speared the deepest of emotion within him. Not lust, this time, but the most intense, most raw *feeling* for her.

He glanced down as Xenia had slipped her hand into the crook of his arm. 'Come, let us walk amongst the lantern-lit gardens,' she invited him with a secretive smile.

He went, but his world had shattered and he knew himself the vilest creature to walk the earth, totally unworthy of Miss Rosington's love should she in fact be innocent of an illicit liaison with Harry Carstairs. For he had done nothing to champion Miss Rosington in public.

It was a warm summer's evening, the full moon casting a glow across the manicured gardens, which led down to the river. Several terraces were cut into the slope, and through the trees he could see a couple of ferries plying a trade across the fast-flowers waters.

'I've waited a long time for you, Perry.' Once they'd gained the seclusion of a copse of small trees, Xenia's little fingers slid inside Perry's coat, seeking his bare skin beneath his white shirt. She rested her head against his chest as she rubbed her right hand gently up and down, sighing her need while he stared dispassionately at the top of her head, preparing to extricate himself, uncaring this time of inciting her rage.

He could not do this. The moment was upon him and he realised that what he'd desired for so many years was ashes compared to what he'd just thrown away.

He'd had his chance in the middle of that public ballroom to state clearly his feelings, to declare his belief in Miss Rosington's innocence. And he'd done nothing.

Now his so-called reward was the lush and bounteous charms of the woman he'd thought he'd desired above all others. A woman without empathy; a self-serving, venal creature with a cankerous soul.

He disgusted himself.

He rested his hand gingerly upon Xenia's coiffure, wondering if she even felt the pressure, her hair was so extreme.

Her hand twined up around the back of his neck and she gave a little sigh of satisfaction. 'Kiss me, Perry,' she whispered. 'Do you know, the last time you kissed me was …'

'Just before you married your first husband. I know. I feared my rage would kill me.' It was true. As a twenty-year-old he'd truly believed he would expire from the force of his feelings. It was the last time he could remember such intensity. But his feelings had been fuelled by rage and pique, not tenderness. No, he did not know how to feel tenderness.

That was why he and Xenia deserved each other. And why Miss Rosington assuredly did not deserve *him*.

He lowered his head. Yes! He'd kiss her, satisfy her desire for a quick fumble in the darkness, and then he'd take her home to her townhouse where he'd spend a night in amorous abandon. He might not deserve Miss Rosington but he deserved Xenia. They were two of a kind: amoral, heartless. The perfect match. His loins should be on fire at the prospect. He'd been living like a monk far too long, lusting after her through two husbands while she'd toyed with him like cat dangling a mouse by the tip of its tail, salivating, savouring the anticipation almost as much as the denouement.

But when his lips touched hers he felt no spark. No flare of desire. No tingling of his fingertips or heat surging to his groin. None of the feelings that had swamped him when Miss Rosington's sweet breath had caressed his heated cheek before her lips had melted beneath his.

'My darling, I've waited so long for this.' Xenia's lust-laden whisper did nothing to elevate his need. He *wanted* to want her. It would be as much punishment as satiation. Like an automaton he caressed the bosom she bared to him, but the feel of her creamy flesh only served to heighten the disgust he felt for himself.

'What is it?' Xenia's question was a drawl of unconcern. 'If it's someone on the path what do we care? We'll draw closer to the shadows.'

As he gazed upon her, eyes closed, her lips moist and parted in lustful abandon, Perry wondered how he'd ever desired Xenia. She was a husk of a human. He'd always known her capacity for cruelty; perhaps it's why Miss Rosington proved so refreshing. Right now Perry yearned for the milk of human goodness. Of the kind Miss Rosington exuded.

And now Miss Rosington was to waste herself on another husk of a human. A man who quite possibly had used her as badly as Xenia had. Miss Rosington had warmth and strength and honour but that counted for nothing when she was positioned as she was: a pawn in the lives of others who would use her as it pleased them.

'Perry?' Xenia opened one eye and frowned. Even the soft moonlight couldn't hide the grooves of displeasure that marred her expression and highlighted her essential hardness. 'Perry, where are you going?' The lazy drawl was replaced by panic. Perhaps she read his feelings. Perhaps he was not so inscrutable after all.

'I'm sorry, Xenia.' He shook his head as he took another step backwards. 'I can't do this.' He prised off her fingers.

'What do you mean?' She could not believe that he no longer desired her; that the curl of his lip and the dull light in his eye represented the alienation he felt towards what she was, what she represented.

But she wasn't stupid and it didn't take long before her confusion turned to an emotion far more predictable than devastation.

Anger. That was always Xenia's preserve. She was not used to being denied what she wanted and she wasn't about to let Peregrine go without a fight. Not without him feeling the lash of her tongue and the heat occasioned by any slight upon her dignity.

She drew herself up and advanced with all the stealth of a she-lion, a creature Perry knew was as ferocious and dangerous as she was impressive in elegance and hunting prowess.

'You've always wanted me, Perry. So what has changed? It's that lily-livered little Miss Rosington with her cheeseparing ways and her cloying innocence, isn't it?' Her face was a mask of hatred.

Perry shook his head. Of course he'd deny it. He'd do what he had to in order to protect Miss Rosington, for she did not need another reason for Xenia to hate her. No, Xenia had never hated her. She had used her, *pretending* that she hated her for a crime she'd known all along she had not committed.

Xenia's lips bared in a rictus of a sneer. 'You wanted her but you didn't get her. Now all you can think about are her creamy, virginal wares? Because that's the kind of man you are, Perry. You're low and vile. Like me. You don't deserve her and you know it.'

'Yes, I know it. But I deserve you, Xenia. Because, as you so rightly pointed out, you are low and vile. Like me. Shallow and heartless. We're two of a kind. We'd deal well together. The trouble is, I've lost the stomach for simply existing as a worthless creature without any redeeming qualities.' He arrested her flailing arms, gripping her wrists, shaking his head as he added, 'Don't lose your temper now, my dear. There are too many people to witness it. I'm sure that when my remorse has well and truly worn off I shall be begging to share your bed.'

She tried to wrench her arm free and slap him. Instead she had to satisfy herself with a gob of saliva that landed on his cheek and which he merely wiped off with the back of his hand while he shook his head in pretended sorrow.

'We are all creatures of our birth, Xenia. You might parade yourself as a lady, but the truth will always out.'

'How dare you!' she hissed.

He did not stay to hear more.

CHAPTER 17

*C*eleste didn't care about the nearby voices or the fact her nocturnal wandering would be a cause for even greater shame. Alone and determined, she trod the path towards the river. She'd barely been alone outdoors other than in her own garden her entire life. This was a rare freedom, and a welcome retreat from the heat and hostility indoors. The moment her aunt had been waylaid she'd taken advantage of her opportunity. What did it matter if she were discovered cavorting naked with a footman on the grassy slope? Her reputation couldn't be in worse tatters. There might even be some satisfaction in having something for which to be honestly condemned.

Goodness, though, wasn't that Lady Busselton's husky purr? The sight of that evil woman disappearing into the gardens with Lord Peregrine earlier had made her want to scratch her eyes out. Well, they deserved each other. She tried to console herself with the thought, but it was hard when the pain of Lord Peregrine's heartless agenda kept intruding like shards of glass piercing her heart. How the two of them must have laughed as she, a naïve little maiden, had played right into their hands.

She stopped. If that was Lady Busselton she heard then she had no wish to venture closer. Swinging round, she started off at right angles, hoping to reach the sanctuary of a copse of small saplings before she was observed, though the couple she could make out just off the path did seem very preoccupied with one another. The woman's heavy breathing and slight moan made her almost retch. Well, if it was them she hated them both. Together they'd hatched a plan to bring about her ruin and because it suited Raphael he'd not championed her. Perhaps he'd even been part of it. She still was in the dark.

Fresh desolation washed over her. All her friends and acquaintances were only too happy to believe the lies. They didn't care that she would soon disappear to Jamaica, never to return. Celeste had never felt more alone in her life, though it was a feeling with which she was becoming increasingly acquainted.

By the time she'd reached a copse of trees a little further away she stopped and turned, and to her surprise realised she'd covered some distance and that her evil nemesis had detached herself from her amorous dalliance and was now standing on the little pier on the water's edge.

From further up the slope, Celeste watched her dispassionately. The moonlight glinted on the woman's cloth of blue and silver, the fine thread with which it was woven gleaming. Gleaming like her gloating smile, no doubt, Celeste thought as shards of impotent fury coursed through her.

This woman was at the root of her unhappiness: her ruin and the fact she would travel to a new world more dissatisfied than she had been before she'd discovered love.

Though whether love on one side only constituted the full definition of the word was debatable.

A soft footfall made her swing around from where she stood on the gravel path that zigzagged down the side of the hill, gazing at Lady Busselton in the distance.

'Lord Peregrine!'

His expression one she couldn't immediately identify.

'I'm not going to hurt you,' he said as she cowered, caught between fear yet at the same time disarmed by another emotion, 'though God knows, I deserve that you should look at me like that,' he whispered as he closed the gap between them, snatching her hand and pulling her into the cover of nearby trees.

'I shan't go with you, my lord!' Celeste tried to pull away. 'I saw you and Lady Busselton just now. I know about the wager you made with her to ruin me. God knows, *everyone* does.'

'Except that *I* didn't ruin you.' His grip on her wrist did not relax until they were beneath a spreading elm and he'd put both his hands on her shoulders. She could barely see his face but she heard sincerity in his voice. Ha! He was a master of deception. Hadn't she followed him like a little lamb to the slaughter?

She was breathing heavily though they'd only covered a few steps. Holding her hand to breast she ground out, 'My ruin is a mystery to me, though it suits Raphael well enough to see me cowed and biddable. Not that as his wife I could be any other way.'

'You do not wish to know why you were lured to Harry Carstairs, or why?'

She jerked her head up. 'You're prepared to tell me now, are you? On the eve of my wedding you'll grant me a tiny slice of the truth?' Her misery was like a heavy cloak weighing her down. Like poisonous sludge in her veins.

'What? So I may have the greater comfort of knowing that while all the word believes me a faithless jezebel, you, who ruined me, can furnish me with a little more of the amusing background?'

'Celeste, listen ...'

'You have no right to address me so familiarly after all you've done!' she shot back. 'Even when you prepared to lure me to your bed with false promises of marriage, you had enough respect to address me correctly. God punish me, for I confess that even without a marriage offer I was prepared to play the part of jezebel with you.'

She stepped back but found herself against the trunk of a tree. Tensing as his breath heated her temple, she cringed away from him as he muttered, his face close to hers, 'Celeste, there's not much time. After tonight I won't see you again. You'll marry Raphael and I will let you go, but only because I know I do not deserve you. ' His breathing was laboured, the workings of his face suggesting some inner turmoil. Guilt? Well, he deserved to feel it but she was not going to forgive him just to ease his burden. She winced as he gripped her shoulder. 'Celeste, you need to know a few things, even if it's only so you won't despise me quite so much. I know how bitterness can eat away at one's soul; and yours, Celeste, is pure and untainted.'

'How can you say that? Look at me now!' She pressed her fingertips into her eyes to stem the tears, staring at him in the dim light. 'Who sent me the note which lured me to Harry Carstairs' address? You did! So you could win your dirty little wager with your ... your lover Lady Busselton. Do you think I have no ears? No eyes? That I am such a fool as to believe that you are the not villain in all this?'

He stopped her tirade with a kiss, pulling her suddenly into his arms and covering her mouth with his, and instantly the poisonous sludge in her veins flowered into joy, pulsing through her body to allow her one final brief moment of elation. Oh, she couldn't deny it was a good deal more pleasant than shrieking her pain like a harpy yet he was toying with her, now, just as he always had.

'Good God!' he yelped, eyes wide with shock as he leapt back, holding his injured lip.

'You weren't expecting that, were you?' she hissed, turning on her heel and adding over her shoulder, 'Goodnight, Sir Peregrine, may you continue to reap such similar rewards from all the unkindness and poison you and your viperess lady friend are responsible for in the world.'

No, he was not expecting that. With admiration, he watched her disappear gracefully around the bend in the gravel path.

It was so true. He didn't deserve her. But he certainly wished he did.

It was an extraordinary sensation to feel so powerful. Celeste wasn't used to it, so it was perhaps the reason she didn't simply stand on the grassy slope and allow desolation and self-pity to wash over her as she stared at Lady Busselton who had remained staring across the river from the jetty, no doubt waiting for her lover to come to her.

It was equally extraordinary to feel rage to this extent. Like a tide, it surged through her, fuelling her with courage and propelling her down the slope, each step she took banishing the caution and duty drummed into her over a lifetime.

Not that such obedience had done her the slightest good, she reflected as she closed the distance between her and the woman who'd taken such pleasure in destroying her life. No doubt Celeste would pay for the folly of engaging Lord Peregrine's lover in a full confrontation, but right now it would be catharsis.

Lady Busselton turned when she heard her muted footsteps on the jetty, her features reordering themselves from wistful into an expression of gloating. She clearly recognised easy pickings when presented in the form of a defenceless young woman.

Her critical gaze raked Celeste in one dismissive gesture, ending at her feet.

'Your shoes are ruined, Miss Rosington.' Her mouth twisted into an ugly smile. 'Ruined ... like you.'

Ruined? Well, that didn't make her defenceless and right now Celeste felt as dangerous and powerful as the she-cat before her. What's more, she had right on her side.

Lady Busselton raised a languid arm to pat a perfectly pomaded curl and drawled, 'Trysting with yet another lover, Miss Rosington, on the eve of your wedding? Why, you're more brazen than I thought.'

Celeste struggled to remain calm as she raised her eyes from her exquisitely embroidered high-heeled shoes, now damp with dew and mud and, yes, all but destroyed. She'd never hated anyone as she hated this woman, with her simpering smile hiding her secret satisfaction that she'd snared Lord Peregrine and ruined Celeste in the process.

Celeste drew in a breath for courage, skimming the outline of her cloth of gold skirts. 'Now that you have won your wager, Lady Busselton, I'm curious. I hoped you could help answer a few questions. Obviously you have been very cunning.'

Perhaps pandering to this woman's vanity was a better approach.

Lady Busselton smiled, the warmth not reaching her eyes. 'Cleverer than you, Miss Rosington. But no doubt you've gained in worldliness lately. I've done you a favour, you know. Lord Peregrine would have eaten you for breakfast and spat you out once he'd had his pleasure.'

'Ah, so there's comfort in the fact I'm ruined only in the eyes of the world rather than in truth, is there?' Celeste's nostrils flared as she fought to keep her voice level. 'You knew there was nothing behind my dealings with Mr Carstairs the night Miss Paige caught us together. It was just a convenient excuse for this … campaign against me. You traded on your friendship with Lord Peregrine's sister, pretending concern for her, hence the need to find the man who'd thrown her over, purely as justification to propose your outrageous wager with Lord Peregrine.'

'And how amusing, my dear Miss Rosington, that *you* engineered your own downfall ultimately, without either of us having to raise a finger or dirty our hands.' Lady Busselton pursed her lips in amusement.

Her arrogance was incredible. Celeste felt another surge of hatred seep through her like poison and longed to run her fingernails down the white evil, smiling mask that taunted her.

'I know that you have wanted Lord Peregrine for a long time.' Though Celeste had nothing definite with which to charge Lady Busselton, she intended to keep talking; and she would do so for as long as it took to gain the satisfaction of a full confession. Lady Busselton was too arrogant not to succumb and Celeste, for her own peace of mind, had to tease out the real reasons for this woman's actions; otherwise she'd go to Jamaica and her grave wondering how her life could have been ruined for a mere wager.

There was so much more to it than that. There had to be. Like who had forced Harry Carstairs against his will to be discovered in bed with a woman? He didn't even like women.

And why had Raphael participated in this wager so ruinous to his intended? Surely not only to make his beloved

Harry appear more manly? That didn't make sense when they were all leaving England within the week.

Celeste bit her lip and though she spoke slowly, her thoughts raced. 'Lord Peregrine wanted you, and it gave you great satisfaction to know it through two husbands. But that was too easy and as you were bored you suggested the wager as a reason to avenge Lord Peregrine's sister.'

'It didn't take much for you to fulfil your necessary role and to take the bait, did it? I daresay you're not in the habit of garnering the admiration of sophisticated, older men, are you?'

Her self-containment enraged Celeste. Yet she sensed Lady Busselton was hiding a secret. There had to be more than she'd confessed, though the woman's implacable smile was giving nothing away.

'You challenged Lord Peregrine to seduce me, supposedly to avenge his sister but when you saw that his heart was now *truly* engaged by me, you had to put an end to it, didn't you?' Edgily, she studied the woman's face, while the litany of *why?* chased itself around her head. Surely the real reason for the wager was at the heart of everything? That was what Lady Busselton was guarding. In the meantime, however, Celeste chose the safety of pursuing a line that would enable Lady Busselton to gloat over her mastery of the situation.

'Therefore *you* persuaded Lord Peregrine to send me that note in order to entice me to Mr Carstairs' home. *You* persuaded Lord Peregrine to manage the servants so that I was drugged and … put in a compromising situation, so that he could then wash his hands of me and I was ruined in the process, without him appearing a party to it. But,' she worried her lower lip with her teeth, 'how? I think Lord Peregrine is more honourable than that. What terrible threat did you use to make him behave like a … cad with no morals? And what role does Harry play in all this?'

The other woman laughed. 'So many tangled skeins to reorder. You'll manage your new estate with consummate skill, my dear. Your new husband will appreciate that.' She ran her eyes up and down Celeste's form while her simpering smile only grew more maddening, 'If he doesn't appreciate anything else.'

Celeste gasped, the wind knocked out of her sails. 'You know?' And then immediately the answer came to her: blackmail. Lady Busselton had blackmailed Raphael.

'Oh yes, I know of the sinful, noose-rewarding peccadilloes of your husband-to-be and Mr Carstairs. Their criminal love for each other played so nicely into my hands for—and I simply can't keep it to myself—yes, it was in fact *I* who masterminded your supposed seduction in order to disgust darling Perry who was becoming, as you so correctly put it, rather distressingly enamoured of you.'

It was as if the ground had fallen from beneath Celeste's feet. For a moment she couldn't speak as the ramifications of the woman's confession sank in. When she'd regained the power of speech she managed, 'Lord Peregrine was not behind my being drugged?'

'Indeed not, my dear. And until recently he believed you really were guilty of having a secret affair with Carstairs.'

'But now?' Hope made Celeste breathless.

'Poor Lord Peregrine has been so confused.' Lady Busselton sighed. 'Yes, he was disgusted when he saw you in bed with Carstairs, but he's not a stupid man. Now he suspects your dear Raphael is the villain; indeed, that quite possibly your husband-to-be set up that unedifying little spectacle to damn your reputation because he needed to keep you shackled to him.'

The false sympathy on Lady Busselton's face sent the bile surging up Celeste's gullet but she didn't interrupt.

'Yes, when he learned what Harry Carstairs really was to

Lord Ogilvy,he believed Ogilvy was complicit in perpetuating the rumour of your so-called amours with Harry Carstairs. He reasoned that only Carstairs would go along with such a sham and that it must have been done in part to make him appear the red-blooded male he was not. Lord Peregrine reasoned your so-called seduction by Harry Carstairs played into Lord Ogilvy's desire to ensure that your marriage to him go ahead, partly by ruining you in the eyes of the man you were becoming so fond of: Lord Peregrine himself.' She laughed softly. 'Sadly Perry's fondness was not returned with sufficient strength for him to champion you.'

Celeste balled her firsts into the folds of her dress. 'You're wrong, Lady Busselton.' At least there was some consolation in what she was about to say. 'Lord Peregrine waylaid me just now to tell me much of what you've already said. Only days ago he proposed that we elope, but then of course the unedifying spectacle in which I played my unwitting role changed all that. Still, just moments ago he declared he wished he deserved me and that he couldn't bear the idea that I'd leave England hating him.'

A twitch of the lips and a flare in her eye was the only indication that Lady Busselton was affected by Celeste's declaration. Then the air of jaded *ennui* was back as she shrugged. 'Ever the charming rake, isn't he? He simply can't bear a beautiful woman to think ill of him. Why, when I proposed the idea all those weeks ago, Lord Peregrine was quite simply taken by the idea of ruining you for a wager, as he had nothing better to occupy his time. He's consumed by the need for diversion as long as it does not impinge on the comforts of life. No doubt the excitement of suggesting an elopement was soon overlaid by the realisation that he'd be shackled with responsibilities for life. Darling Peregrine prefers his pleasure with no responsibilities.' Concern flashed across her face. 'Do be careful, Miss Rosington. I fear you are a little too close to the edge.'

A spasm of fear tore through Celeste at Lady Busselton's sudden advance, which forced her to step back. Finding no purchase on the jetty for her right foot, she gripped an upright post for balance as she felt the cold air from the river swirl up her skirts.

'My dear, a lucky save. Are you all right?'

The spasm of dread that gripped Celeste held her prisoner as Lady Busselton's small, surprisingly strong, fingers, dug into her shoulder. 'Here, let me help you.'

Celeste tried to shrug out of her captor's grip, for there could be no doubt that that was what Lady Busselton was, now that Celeste had her back to the water and nowhere to run. Lady Busselton's hand was heavy on her shoulder and Celeste was in a precarious position, even though she'd managed to return two feet to a solid footing. She clung more tightly to the post while trying to edge past and make for land. 'So not only did you propose the wager …?' She had to learn as much as she could, for she *was* going to get out of this situation and she was going to set the record straight. The world would not judge her the way Lady Busselton intended. Lord Peregrine would learn the truth about this evil woman. She tried to hide her fear and to distract her as she slipped past. '*You* engineered my supposed seduction by drugging me? *You* blackmailed Raphael and Harry? *You* were behind everything?'

'Not without help, of course. I wasn't at Harry Carstairs' home, if you recall.' She smiled. 'I must say, though, that when Harry was finally discovered a few days ago by my servant, cowering in a staging inn where he'd apparently been hiding for two weeks, I was rather persuasive when I suggested I'd only keep Carstairs' and Lord Ogilvy's ugly secret if they implemented a couple of simple little tasks for me.'

'You truly are evil!' Lady Busselton's satisfaction was more than Celeste could bear. Despite her precarious position, she managed a satisfying slap to the other woman's face, and then a couple of steps towards the shore as Lady Busselton put her hand up to her injured cheek.

One more elbow thrust and she could make good her escape.

'Oh no you don't!' The strong, elegant fingers were grasping for her. Celeste tried to twist her way past the woman, but her full, hampering skirts made her an easy target.

Then Lady Busselton's hands were on her shoulders again and her face was inches away, the hate and malice in her expression far more terrifying than her jaded self-possession.

For possessed this woman undoubtedly was: with the desire to punish Celeste for winning the love of the man Lady Busselton had sought to make her own.

'Let me go!' Celeste thrust out her hand in self-defence, but Lady Busselton was a formidable opponent and Celeste's only experience with her fists was as a ten-year-old in a fight Raphael easily won. The older woman was surprisingly agile, avoiding Celeste's grasping hands as she used her body as a barrier to imprison Celeste between the edge of the jetty and herself.

'You're more than evil! You're insane!' Celeste gasped as a satisfying counter-offensive knocked Lady Busselton's galleon right out of her coiffure. It landed on the ground between them, and was quickly trampled beneath Celeste's feet as they tussled with each other, hampered by wide, heavy skirts and closely set in-sleeves, which prevented much in the way of arm movement.

'Look what you've done! By God you'll pay for that, you

little slut!' Furiously Lady Busselton responded with a sound blow to the side of Celeste's head, which turned the world dark for a second and completely disoriented her.

They were now closer to the far end of the pier, some three yards from the riverbank, against which the Thames lapped like a hungry creature in the dark. The wood creaked and the little edifice rocked unsteadily beneath them. Lady Busselton's eyes flashed in the light of the moon and her mouth was set in an ugly line as she gained the upper hand, manoeuvring Celeste into a vice-like grip and marching her backwards to the edge of the jetty.

Oh God. Without doubt Celeste knew what was about to happen next and fear flooded her.

'Why do you hate me so much?' she gasped. 'I did nothing to hurt you.'

'You know exactly why. You did not play by the rules and Lord Peregrine fell in love with you.'

'He didn't! He was only playing with me. If he truly loved me, he'd have championed me like you said! Now let me go!' Celeste sobbed. 'Surely you're satisfied with what you've done to me?'

'What? And let you run to your dear Lord Peregrine with your pitiful sob story about what a dreadful woman I am? I know the effect your simpering smile and heart-rending tears will have. All right, if it's what you wish, then I'll release you, but not so you can go where you *want* to go.' The grim satisfaction in her tone sparked deadly fear within Celeste as she realised what she meant. Lady Busselton's face loomed up in front of hers and her voice was overlaid with satisfaction. 'I didn't intend for this to happen but you, my dear, struck the first blow.'

Celeste could feel the cold air from the river rising up, the clammy mist like damp fingers stroking the back of her neck as her evil nemesis held her over the water.

'Lord Peregrine loves me more than he'll ever love you!' In a final burst of energy Celeste, shouted the words at the top of her lungs as she thrust her knee up in a final bid to push back her captor. But the action merely unbalanced her, while making no impact on Lady Busselton, protected as she was by multiple petticoats and panniers.

'Let him prove it now,' were the last whispered words she heard, as Lady Busselton simply removed her hands from Celeste's shoulders.

And then Celeste was falling. Falling with nowhere to go but the dark, swirling river, four feet below.

CHAPTER 18

*P*eregrine's encounter with Miss Rosington was more unsettling than he could have believed. More unsettling than the vituperative glance Xenia had levelled on him as she swung away. That, he knew, augured ill.

He turned back to the ballroom with heavy heart. After Nelson's sobering information, he didn't know what to think with regard to Xenia being possibly complicit in her father's crime. He'd known Xenia for ten years. Yes, she was vain and sometimes heartless, but surely not to the point whereby she'd orchestrate a plan so elaborate that it encompassed blackmailing Carstairs and Ogilvy into ruining the woman who'd in fact risked her very reputation to aid Carstairs when he first fled.

Deep in thought, he trod the winding gravel walkway that led to the house. Xenia's motives in bringing Carstairs to heel, however, suggested this was so, though at the heart of it all was the murder of so many slaves. The mere concept of slavery made him ill, though he conceded his views were coloured by his personal relationship with Nelson.

Not for a moment did he doubt that Nelson was telling the truth when he claimed a cargo of slaves had been deliberately thrown overboard, as opposed to having died of natural causes.

Sadly, Nelson was probably perfectly correct when he argued the crime would be regarded as insurance fraud not murder.

But it *was* murder. These slaves, men and women, torn from everything they knew and loved so as to serve the commercial needs of a new white, English slaver, had been relegated to less than the sacks of grain or coffee or whatever other cargo Captain Higgins carried aboard his vessel.

If Captain Higgins was in fact guilty of this shocking crime, then Peregrine was coming to believe, with growing certainty each step he took, that Xenia, who benefited so greatly from her father's largesse, *was* complicit.

He stopped a few yards from the house to gauge the merits of returning to the ball. What entertainment was to be gained when he'd completely lost the desire for life in general? The strains of the string orchestra drifted out of the double doors, overlaid by the soft murmur of guests enjoying themselves, but Perry could anticipate no such enjoyment in the future.

Miss Rosington was leaving and he was letting her go. Ruined. Admittedly, she'd not been ruined precisely on account of him; but just as Xenia was complicit in her father's terrible crime, Perry was complicit in everything terrible that had happened to innocent Miss Rosington and he'd done nothing to champion her.

He was as worthless as his worthless uncle, and no doubt he'd go the same way: defeated by the aimlessness of a life lived for the bottle, the horses and a handful of worthless women.

The only woman who came instantly to mind and who

did not fit that description was Miss Rosington, but some compensation Perry would be if he made up with her. After the first flush of enthusiasm he'd prove to be no better than he always feared. She'd soon wish she'd stuck with her twisted cousin after all.

Perry turned to glance down the hill. The night was still with the waxy moon bathing the gentle slope in a milky glow. He half expected to see Xenia planted in the midst of it all, glaring at him. That would be a frightening sight. Xenia was malevolently creative when it came to concocting punishments for those whom she believed had wronged her. He shuddered. Poor Miss Rosington—though it would seem the man she was soon to marry was just as creative.

He noticed the slope was bare of all but the copse of trees where he and Xenia had briefly had their tryst; though turning, he glanced over his shoulder in the foolish hope of seeing Miss Rosington gazing at him with forgiveness in her eyes.

That wasn't going to happen. The viper's bite with which she'd sealed their association left him in no doubt as to her feelings for him.

Well deserved.

Still, he continued to stare across the moonlit-bathed slope for one final glimpse of the woman who continued to haunt his dreams with what might have been.

As he turned back towards the house he heard a cry. An unusually shrill, feminine cry for a ferryman, he reflected, as he retraced a couple of steps, to squint into the distance towards the river.

A light in the middle of the murky water drew his eye to a ferryman holding a lantern.

He shifted his gaze. This was not where the cry had issued from.

The cry came again, more urgent now, and the familiarity

of the tone propelled him down the slope, scanning the middle distance before he saw the two figures on the jetty.

Two people on a jetty. It wouldn't have been such a remarkable sight had he not observed by their wide skirts and high hair that they were two women and they were alone.

And ... dear God, that they were fighting.

Fighting with their fists.

He broke into a run as foreboding tore through him. Xenia was not someone he'd suggest Miss Rosington should approach, unchaperoned at the best of times. But alone, when Xenia had orchestrated Miss Rosington's downfall. Why, Xenia was ....

Evil.

Xenia was ruthless. She'd stop at nothing to get what she wanted or to safeguard what she had.

And that, it appeared, was Perry. In making clear his preference for Miss Rosington's fresh innocence as opposed to Xenia's more brazen charms, he'd put Miss Rosington at tremendous risk.

As he drew rapidly closer, the exchange between the two women came in clouds of sound. Xenia's husky accusing tone floated on the dew-laden breeze like the swirling river mist; Miss Rosington sounded panicked.

Oh God, why had he not done more to protect her? He'd thought it punishment enough that he'd have to live with himself and his guilt after she'd gone, but he'd had no idea his inaction would have such devastating consequences. Miss Rosington had landed herself in the greatest peril but that was only thanks to him.

As the cool wind fingered his cheeks while he covered the distance between them as rapidly as he was able, he assessed the scene for whatever succour might be at hand. The ferryman plying his trade from the far bank was holding his lantern aloft, illuminating the detritus from upstream carried by the fast-flowing current. *It mustn't come to that*, he told himself, urging ever-greater haste as Xenia's clipped, nasal tones cut the crisp air. 'Lord Peregrine still believes your dear Raphael is the villain; indeed, that your husband-to-be set up that unedifying little spectacle to damn your reputation because he needed to keep you shackled to him.' Her smug satisfaction sickened him.

Was he really such a fool that he'd not been able to see what was in front of his nose? Xenia had orchestrated *everything*. Of course she had, and he'd been too blind and stupid to see it.

'If Lord Peregrine believed that, then why did he not … do anything to at least ease my pain?' The anguish in Miss Rosington's tone cut him to the core. 'Even if he had no feelings for me, why did he not reassure me that he did not believe this evil lie?'

He was nearly there but he staggered a little as shame ripped through him. Disgust, too, that he'd not taken the noble path of backing up the respect that had motivated him to offer for her hand in marriage with his belief in her innocence in the face of her denial.

'Why? Because Lord Peregrine has no honour and no conscience. He's like me, my poor Miss Rosington.'

With only a few yards to go Peregrine raised his head to catch his breath and saw the prurient gleam of something akin to madness in Xenia's eye as she suddenly gripped Miss Rosington's shoulders.

Dismay flooded him. Every second counted. Miss Rosington's life was at stake and no one was more culpable in her current dire predicament than Peregrine was. Stealth was required. His sudden appearance might well be the catalyst to delivering the *coup de grace*, though surely Xenia was not as evil as that?

He faltered, though Miss Rosington's response was enough to knock him to his knees. 'I believe I could have made him a man of honour and conscience—if you'd have let me.'

Such sweet words. And she truly did believe that. God almighty, Peregrine had never been so struck with pained remorse as he was in that moment. But this was no time to slow his surprise attack. He needed to deflect Xenia. Anything to prevent her from carrying out her dastardly intent. It made little difference whether Miss Rosington could swim or not. The weight of her clothing would send her to the bottom of the river in seconds.

And then Xenia struck.

Struck with no more effort than a slight pressure as she released her grip and stepped back.

A shocked silence, Xenia's satisfied grunt and then Miss Rosington's strangled scream of terror as she disappeared from sight punctuated the still night air as Peregrine tore past his former paramour, pushing her aside as he stared over the side of the jetty and into the water.

But the murky depths below were soundless as he cast about for something that would indicate where she'd gone.

Another cry, more distant now, filled him with relief and as his gaze raked the river he saw her bobbing in the water, caught up against a large plank of wood that was travelling at speed with the current.

'Out of my way!' he snarled as he became aware of Xenia at his side, saying something. He didn't care what. He was too busy assessing how best to utilise the few resources he had available to save the one thing he'd discovered in his life worth saving.

Hailing the ferryman in the distance at the top of his voice while he tore off his coat and shoes, in the next moment Peregrine had plunged into the detritus-laden depths and was plying a good strong stroke in the direction of the panicked whimpers.

Thank God Miss Rosington had had the good fortune to discover a log to cling to and the foresight to hang onto it.

The water was bitingly cold and his clothing hampered him but how would Miss Rosington cope with her many restrictions? It was a miracle she'd not sunk to the bottom like a stone.

'Don't let go!' he gasped at the top of his lungs. 'There's a ferry nearby. I'll save you.'

Suddenly he was nine years old again and his mother was flailing in the cold, muddy lake, just out of reach, her skirts billowing as they took in water, her panicked expression marring that beautiful, beloved face that had always brought him such comfort.

Before the nightmares began.

The nightmares that reminded him that he'd been the only one close enough to have aided her, only he'd been too weak and too afraid.

I'll save you. Empty words, or could he? Could he reach her before Xenia's evil and the water's voracious appetite swallowed her up forever … before Perry, too, was subsumed into a swirling hell from which, he knew, this time, there would be no reprieve.

He heard her choked gurgle as she took in water, just as he heard the thump of an oar against the side of a boat, and then suddenly she was gone.

Disappeared beneath the surface in a billow of skirts, like his mother.

It was hopeless in the darkness yet still he dived beneath the surface, his hands flailing in the filthy depths, grasping helplessly, hopelessly.

Until they snagged upon something feminine: trailing hair. And skirts. He gripped both, propelling himself upwards with all his might, lungs near to bursting; a final effort enabling him to break the water with a cry of triumph.

'A king's ransom if you can get this woman into your boat,' he gasped in case the ferryman needed any incentive. 'A king's ransom if you can deliver me from the gates of hell.'

CHAPTER 19

'*P*lease, Celeste, *try* and wake up, dearest.'

She'd heard the words before but had been too weary and disinclined to respond. No, Celeste never wanted to wake again. Far better to revel in a soft bed with warm coverings and exist in the dream world of her creation. Lord knew, reality was not a desirable place right now.

'Celeste, *please*.'

With a sigh, she fluttered open her eyes to see Aunt Branwell sitting on the chair at her bedside, bending over her and smoothing back her hair.

'Is it my wedding day?' she asked, pain knifing her side.

'Your wedding day was yesterday.'

'Yesterday?' Shocked, she blinked her eyes open. 'So I am married?' *How had this happened?*

'No, my dear. You've been very ill. But Celeste, there's someone who wishes to see you. He's been waiting here a long time. In fact, for almost two days. Really, he is *most* anxious to speak to you.'

A myriad of characters Celeste had no wish to see floated into her mind as possibilities. '*He?*' she asked suspiciously.

'Lord Peregrine?'

And of all the people who epitomised the hideousness of her situation, Lord Peregrine was the worst. She shook her head. 'I won't see him.'

To her surprise her aunt seemed upset. 'Surely you wish to at least thank him? He's been in a fever of agitation ever since he brought you here, returning every few hours and waiting for you to wake. For a while we wondered if you'd even survive.'

'Survived? *Who* brought me here? What do you mean?' Celeste tried to clear her brain as she rose onto her elbows. '*Who* brought me here?'

Her aunt soothed her back down upon her pillows. 'My dear, the whole town has been agog with the revelations his lordship made public about you—'

Gasping, Celeste rose up again, clutching the covers to her chest and looking around her wildly. 'Where's Raphael? He believes in me, doesn't he? He hasn't reneged? Surely he knows what is fact and what is not? He's taking me to Jamaica. It's the only future I have left. If he casts me aside there's not a man who'll take me on, and I won't live my life in this country under a cloud of ignominy.' Even in the midst of panic, Celeste knew exactly how vulnerable she was as a woman, not in control of her fortune. No, her fortune and thus her future were in the hands of the men who pulled the strings, and if they chose to cast her to the wolves of public opinion her life would be untenable. She could not—*would* not— live it as a ruined spinster.

'Has he not done enough already to destroy my life?' she sobbed. 'What are these revelations you speak of? I have done nothing wrong, I promise you! Where is Raphael?'

'Raphael has gone to Jamaica, my dear.'

She gasped again, pain tearing through her. It was too much. 'Without me?'

Her aunt pushed down her shaking shoulders in an attempt to soothe her, but Celeste raised her voice above her ineffectual protests, her breath catching in her throat as the door opened and Mary squeaked, 'Miss, I couldn't stop him. He *would* speak to you!'

And there was Lord Peregrine, tall and dark and brooding, dressed all in black today, which reinforced his satyr-like presence as a cruel reminder of all that was wrong with her life.

Rage galvanised Celeste into action. By God, if Raphael had left her it was because of this man who'd now returned to gloat. Seizing the candlestick by her bed, she hurled it at him as she gave vent to a cry encompassing every cruel hurt he'd inflicted on her. 'How dare you show your face?' she screamed. 'Ha! It's only a little scratch, though I wish to God my aim had been better.'

Checked, he raised his head, eyes wide with surprise as he wiped the blood from his cheek, then continued his advance, while Celeste's rage coalesced into a life force of its own. Casting around for something else to hurl at the viscount while her aunt attempted to wrest from her the book that was her next intended missile, it was cold comfort, but comfort nevertheless, to express her anger. 'Get out of my sight! You've ruined me, stolen everything that constituted a life worth living and now you've returned to rub my face in the power you yield over me—'

'Stop Celeste! You don't understand!' Her aunt was flapping about her like a flustered hen, the fringes of her Kashmir shawl tickling Celeste's nose as she tried to silence her niece's tirade. 'Lord Peregrine brought you here. He rescued you from the river, he saved your life and then he broadcast to the world the cruel manner in which you'd been used by Raphael and Mr Carstairs and, worst of all, that evil woman, Lady Busselton!'

Her words only registered after Celeste had released the book, which Lord Peregrine caught deftly. Amidst the flurry, he'd now insinuated himself at her bedside, gently returning the book to her, his hands covering hers as he repeated the title of her reading matter with clear amusement: '*A Discourse on Maidenly Virtues* by the Reverend B. Attwell. A jolly fine choice of reading matter to throw at my head. But hush my love and, even if it's the only time in the years to come that you listen to me, pay heed now.'

He smiled at her shock, his deep, but gentle tones cutting into the silence created by her sudden obedience. 'I came here anticipating heart-melting gratitude and instead I've sustained a shattered cheekbone, yet I hope you're impressed at the manner in which I've reined in my temper. I had no idea you were such a spitfire beneath the demure exterior.'

Still mute with shock, Celeste did not miss his subtle nod of dismissal, which to her amazement had her Aunt Branwell obediently quitting the room; a fact which Lord Peregrine immediately took advantage of by lowering his face to whisper with unconscionable familiarity, 'Though such spirit augurs well for our future, my little termagant.'

Celeste managed to inject the right degree of disdain into her voice, despite the fact she was shaking. 'Oh, so you've come in for the kill have you, my lord?' she responded haughtily. 'My reputation is in tatters, I am ruined, and now you're here to propose I become your mistress. Well,' she shrugged as if it were of no matter, 'Raphael has left me now. I have little choice other than to join your sister in a nunnery or live out my days a scorned, pitiful creature or, as you've just suggested ...' she hoped her eyes flashed fire, because the thought was as hideous as it was secretly exciting, 'lower myself to the basest level to which any creature could ever reduce herself and ... become your mistress. But, let me warn you, it's a proposition you should seriously reconsider since I swear I will devote my lifetime to making you pay for what you've done to me.'

'Celeste, please— ' He stopped midway to putting his finger to her lips, adding with a wry smile, 'For fear of having my middle digit nipped in two, let me explain first why I'm here, though perhaps it would make more sense if I tell you what's happened during the twenty-four hours you've been blissfully unaware of your surroundings.'

'Blissful is hardly a term I would use to describe any aspect of my life right now.'

'No? Well, for the moment mark it down as an aspiration I would hope to entertain you with. Hear me out, I beg of you.' He attempted to take her hand, and when she snatched it away, sighed and continued patiently, his hand lying across her knees in the most familiar fashion, which made her insides cleave with a longing she swore she'd fight for all time. 'First of all, I'd hope that if Charlotte can make an about-turn and decide that holy matrimony is vastly preferable to a nunnery, then perhaps you can too.'

'Good God! She's marrying Mr Carstairs after all?'

'No, in fact ...' Lord Peregrine looked rather bemused. 'She's marrying Sir Samuel.'

'Sir Samuel ... Wray?' Celeste leaned forward, eyes gleaming, sharing in her companion's clear bewilderment as she forgot for a moment her own predicament. The familiar scent of ambergris that wafted from the man beside her was a harsh reminder of the intimacy she'd once enjoyed in his arms; an intimacy he'd traded upon in order to use her so badly. Before she could snatch away her hand again, he brought it to his lips.

'Celeste, I'm the first to admit I'm guilty of gross wrong-doing.' His voice was filled with remorse, and in the pale sunlight that sliced across the bed she saw it reflected in his beautiful eyes. She shivered. He looked so sincere she was almost taken in all over again. 'I agreed to Xenia's wager before I even met you, and because I thought you were in fact a wily fox parading as an innocent dove.'

She tossed her head. 'The knowledge that I wasn't didn't stop you continuing with the wager, did it?'

'I was trying to protect you—'

'A fine way of showing it!'

'You must believe it's true,' he protested. 'Xenia was determined to see you destroyed. It became ever clearer all the time I was falling in love with you, and as her hatred of you grew, so did my desire to protect you from her. First, though, I needed to find out *why* she had you in her sights. I couldn't voice my suspicions to anyone, but please believe me when I say that at no stage did I ever set out to deliberately embroil you in scandal, as Xenia would have me.'

Celeste wished she could be immune to the tingling desire his words and the gentle caressing of her hands was having on her. She drew in a laboured breath, expelling it in a tone that did not hide her hurt.

'You were quick to believe I was guilty of … having an affair with Harry.'

Lord Peregrine made a noise somewhere between a snort and a sigh of exasperation. 'It was difficult to immediately discount what was in front of my very eyes, Celeste.'

Celeste acknowledged this with a brief nod. He went on, 'Lady Busselton knew that Raphael and Harry had a terrible secret they needed to hide from the world. She also saw I was becoming exceedingly interested in you, so when Harry was conveniently discovered just after she'd learned of my plans to marry you, she blackmailed Harry to tarnish you.'

'And you believed what you saw.'

'Of course I did! What other explanation was I offered?'

'My assurances of innocence were not good enough?'

Lord Peregrine rolled his eyes. 'Lady Busselton had thought of every contingency—'

'Including sending me to a watery grave if I didn't go quietly to Jamaica with Raphael.' She gasped as a sudden flood of memory overtook her. 'Dear Lord, Lady Busselton tried to kill me! She pushed me into the river.' Celeste stared wildly at Lord Peregrine. '*You* fished me out of the river?' She shook her head. 'It's all coming back to me. Forgive me for being so stupid, but a great deal has happened to me over the past few days and there's a lot I'm trying to come to terms with. Not least that my intended has deserted me and I have no idea what's to become of me.' She ended on a sigh of despair as she collapsed back onto the pillows.

'That's one of the reasons I'm here now—'

'Yes, I know,' Celeste responded on a note of resignation. 'I suppose Aunt Branwell sees it's the only way I shan't be a burden on her limited resources. She was remarkably civil to you, I thought.'

Lord Peregrine gripped her hand tighter. 'I was hoping that—'

'Hoping? When you've called the shots from the start, my lord?' She shook her head. 'Just as long as you choose a bower for me that's not a tiresomely long walk from the debating societies and the galleries. I shall have to go veiled, of course, for fear of my former friends throwing stones at me.'

'Good God, Celeste, please don't talk like this. What if your aunt should hear you?' Then his mouth dropped open. 'Why, you really believe it, don't you?'

'Believe what?'

'That I'm here to make you my mistress.'

She blinked at him in an attempt to clear her head. 'Why else would you be here?'

It was his turn to blink at her. Stupidly. 'Do you consider me so beyond redemption that I'd even consider suggesting such a thing to … a paragon like you, Celeste?'

She snorted. 'Paragon? Go outside and quiz any bystander and they'll give you a different epithet to describe the poor, fallen Miss Rosington.'

Outraged, Lord Peregrine rose; and without ceremony hauled Celeste to her feet, dragging her, shocked and protesting, to the window. 'Is that what you really think, Miss Rosington?' he asked, an edge to his voice as he forced up the sash and thrust his head outside.

'Lord Peregrine! Stop!' she cried, as he cupped his hands around his mouth and shouted into the street. 'Ahoy there! Yes, you madam! And you, too, sir! Pray attend to me a moment. Do you recognise me? Yes? And this is Miss Rosington!'

Cringing with embarrassment, Celeste tried to withdraw, for a small group of people, both well dressed as well as street urchins, had gathered below. About a dozen from all walks of life were staring up at her, and she with her hair about her shoulders and barely respectable with a shawl wrapped about her.

But Lord Peregrine wouldn't let her go, and was about to address the crowd when a young woman in a simple home-spun dress called out, 'Lor' is that really you, Miss Rosington? You survived yer dunkin' 'an all?'

The young woman beside her grew excited as she added her voice, 'So that evil Lady Busselton's wicked wager came right back to bite her on the bum, eh, Miss?'

Celeste turned a shocked and enquiring look upon the viscount beside her, swinging back when she heard a familiar voice. Focusing her gaze, she identified young Mr Danvers in the crowd. He doffed his Derby hat and bowed deeply. 'I can't tell you how glad I am to see you've made a full recovery,' he declared upon rising. 'Lady Busselton got everything she deserved, and I'm only ashamed to have once considered her my friend.'

'Got what she deserved—?' Celeste began, turning again to Lord Peregrine, but one of the younger, rowdier men in the small crowd pushed his way forward, making a rude gesture as he snorted, 'She and her father, both! The slimy captain put a bullet through his head and seems like his daughter went and throwed hersel' in the river, just like she'd a gone an' done to you. Gone to hell, the two of 'em, wiv respect. Not that what the cunning plan they hatched weren't worth the entertainment it brought, an all—beggin' yer pardon, Miss.'

'Lady Busselton's dead?'

'Hardly a tragedy you'd shed tears over, considerin' how she used you to shift the blame from her own doin's,' the young man called up. This was endorsed by a chorus of voices.

Celeste could barely formulate a coherent sentence. 'All of London knows … everything?' she whispered to Lord Peregrine.

'Bar a few minor details,' he murmured. 'As you know, Lady Busselton was very desirous of locating Harry Carstairs and she'd hoped to use you to flush him out of his hiding place, since he'd witnessed a shocking event aboard the *Batavia*.'

'I knew he was in danger but I wasn't sure what he'd witnessed,' Celeste whispered quickly. 'Raphael said something about a murder.'

'The murder of over a hundred slaves, in fact. The captain had them thrown overboard so he could claim the insurance.'

Celeste's mouth dropped open. 'Captain Higgins killed them all?'

'He ordered his crew to do the evil deed, not knowing

Carstairs had witnessed it, until one of Lord Ogilvy's servants told one of Lady Busselton's servants that Carstairs had been overheard telling Lord Ogilvy.'

Celeste liked the low timbre of Lord Peregrine's intimate murmur but another shout from the crowd recalled their attention.

'So have yer asked Miss Rosington to be yer bride yet?' A young lad with carroty hair sticking up from his ears beamed at them from below. 'Considerin' you saved 'er an all, an' at you was the one wot made all them declarations in the papers and in the street bout her bein' innocent of everyfink wot evil Lady Busselton were in fact guilty of?'

Celeste drew back from the window to face Lord Peregrine, barely able to contain her astonishment. 'I can't imagine what he's talking about?' Her voice sounded choked with embarrassment to her own ears.

With a brief caress of her cheek, Lord Peregrine leaned further out of the window to address the young man. 'Miss Rosington is a little behind the news, my good people. She's only just regained consciousness, so I haven't in fact yet asked her the question that brought me to her bedside.' He turned and fixed Celeste with a level gaze, adding in a murmur, 'The question that I intended to ask shortly and with all due ceremony.'

'Well, ain't no time like the present!' the red-headed urchin called out, his thumbs jammed in his waistband while the tow-headed lad beside him shouted, 'Go on then, ask her! Yer made enough noise all about London town yesterday when you were singing 'er praises and shouting down them wicked creatures that wanted her to look bad.'

Celeste stared. There really were no words to coherently address the myriad of questions she had for Lord Peregrine. But as he angled his face towards hers, the softening of his ascetic features a prelude to what she knew was coming, she was more than ready for the words that followed: 'Celeste, my darling, in case you haven't already realised it, the entire reason for my coming here today was to ask you to marry me.'

She closed her eyes to receive his kiss, her lips forming the only answer she knew would make her happy. And as her ears thrilled to hear the crowd outside shout their approval, her heart beat with an exquisite rapture she'd not imagined she'd feel in her lifetime.

THE END

If you enjoy stories where the hero and heroine must reconcile misconceptions about the other, you'll love **Her Valentine's Secret.** It's about a beautiful French emigree in London in the aftermath of the French Revolution who is torn between her desire for vengeance and her heart's desire.

A GEORGIAN ROMANCE - BOOK 2

Her Valentine's Secret

A beautiful French emigree in London in the aftermath of the French Revolution is torn between her heart's desire and her desire for justice...

Lady Athelton's St Valentine's Ball is a place for love, not vengeance.

Nevertheless, the once carefree Lisette plots to use the infamous gathering in her quest for justice.

But Lucien Monteil, handsome Vicomte and darling of post-revolutionary France, is more than the man who betrayed her father, sending him to the guillotine. He's also the man who stole her heart so many years ago.

Now Lisette must fight the rising tide of her passions, torn between her heart's desire and her desire for justice.

Read this exciting tale of betrayal, love and redemption, and be transported to a gilded age where truth and honour rise above petty vengeance once hearts are laid bare.

Read an Excerpt

"My love, he has come." James's breath chilled Lisette's cheek, his urgent murmur forcing her to turn her head in the direction he indicated.

Lucien Monteil.

Older and more handsome than she remembered. Devastatingly so.

With a shiver of anticipation, she touched the locket concealed below the line of her bodice, and steeled herself to betray no emotion as her cousin rose from his ironic bow and melted into the sumptuously dressed crowd. James had alerted her to their quarry, yet there'd been no danger she might fail to recognize Lucien. In seven years, he'd had not changed. It was she who was now unrecognizable.

"The Vicomte de Monteil grows handsomer by the year." The dowager to whom Lisette was speaking followed her gaze to the landing halfway up the sweeping staircase where, with one elegant hand upon the banister, the young vicomte had paused to rake the occupants of the ballroom with his cool gray eyes.

"You have met him?" With an effort, Lisette maintained her public smile—light, amused, deferential—as she went on to compliment the latest addition to their group, young Madame Pasquier, on her feathered headdress, before nodding at the flirtatious and possibly inebriated Comtesse de Silvain, who raised her champagne coupe as she passed by on the arm of an ageing British Rear Admiral.

Lord Athelton's ballroom was bursting with French émigrés tonight. They were easy to spot amongst the English. They possessed a certain style, a sophistication and elegance in their dress and manner, though it was not that alone which set them apart. There was, too, an edge to their gaiety—those who'd chosen gaiety as their façade. A more diligent observer would have noticed in some the fragility of a smile; the haunted look in the eyes of others for whom pleasure-seeking was a recourse against the violence and blood-letting they'd so narrowly escaped. Lisette did her best to conceal such signs, but the memories of what she had lost were always with her.

It was why she was here tonight.

"Alas, a desire as yet unfulfilled," replied the dowager with a disappointed moué, before Madame Pasquier took up the adoring refrain Lisette was weary of hearing.

"There he is talking to the Duc de Joubert. Monteil saved his life, you know. But then, of course you do." She fanned herself rapidly as she added with a sigh, "And I see Monsieur and Madame Lafour are discreetly awaiting an opportunity for an audience. I believe he diverted the tumbrel taking them to Madame La Guillotine and put them on a boat to England. He is deserving of the gratitude he receives."

"And the title and enormous riches he has since acquired." Lisette tried to keep the acid from her tone before downing her champagne to hide her outrage. Monteil's reputation as a hero of the revolution only added injury to insult, when she knew the truth of his villainy. His perfidy. She toyed with her crystal glass. "I knew him when I was still a child." She cleared her throat, adding, "When he was penniless."

Madame Pasquier's eyes flashed with excitement. She tilted her head enquiringly. "Was he as handsome and noble then?"

Lisette was familiar with such signs of excitement when the vicomte's name was mentioned. The girl's cheeks were suddenly flushed, and her intake of breath pushed up her breasts beneath the sheer fabric of her daring Empire-line dress.

Scandalous, her own mother would have said just years before. But that was another age, another lifetime ago. The new millennium that had ushered in such fashions—"and an uneasy peace—seemed a world away from the heavy brocades and corsetry of the previous century.

Just as Lisette's new life under her distant cousin James's protection was a world away from the security, comfort, and wealth she'd known living with her mother and father in the ancient family chateau near Lyons.

"Was he always so handsome?" Lisette repeated the question as if weighing up her reply. "I thought so when I was thirteen." It was still difficult to speak of the past. "He worked for my family." Out of the corner of her eye, she watched Lucien's progress as he wove his way amongst the knots of revelers who crowded the room.

Oh, he was good.

End of Excerpt

NOTE FROM THE AUTHOR

Thank you for taking the time to read *Wicked Wager*.

If you enjoyed it, you have no idea how helpful **writing a short review** of even just 11 words or more would make.

Were you intrigued by the mystery? Did you enjoy the romance and the redemption? Reviews help make a book discoverable and are more important than ever for authors these days.

You can also:

- Sign up to my newsletter and get a free book here.
- Like me on Facebook here.
- Follow me on BookBub here.
- Visit my Website here.

Thank you and happy reading!
Beverley Oakley

OTHER BOOKS BY BEVERLEY OAKLEY

HEARTS IN HIDING Series

SCANDALOUS MISS BRIGHTWELLS Series
DAUGHTERS OF SIN Series

GEORGIAN MYSTERY ROMANCE Series

Wicked Wager
Her Valentine's Secret

FAIR CYPRIANS OF LONDON Series
Saving Grace
Forsaking Hope
Keeping Faith
Wedding Violet
Christmas Charity

The Daughters of Sin series follows the intertwining lives and sibling rivalry of Lord Partington's two nobly born - and two illegitimate - daughters as they compete for love during several London Seasons.

With Hetty and Araminta both falling for men on opposing sides of a dastardly plot that is being investigated by Stephen Cranbourne, a secret agent in the Foreign Office, there's lashings of skullduggery and intrigue bound up in the central romance.

What Readers are Saying About the Series:

"...lies, misdeeds, treachery, and romance. What an impressive story! Ms. Oakley has a unique way of telling her stories, bringing unknown heroes/ heroines into the spotlight, as they navigate a world of espionage, and intrigue, all while trying to survive and find their HEA. Magnificent and mesmerizing!" ~ **Amazon reader**

"Full of secrets, murders, intrigues. You feel you know the characters and want to strangle some of them, especially Araminta!!! I have since read all in the series and can't wait for Book 5... This is a series I will read again and again." ~ **Amazon reader**

Below is the order of the books:
Book 1: Her Gilded Prison
Book 2: Dangerous Gentlemen

Book 3: *The Mysterious Governess*
Book 4: *Beyond Rubies*
Book 5: *Lady Unveiled: The Cuckold Conspiracy*

GET A FREE BOOK

You can get Her Gilded Prison - Book 1 - for FREE by joining my newsletter. Just visit: www.beverleyoakley.com

Four very different sisters compete for love during an exciting London season: a celebrated actress with a heart of gold, a shy yet daring wallflower, and the artistic, illegitimate daughter of a nobleman. Caught up in a high-stakes game of intrigue and deceit orchestrated by their sister, the ton's reigning beauty, each must play their part to bring a dangerous traitor to justice while finding a man deserving of their love and special talents.

Buy the complete series as a Box set and save.

GET A FREE BOOK

Would you like to know when I have new releases as well as get the romantic start to my Regency-set 'Dynasty'-inspired *Daughters of Sin* series?

Get a FREE book when you sign up to my Newsletter.

ABOUT THE AUTHOR

Beverley Oakley is an Australian author who grew up in the African mountain kingdom of Lesotho, emigrated to South Australia when she was young, and married a Norwegian bush pilot she met while managing a safari lodge in Botswana's Okavango Delta.

Her romance writing career began as a way to amuse herself in the 12 countries she's lived as the 'trailing spouse' of a pilot husband, and when she worked as an airborne geophysical survey operator in the back of low-flying Cessna 404s and CASA 212s – often the only female crew member – in remote locations around the world.

Her *Scandalous Miss Brightwell* series was nominated **Best**

Historical Romance by the *Australian Romance Readers Association*. She is also the author of the popular *Daughters of Sin* series, a Regency-era 'Dynasty-style' family saga laced with intrigue.

Under her real name Beverley Eikli, she writes Africa-set romantic suspense, and psychological historical romances. Her Napoleonic tale of espionage and intrigue *The Reluctant Bride* won UK Publisher Choc-Lit's **Search for an Australian Star** competition and her Regency tale of redemption *The Maid of Milan* was shortlisted in the *Top Ten Reads of 2014* at the **UK Festival of Romance**.

Beverley lives north of Melbourne (overlooking a fabulous Gothic lunatic asylum) with the same gorgeous Norwegian husband, two daughters and a rambunctious Rhodesian Ridgeback.

www.beverleyoakley.com
beverley.oakley@gmail.com